Ryker Chronicles:

Blood Moon

By Jeannette Savage

A child of the wolf that hath borne the mark,
The essence of five, doubled and bound,
'Neath Beltane's blooded moon,
Secures the conduit to their fate.
The gates long closed by hands of men,
Shall open once more.
So that providence, chaos,
Or annihilation may rein.

ISBNe: 978-0-578-21566-2

Cover artist: BookStarsDesigns by Panagiotis Lampridis.
https://www.fiverr.com/v4/perseus/user_page/okomota

Published in the United States of America.
An ODDwall Publications and Nyna Productions product.

Acknowledgments

Thank you to everyone who participated in the making of the Ryker Chronicles: Blood Moon. To my husband and son, who supported my creativity and gave me the time to work, as well as infinite understanding and creative input. To my sister, Thylene Mendez with Nyna Productions, for whom I could never have braved the marketing world without, who offered her unyielding support. To BookStarsDesigns by Panagiotis Lampridis for the magnificent cover design, who took my jumbled vision and created something wonderfully coherent.

And finally, a special Thank You to: Gabby Waltermeyer, Fela Gutierrez, Brittany Kunkle, and Richelle Biancone!

To my readers: If you are picking up one of my books for the first time, start with Book 1 of the Ryker Chronicles (this book). I do not recap earlier works in the series unless it directly applies to the storyline, so if you pick up the book out of order, there may be some confusion as to who some of the characters are, and why they behave the way they do. My installments so far are as follows:

Book 1: Ryker Chronicles: Blood Moon
Book 2: Ryker Chronicles: Dead Man
Book 3: Ryker Chronicles: Old Wounds
Book 4: Ryker Chronicles: Lillian's Scourge
More on the way…

Prologue

Kane Blackmoor couldn't shake the needling pain from his limbs. Blood was splattered on his arms and chest, gluing his fingers together as red lights strobed above him.

The alert system blared military protocol but there was no one left alive to respond. He examined the wreckage: bloody corpses scattered across the otherwise pristine hallway, martyrs only of their vile pursuits.

In a room up ahead, his sisters cried out.

Relief coursed through him as he followed the noise. If nothing else, he would break them out of this nightmare.

As he kicked the door open, they hushed.

"Kane?" Clara called, smelling him over the chemicals.

He tore a set of pliers off the wall and sheared the locks open. "Clara, Aurora, I'm here."

Aurora emerged, followed by Clara, the elders, and shifters from another pack. His kid sisters clung to his patient gown, their little fingers flexing and clutching in fright.

Little Clara stifled her tears with a fist.

A stout man with a wide face and intense, beady eyes grabbed his shoulder. "Thanks. The name's Vorrin."

"Kane," he responded. "You know the way out of here?"

Vorrin gave a nod, his smile exposing two rows of yellowed teeth. "Like the back of my hand. Follow me."

Kane yielded, allowing the stranger to lead them to the exit. He couldn't recall the last time he felt soil beneath his feet, tasted a burbling river, or heard the trill of birds in spring.

It'd been too long.

He followed behind the group with the girls at his side, twin brunette locks bobbing around their beautiful faces.

He always thought they'd looked more like their mother, so different from their father's gruff, dark looks. The alpha had a way of commanding a room, something Kane missed fiercely of their father.

It was the lab.

They destroyed *everything*, killed their parents and took them from the farm, desecrating Kane's entire life.

He felt the unnatural energy flowing through his limbs, waiting for him to change so it could take over again.

And he hated it.

An exit came into view, a hundred feet from their group. Before the shifters in front cleared the entrance, bullets ricocheted down the hall from behind, barely missing as Kane and the others dodged medical equipment. Kane prayed his sisters knew how to change. "Run!"

The adults dropped to all fours, dashing to freedom.

Security bars began their descent, and once they closed, the group would be trapped. Kane could change at any moment, but his sisters might not. They'd spent all but a year of their life in the lab, forbidden from doing just that. "You *know* how!" He glanced back at their pursuers. "It's in your blood!"

Aurora barreled towards the exit, desperate to escape. Her limbs rippled as she forced the transformation, chestnut fur sprouting from her pores as she landed on all fours. She cleared the door and was caught by one of the elders.

Clara stumbled, losing momentum. "I can't!"

With no time left, Kane gripped the front of her gown and ran full-force, sliding the last ten feet under the grate. The fabric tore in his fist and he realized Clara was not with him, but still inside the lab.

"No!" He reached an arm through the bars and pressed her forehead against his. "We'll come back for you. I swear it."

She wept, gripping at his gown with skinny fingers. "Don't leave me!"

A second security door rumbled to life.

Tears streamed down his face as he kissed her forehead. "I love you, Clara." The metal forced him to let go as military personnel closed in on his sister.

Gunfire shattered against the panel. She shrieked, and a deafening silence followed.

Kane froze in the quiet, unable to tear himself away, and equally unable to accept that Clara was dying, alone and scared, just on the other side of the door.

The building reinforcements were impermeable with the safety features engaged. A scrap of Clara's gown was the only thing he had left of her. He trembled with the last remnants of the serum and leaned against the grate, his tightly wound body pressing into the cool metal.

Kane's breath slowed as he closed his eyes.

The lab had killed his parents and stole the three of them away for seven long years. Now Clara was dead, too.

She hadn't even seen her ninth summer.

The scientists deemed his transfusion a success. Kane had been the first shifter to accept the serum without succumbing to the flames. And he'd made sure to tear them all to pieces with the gruesome power.

Subject 783, they called him.

Kane threw a fist at the door, fury and grief mingling. He could not summon the inhuman strength again, not so soon.

Not yet. He turned slowly to see the others assembled at the edge of the woods. The wind tugged at the cloth until he released it, letting it flit jubilantly into the forest.

They had to get away from this place before sunset. Aurora and the rest would follow him to the ends of the earth and this time, he would be strong enough to protect them.

Kane's knees buckled with the change, his heels lengthening as he hunched to meet the earth. A tail sprouted and his every follicle burned. Bones cracked and popped, and his jaw lengthened into a dark, familiar muzzle.

He dashed forward, tearing past the others with such speed, they swayed with the current before following. Aurora and her tawny nose appeared in his peripherals, as determined as he.

They ran far from the horrors of the lab, the sirens fading into the distance, leaving it behind for good.

When the elders eventually began to tire, Kane slowed, giving them reprieve. He would never allow them to endure such pain and suffering again.

It was the least he could do in Clara's memory.

8 years later

Chapter 1

Danny scuffed a stray rock beneath his boot. "Are you fucking kidding me?"

Gabriel Ryker's dark glower made him nervous, more than nervous, if Danny were being honest with himself. His new alpha sat at an oak table in the war tent, tapping his thick fingers against the grain. "You've got a problem with it?"

"Naw, man. Just didn't think I had to babysit. What's it matter, anyway?" He sighed and looked up at Ryker, who shot him another murderous look from beneath heavy, dark brows.

The silence stretched into a long, awkward moment, even the guard at the entrance shifted. "Get out there and do your fucking job, Danny, or I'll have your pelt mounted on my wall."

He threw up his hands in mock irritation. "Fine! You don't have to tell me twice." Before the unforgiving alpha changed his mind, he withdrew from the tent and stormed into the thicket.

Once out of sight, he grinned to himself. Danny had successfully infiltrated Ryker's camp and gained the alpha's trust. Now, he would be spying on the man's human daughter, though by the sound of it, she wouldn't be human much longer.

Get in deep, get the intel, lay low. Those were the orders from his true boss, agent K. That's all Danny knew about the lean suit that captured him and offered the job. He took it, happy to avoid the terminal fate the rest of his pack suffered.

Every mongrel for themselves.

Danny was still free to roam, get in trouble, screw bitches, whatever piqued his interest. He just had to report to agent K, and now, Gabriel Ryker: an alpha who enacted punishments that often far outweighed the crime. As long as Danny kept his head down, it would remain on his shoulders.

The final step was to penetrate this budding pack before Ryker's daughter arrived. Agent K would help him mimic the first change in a shifter.

He just needed to stare in horror, add in a few screams, dial up the pain and they'd welcome him with open arms, believing he was a newly-turned stray.

7

The pack needed the numbers, and this was the perfect opportunity to join their ranks. Danny smirked to himself, crossing through the brambles to the rally point.

Chapter 2

As a crescent moon lifted off the horizon, Matt and I wandered through the city in a fog to find another bar, one that didn't remind us of work.

This was a regular occurrence for he and I.

Today, however, tension hung on his every word. He was extremely polite, for a stuffy bartender, too polite to ask me out. But I had a feeling that tonight, he just might take that leap.

His mild slur pierced the quiet as we lingered on the sidewalk. "Let's get something to eat."

"Dolly's is open," I suggested, probably slurring a little myself. I pulled my hair up into a rough bun, trying to straighten it after too long without a hairbrush. "The food's good enough."

"Sure thing. My treat." Feigning distraction, he reached for my hand. I pulled away, leaving him grasping at air. "You feeling alright, Amy?"

I scoffed. "Course, let's go."

Down the street and around the corner, we entered the diner, rowdy patrons feeding coins to an outdated jukebox. Bikers, laborers, and miscreants argued with one another, while servers took their orders.

"Two house burgers!" Matt's false confidence carried easily over the crowd. "All the trimmings!"

My head throbbed from the whiskey, and the noise didn't help at all. "Some water, too," I said in the waitress' direction, hoping it would take the edge off of the hangover that was already on its way.

Our server nodded, returning with two glasses of water and a basket of fries. "Anything else?" She glanced at Matt, then me. "You okay, darlin'? You don't look so good."

I waved the sentiment away, hating her false concern over my wellbeing. I wasn't buying it. "I'm fine." She shrugged and disappeared into the throng of patrons. I caught a look from Matt, whose steel eyes flashed with worry. "*What?*"

"You sure you're okay? You're *really* pale."

Chugging the water, I slammed the glass onto the coaster. "What the hell are you going on about? I'm always really pale."

10

His hands shot up defensively. "Nothing. If you're fine, you're fine. Sorry." He took a swig of water and avoided eye contact, his lean jaw ticking with what looked like irritation.

Sometimes Matt reminded me of a skittish rabbit, sweet guy, but no stomach for confrontation. I knew not to push too hard. "No, *I'm* sorry. I guess it's been a rough night for me. Let's just have a good time, alright?"

He raised his glass and clinked it against mine, meeting my eye again. "Deal." With an easy smile shared between us, we drank to surviving another workday.

"Did you see Bruce kick that sleaze out?"

Matt shook his head. He leaned forward, honing in on me. "What happened?"

"A drunk guy came in and grabbed Mira's ass. Tammy almost called the cops before he booted him out the door." I shook my head. "Can't believe some of the losers that walk in."

"No kidding. Mira's alright though?"

"Yeah," I said, "she's used to it."

It was his turn to shake his head. "She shouldn't have to be. Some of those assholes think they're smooth, coming in already pickled from another bar. They don't understand why I cut them off, even if they are acting like total idiots."

"Right?" I snagged a fry. "Seriously, 'Look in the fucking mirror, you're drunk.'"

11

Matt and I laughed, my stomach cringing at the effort. Though his cheeks were flush from the whiskey, his face sobered. "Hey, Amy?"

Here it comes...

"You know." He paused, glancing around the bar and lowering his voice. "I really enjoy hanging out with you after work. Do you, um." Matt mustered all he had. "Will you-"

My gut churned, threatening to spew.

I didn't have time to explain as I lurched from the seat and dashed to the exit. I probably looked like I was fleeing the scene of a crime, but I couldn't care less. Holding back vomit, I barely made it through the double doors before emptying the contents of my stomach onto a dry patch of earth. Leaning against the brick wall, I spit out the remaining bile.

Matt was right behind me, in hot pursuit. "Did you have too much to drink?"

"I only had a shift drink."

He tried to stroke my back, and I brushed him off. After my fountainous display, I'd hoped he'd leave me alone.

A stabilizing minute later, we returned to the booth, my cheeks still burning with the blood that had rushed to my face. The server had refilled my glass and I took a long drink, trying to eradicate the foul aftertaste.

"Amy." His voice strained with the weight of his next words. "I like being around you. A lot-"

"Matt." I stopped him there with a quick wave of my hand. "I don't date. Anyone."

His mask of hope fell as I continued.

"You're a great guy, really. Tons of fun, don't get me wrong. I just don't think I'm- ready to be in a… relationship." *What a dirty word.* "It's- not something I do, and I- I hope you can understand."

The unspoken friendship between us crumbled as his gaze dropped to the table.

Our waitress set two plates in front of us. "Two house burgers, all the trimmings! Give me a holler if you need anything else, cuties."

"Thanks," we both said in entirely different inflections.

When he finally looked up, it was as if we'd never had the conversation. He grinned at me. "Let's eat." Matt set himself to devouring the burger as if someone dared him to.

As I picked up my burger, a pack of somber men entered the bar. They were out of place in the swarm of ruffians, dressed in thick denim and cotton shirts; the earthy hint of soil followed them in. The biggest one sat at the bar and ordered a drink.

Turning his head to rub his black goatee on a sleeve, he caught my eye.

The stranger's frost blue gaze seared into me, lasting an eternity. But before I realized I was staring, he'd already turned back to his friends.

Matt waved a hand in my face. "You sure you're alright? You've been kind of spacey all day."

I dropped the burger as my stomach clenched, threatening to betray me again. I moved to stand, my body trembling. "Maybe I'm not feeling well. I should probably go home."

He stood and offered a supportive hand. "Let me drive. You don't need to walk or-"

Unable to hold it in, I barreled past incoming patrons and wretched over the scummy patch of dirt. Levering up from the wall, I took a heavy step in the direction of my apartment.

Matt fluttered about, trying to persuade me back inside. His pleas absorbed less of my focus, eventually bothering me no more than the hum of fluorescent lights. "I'm going home."

"I'm calling an ambulance. You need help." He pulled out his cell but never made the call.

Before his fingers punched in the numbers, several figures surrounded us. One stole the phone from Matt.

My head throbbed and I couldn't focus, the effort alone was dizzying.

Prickling needles rippled over my skin and through my core, making it impossible to think. I might have otherwise been bothered that someone was lifting me into the bed of a truck, or that several pairs of hands held me down.

At this moment, I cared for none of these things.

My bones protested and a stabbing pain coursed through my spine. Every pore opened all at once as time abandoned me. This bright, hot pain was now my reality.

As suddenly as it came, sensations rushed in, leaving the world a swirling kaleidoscope. Faces clustered in my vision, none of them familiar.

The air was bursting with flavors that tickled my tongue.

One in particular drew my focus.

I stood on shaking limbs as unfamiliar hands tried to keep me still. I shook them off and leaped onto the concrete. My nose led me towards the tantalizing scent, and on either side of me, a rhythmic pounding matched my pace.

Bright spots of liquid trailed the ground, leading me to a delightful aroma. A splash of fluid, warm and wet, drew me even closer. As I arrived upon a dying creature, I caught a whiff of the source. Pulsing fluid hit the grass and soaked into the earth.

The creature's eyes widened as I stooped to taste.

Before my tongue reached the wetness, a dark mass struck me hard, propelling me away from the animal. My head rattled, and the illusion swam into muted clarity. A man in a suit lay bleeding to death beneath a shrub, gasping for air.

15

But I couldn't focus on him as a massive black wolf stared down at me with frigid eyes before everything swam out of focus.

Chapter 3

Secret Agent Morgan Lazaro had a lock on the target.

After observing her for nearly a week, he had a handle on her schedule and acquaintances. They couldn't be called 'friends'. Everyone in her life was kept at arm's length, which impressed Lazaro, though he'd never admit it aloud. If he didn't know better, he might say she was undercover.

But he did know better.

Fifteen years prior, Lazaro had trained under his mentor, agent Bell, when they were summoned to the scene of a domestic violence case.

The FBI didn't normally process these cases, but this one was a doozy. The mother's corpse was found in the marital bed, torn in more pieces than not. The father, of course, was missing, along with one of their two children. The other was found wandering the neighborhood, covered in her mother's blood.

The police had assumed foul play on the father's part and the FBI believed he had links to a crime syndicate in the area.

The sole survivor, Amy Ryker, was admitted to the foster care system shortly after her eighth birthday. No other family was located, so Lazaro and his mentor facilitated the transition, keeping tabs on her in case the father returned.

Amy was a slippery kid, running away from every foster home she was placed into. But Lazaro continued to monitor her movements well after the bureau ended the search.

He'd introduced himself once, on the day her mother was murdered. The girl was traumatized, and never spoke a word, but Lazaro became protective over both her and the case.

Over the years, she'd blossomed into a beautiful young woman. Lazaro felt a strange sort of pride in that, something that had snuck up on him with age. When she eventually settled down in the city, Amy finished her education, got a job, and accepted civilian life, albeit grudgingly.

Her file found its way to his desk again, after so many years on the shelf. The director wanted him to keep an eye on her, choosing Lazaro because he was already familiar with her case.

Perched outside her usual haunt, he kept watch.

Tonight, the bar closed early. Matthew Pierce, another bartender, invited her out. Even from five hundred feet away, Lazaro could tell he was smitten. But his girl was a firecracker,

18

and unbeknownst to Pierce, he didn't have a chance in hell. Hoisting his elbows up, Lazaro peered through the binoculars.

The show was starting.

Amy and Pierce entered the restaurant, the same, dingy hole-in-the-wall they always went to. *A little predictable, don't you think?* Lazaro scoffed at Pierce. Anyone could see she wasn't interested, but the lanky idiot looked oblivious.

The waitress came and went, but he sensed there was something else going on.

Amy's skin had turned a shade darker than snow. She tore away from the table and emerged out the front doors, vomiting onto a patch of dirt.

Pregnant? Lazaro quickly dismissed the thought. No one got close enough to be considered a romantic interest. He wondered offhandedly if she were still a virgin. No, she wasn't pregnant.

Pierce comforted the target, her flesh pallid.

Leaves crunched behind Lazaro.

"Quite a view, huh?"

Impossible, he thought, rolling over and pulling out his pistol. *No one's ever blown my cover before.* The man kicked the weapon from his hand and caught his wrist underfoot. A sickening crunch echoed off the trees as pain lanced through his arms. But his training served well. Pulling another sidearm from his holster, he aimed at the intruder's head.

The stranger was inhumanly fast. He grabbed Lazaro's good wrist and snapped it backward, another hand went down onto… no, *into* his stomach, pulling out a twisted ribbon of organs.

At first, he didn't feel anything, pinned between the earth and this intruder. Lazaro's head buzzed as he came to the slow realization that he'd been gutted.

"Sorry fucker, bad luck." The attacker threw Lazaro's innards back at him, hand glistening with blood. *His* blood. He didn't often get greedy, but at the moment, it couldn't be helped.

He refused to die until he knew who bested him. "Who are you?"

"That's classified." The stranger chortled to himself, snatching the guns. He glanced back only long enough to grin at him with long, sharp teeth, then disappeared in the underbrush.

Lazaro lay in a growing pool of his own blood. *So, this is how it ends.* Unable to feel the tips of his fingers, his eyesight darkened, and focusing became difficult.

Suddenly, a figure crashed through the bramble: curious, starving, and coming right at him.

It was a dog. A massive, white dog.

Maybe it smelled his blood and escaped its owner. With the last of his energy, he raised an arm, shielding himself from an attack that never happened.

Lazaro watched with fading interest as a black mass struck the dog, knocking it off course.

At least he didn't have to watch himself get devoured before he died. Lazaro's sigh was wet as he resigned himself to fate.

His vision blurred and darkness overwhelmed him.

*

A bleating alarm yanked him from sweet oblivion. Lazaro tried to bat the sound away, but his arms didn't respond.

"Hold still," a hushed voice murmured.

"Where-" Pain rushed back. With his body wrecked, he could feel every pulse of agony. The EMT's had strapped him into some sort of body suit, likely the only thing keeping him in one piece.

"You're safe, agent," the voice responded. "We're going to take good care of you."

In Lazaro's line of work, 'take care of' didn't quite mean the same thing. Since he'd failed the mission, only one thought

21

entered his mind: would they neutralize him? Surely, his injuries were severe enough to keep him off the field, and he knew too much to simply be retired from the bureau.

"We need another transfusion!" someone shouted as alarms rang out.

So, he was in a hospital.

Lazaro wondered if director Aldridge heard of his failure yet. *Probably,* he thought, relaxing into the pillow.

A pinprick kissed his inner elbow, and rapture coursed through his veins. Lazaro relinquished his grip on the living world, falling into a velvety void, free from suffering.

Chapter 4

I bolted upright in bed as someone clanged pots and pans in the kitchen. *Matt???*

Flinging the covers off, I froze, my whole body searing with pain. I bit back a scream and gingerly set a foot on the hardwood as invisible shards of glass shot through my heels.

Another bang made me rush. I stumbled against the wall and flung the door open.

A massive stranger was rifling through my kitchenware, cursing under his breath. I seized a wooden baseball bat – set aside for just this purpose – and aimed it at the hulking figure. "What the *hell* are you doing here?"

The trespasser froze. He was huge: rippling muscles that strained a deep tan, evidencing years in the sun. Setting down a pair of tongs, he turned. Ice blue eyes met mine, sending a shock of recognition through me.

"You're from Dolly's."

He stroked a sable goatee, his voice as deep and full as his chest. "The name's Kane."

"What are you doing here?" I asked with an edge, wondering if I'd forgotten my own rule and brought him home. *No one* was allowed in my apartment. Under any circumstances.

"Give me five minutes, and I can explain."

I shook the bat, threatening violence. "You have thirty seconds, or I'm going to shove this thing so far up your ass, you won't shit right for a week."

A smile spread across his face, exposing strong teeth. "It's not what you think. I promise I-"

The fire alarm pierced the tension between us.

Whipping back into the kitchen, he tore it off the wall and silenced the chirping, then snatched a pan off the stove without a mitt. The pan burnt his hand and he hissed another string of curses, letting it crashed to the floor. Scrambled eggs speckled my kitchen cabinets.

I lowered the bat. "You going to clean that up?"

"Gladly." He snagged a roll of paper towels, ringing a square under the tap. He hunkered to wipe egg spittle off the floor, my kitchen barely accommodating his size. "What do you remember from last night?"

It gave me a moment to assess him. He had a tangle of black hair, pulled into a ponytail. The hair followed his jawline

24

and that irritating goatee; it implied a meticulous demeanor, despite his wild locks. "I can't remember anything, other than Matt- You took his phone," I raised the bat again. "Why?"

"He was about to call the cops. It was for the best." He glanced up and seemed to see my skepticism. "No one hurt your boyfriend."

"Matt is *not* my boyfriend," I spat. "Why are you here?"

He stood, and would have loomed if he came any closer. "You're changing." Kane tossed the paper towel in the trash. "I can't let you roam around without knowing what you are."

"What do you mean?"

Not answering right away, he rinsed and scrubbed the pan. "Do you remember your motorcycle accident?"

"That was over a year ago," I argued, but remembered. I'd tested the limits of my Ducati in an attempt to feel... *something*. Anything at all. The wheel destabilized and I was launched into the concrete at a speed few survived.

Not only did I beat the odds, but the doctors were perplexed at my recovery. I was discharged in a day with nothing but a crooked scar on my shoulder blade.

Afterward, thrill rides were out of the question. I gave up the adrenaline-junkie lifestyle for the promise of a bed and a steady income, learning to ignore the aching emptiness inside me. There was something missing, but I chalked it up to having an awful childhood.

25

"I pulled you from the wreckage, myself." He dried his hands, raising an eyebrow. "You still have the scar, don't you?"

Lowering the bat, I rolled my shoulders and felt the tightness of the skin. "*You* did that?" I reached an arm back to rub the mark.

"I did," he confessed, looking a bit guilty. "-but I wasn't in the form you see now."

He's insane. I raised the bat again. "You've had your thirty seconds. Get out."

"It seems strange, I know. But give me a sec-"

"I said 'Get out'!" I took a step forward and swung at his pretentious chin.

The bat froze mid-strike. My arms halted long before wood connected to bone. The stranger's hand clasped the fat end of the bat, making it creak. Black fur rippled over the skin as nails pursed into claws that splintered the grain. "I'm not leaving until you understand." He spoke calmly, but a growl reverberated through his teeth. "Trust me, Amy."

I let go and backed away. "What are you."

"*We,*" he said, lowering the bat. "-are shifters." Kane let the splintered wood drop to the ground. As it clattered against the tile, his hand resumed an ordinary appearance.

"You're not human."

"Some might argue. But that means you aren't, either." He took a seat in my favorite chair, which groaned beneath his weight. "I could do with some breakfast. You hungry?"

Hardly comprehending what had just transpired, I could barely form words. "… breakfast."

Kane nodded, arching a brow.

My voice was small when I finally found it. "Sure. Let me- um, get changed." I slid into my bedroom and locked the door, leaning against it.

My phone flashed a full-battery light on my nightstand.

I *could* call the cops, but they wouldn't hurry, not on this side of town. I allowed my breathing to slow and racked brain for a better plan. When none surfaced, I glanced down at my clothes and noticed they were not the ones from yesterday.

Rage spiked through my core. Did he *dress* me?

I tore through the drawers, looking for a new pair of clothes. My favorite bra was missing, too. It hadn't been thrown in the hamper but was just- gone.

Slipping on a black t-shirt and a pair of jeans, I tucked the phone and wallet into their respective pockets.

I donned my leather jacket and some running shoes, then clipped a Gerber to my belt.

This fucker had some explaining to do, alright.

Storming into the living room, I almost ran into him. He reached out to steady me, appraising my outfit with the same, infuriating eyebrow.

"Don't touch me," I snapped. "*You've* done enough."

Kane's face softened in confusion. "What do you mean?"

I counted the ways. "First off, I can't recall most of last night. Apparently, you brought me back here when I was unconscious and *dressed* me. And you've been slinking around my apartment all morning!" I almost threatened him again but thought better of it.

"After you changed, the clothes were trashed," he said, scratching the back of his neck. "If you woke up naked, you'd have ripped my throat out before I got a chance to speak."

"Then speak."

He opened my front door. "Breakfast first."

I rolled my eyes. "What *is* it with you and breakfast?"

"Our kind eats a lot. You must be starving after last night. The first change is usually the worst."

"Where are we going."

"Bob's. They give us a discount."

"So, you're cheap."

"Economical," he corrected. "We deliver produce, and they cut the bill in half. We still run it up every time, but it's nice to have someone else cook once in a while."

I ducked through the doorway. "Cause you suck at it."

28

Kane's face went blank for a moment, and then he erupted with a booming laugh. I marched into the lobby, ignoring the hysterics. He followed after, cooling from the outburst and shooting me a grin. "You're probably right."

The fair-haired building receptionist offered a nod as she caught my eye. When Kane came into view, her features dropped into a jealous glower, marring her porcelain mask.

She could keep him.

But Kane wasn't bothered by her reaction and, in fact, didn't seem to notice at all.

As he moved to open the door again, I intercepted. "Quit this shit. I'm not helpless."

He blinked and allowed me to pass.

"I would never assume." Kane followed after, jogging in easy strides to catch up. "You seem capable. I didn't mean to offend you."

Scowling, I stood on the street corner and waited. He pulled out a set of keys and hit the fob. The most obnoxiously huge F-450 flashed its lights, "Really?"

"What can I say? We live on a farm." Kane rounded the behemoth and opened his door. He glanced over the hood at me. "Are you coming?"

Wondering if I was about to make the biggest mistake of my life, I stepped over the threshold of control. Anticipation spiked in my chest, that old thrill I'd learned to live without.

29

I opened the passenger door and hoisted up onto the bar, sliding into the truck. The scent of fresh plastic and leather filled my nostrils.

Kane slid in as well, his finesse defying his bulk.

I pulled out my phone as if to text someone and asked, "where is this place?"

He started the engine and pulling away from the curb. "About 30 miles from here. It's North, off of 26. Want the cross-street?"

"Nah." I feigned nonchalance, Googling 'Bob's' for the address. Sure enough, there was a restaurant with that particular name off of 26, just like he said. "What do they have?"

He kept his eyes on the road and turned onto a bridge. "They've got a great variety. I'd be surprised if you can't find something to eat."

Silence rode with us for a time. I watched his casual motions, flicking the turn signal, guiding the beast through morning traffic. Had I imagined his hand changing like that, morphing into something... monstrous?

'Shifter', he'd called it.

I must be insane.

After twenty minutes on the road, he took an exit and rolled onto a gravel drive. We pulled up to the humble, one-story building. It was already packed with customers and, despite the foot traffic, he found a parking spot with ease.

My body was stiff from sitting in the same position. I unbuckled gingerly and slipped out of the truck before he could hold the door open for me again.

The air was full and fresh, so far from the city, and steam wafting from the restaurant made my stomach clench with a gnawing hunger.

"You're a farmer?" I asked, breaking the tenuous silence.

Kane nodded without hesitation. "We've planted the radishes, most of the greens have taken root, and the strawberries will be blooming soon."

We approached the double-doors together, and I was hard-pressed to keep up with the even stride of his long legs. "Have you been a farmer long?"

His jaw ticked, almost getting the door again. He caught himself and waved me forward. "Most my life."

I pushed inside on my own.

A stout man with a balding scalp and a friendly demeanor greeted us. "Morning, Kane! Just the two of you?" He glanced between Kane and I, curiosity wrinkled his forehead, but a warm smile broke across his face.

Kane reciprocated the smile, glancing to me. "Yeah, the others won't be joining us today. Robert, I'd like you to meet Amy. Amy, this is Robert." I shook the man's hand out of

31

sheer obligation, but he seemed like nice enough. "We've known each other for, what, six years now?"

"Seven, come August." Robert extended his arm to the restaurant beyond. "Would you like a booth? Or we could get your room ready if you'd prefer." He winked at us.

"A booth is fine. Thanks, Bob."

Robert led us to a seat near the server door. "It's always my pleasure. Kelly will be with you shortly." He adjourned to the front entrance, where more patrons flooded in.

Some of my lingering suspicion faded. Kane seemed to be telling the truth, from the restaurant to his familiarity with the owner. I leaned forward and eyed him. "A *room*?"

He chuckled. "Bob keeps the second event room reserved to accommodate our rowdy group. We come here a lot." He flipped open a menu and scanned the contents.

Sighing, I opened my own. The menu was heavier than expected, and the prices were outrageous. "Holy shit. I don't have the money for this."

Kane glanced over the menu. "Order what you want. I've got the bill."

I didn't like it but was too hungry to argue.

Breakfast, Lunch, and Dinner were served all day, and besides the traditional fare, they served select dishes from around the world. I considered a cheeseburger and recalled last night. "So, what happened to Matt?"

He lowered the menu slightly, still panning. "Hm?"

"After-" I couldn't put it into words. "He wasn't hurt?"

Kane turned his attention to me. "He got home safely. Gary made sure of it. Give him a call if you're worried." He glanced down at the menu. "You know what you want yet?"

I considered his offer, then thought better of it. "There's just so much to choose from."

"You should eat something high in carbs."

"I don't like carbs."

Kane's eyes flickered up with amusement. "You better get used to them. We need a lot more than the average person. Expect to triple your intake."

"You're kidding."

"I wish. You don't want to know how much it costs to feed twenty-one ravenous shifters. We burn a days' worth every time we change. So, eat up."

"Change." I tasted the word. "That's what you did back at my apartment. When-"

"You tried to hit me with the bat?" Kane finished. "Yeah, very hospitable of you." A sly grin spread as he twisted his goatee, then he went serious again. "Once you master your second form, you can do it too. I have to admit, though, that was a pretty good swing."

I remembered the sickly crunch of wood and shivered. "Not good enough."

33

"You're stuck thinking like a human, but if you'll let us, we can teach you how to control the change. We're-" He held up a finger. "One second."

A peppy brunette sauntered to our table and placed the waters down. "Hey, Kane. Good to see you again!" She smiled widely, her eyes glazing over his figure.

"Good to see you too, Kelly," he said, turning back to me. "You know what you want?"

Kelly's head snapped in my direction, her eyes narrowed so minutely, most people wouldn't have notice. I didn't miss a beat. "I'll take the pot roast, with a coffee."

She jotted my order on her notepad, the pen scratching angrily into the paper. "Cream and sugar with that?"

"Cream, thanks."

She turned back to Kane with less hostility. "And for you?"

"A black bear steak, fish and chips, turkey dinner, and a chicken stir-fry. I'd also like a Rouge and an extra plate."

She gathered the menus and scribbling the order down. "Will do! I'll get your drinks." Kelly sashayed to the kitchen with a little extra sway in her hips.

"A beer? It's hardly eleven."

He shrugged noncommittally, opening his silverware with meticulous fingers. "Why not?"

"I'm a bartender and nobody comes in this early."

"We don't get drunk," he explained with a wink, a crooked smile forming. "At least not easily. It would take a lot more than a beer to floor me. You're a shifter now, too, and there are certain things you'll have to get used to."

"What does that even mean?"

"Let's start with last night. Can you remember anything that happened after leaving Dolly's?" His cold stare bore into me until I was forced to glance at my place setting.

Fiddling with the silverware, I focused on what I remembered. "Matt tried to call an ambulance, then, everything hurt." My stomach cringed. "It was like white fire and hot needles in my gut."

"That's a good way to describe it actually, but the pain only emerges when you resist. Since you *will* change again, you need to learn how to control yourself."

I tore my napkin to ribbons, making a pile of confetti. "So, I'm just some freak now, is that it?"

He gave a hearty scoffed. "Not in the least. Since your accident, we've been keeping an eye on you, waiting for signs of the change. Not everyone does, even if they're bitten. It took a year to manifest itself. Last night, you released a pulse of energy. We felt it and came as soon as we could. But by then, you'd already begun changing. It started with nausea and the pain. After that, you were on your feet again." Kane rubbed the back of his neck again. "You almost tasted human blood."

35

My head shot up. "What?"

His voice dropped lower and he leaned in conspiratorially. "There was a human. He'd been ripped open and was bleeding to death. We didn't know until you led us to him. I stopped you from going rabid, myself."

"What does that mean?"

"Literally that: rabid. You'd stay in your secondary form, murdering until caught or killed. Something about eating human flesh, especially during the first change, can shut down rational thought. They stay in their second forms indefinitely. I haven't heard of a rabid shifter recovering."

"I would never do that," I said, aghast.

"Right, but your secondary form is another matter. We stem from humans, but the genetic material changes. Shifters made from a bite take longer to adjust."

Before I could ask one of my numerous follow-up questions, Kelly came back with the drinks. She placed the beer and glass in front of Kane, cracking the lid, and plopped down a carafe and creamer in front of me. "Here you are. The food will be out in a minute." She left us alone again.

"What exactly do *we* turn into?"

He poured the beer into a frosted cup. "Similar to a wolf but bigger, and much stronger."

"A werewolf?!" I almost shouted, then lowered my voice, "You're saying I turned into a *werewolf* last night?"

"No." Kane rolled his eyes at my outburst. "We're shifters. The term 'werewolf' has been overused at best. It also implies we change with the phases of the moon. That's a myth. We resemble something closer to a Native American skinwalker, and even that lore is shrouded in stigma and misrepresentation. It's impossible to live among humans for long, so we group up and stay rural."

"There's a lot of shifters then."

"Nobody knows. There are half-a-dozen packs that I'm familiar with in a thousand miles, but we've got our share of enemies." His voice dropped to a murmur. "That's why I'm here, to make sure you don't get taken."

"Taken by who, exactly?"

Kane didn't have time to answer before Kelly came back with the food, setting each plate down in succession. "The steak, fish and chips, turkey, and stir-fry. And the pot roast." The plate clinked in front of me. "If you need anything else, let me know!" Her gaze lingered on him as she left.

The pot roast caught my attention, and my mouth watered, but I added cream to my coffee instead. "That girl is all over you. What's that about?"

He speared a bite of vegetables. "Jealous?"

"Hell, no. Why would you think that?"

"I'm joking, Amy." His eyes slid to the window. "Humans are hyper-aroused by us. We appeal to them on a fundamental level. Maybe it's the hormones. Your friend Matt, for instance, did he make a move before last night?"

I shook my head. "Now that you mention it, no. I felt it coming, though."

"It's not his fault." He took a bite. "Eat. You're starving."

Kane wasn't wrong. I sawed off a chunk of the roast and took a bite of my own. Before realizing it, I polished off the meal, considering licking the grease off the plate.

I glanced at his feast guiltily.

He pushed fish and chips in front of me. "Here. Have this."

Snatching the plate, I made a sandwich out of the two fish patties and chewed with delicious abandon. Between desperate swallows, I took another swig of coffee.

"See what I mean? Just don't forget to breathe."

I ignored him and pulled the third plate forward to gnaw on the gamy steak. "You weren't kidding."

"No, but it's normal. You see why we live on a farm?" He took a bite of stir-fry. "You should stop by to meet them. Our place isn't far from here."

I jabbed a slice of turkey off a plate with my fork. "What're they like?" I asked with a full mouth.

Kane's methodical chewing slowed. He swallowed before speaking. "We're all adoptive family, in a way."

The word made my heart skip a beat, but I smothered that old hurt with my usual nonchalance.

"There's my little sister, Aurora. Johnny, her boyfriend, and his father Mortimer. Johnny's great with computers, taking after Mort in the best ways. Then there are the elders, Moira and Solice, practically inseparable. Serena keeps everyone's head on straight and Greg's a big softie, but solid in a fight. We've got Crystal, Jean, and their kids; David, Emily, and *their* kids. Kyren is my second, and Maxwell, his mate. Gary was with me at Dolly's last night, along with Jean. Then, there's Danny." He paused. "He's still getting used to living on a farm, I think." Kane almost said more but seemed to wait for my response.

I chewed on the turkey. "That's a lot of people in one house."

He chuckled. "True, but thankfully it's big enough to accommodate everyone. I had the farmhouse expanded a few years ago so we have room to grow." He watched me absorb the information, then asked, "would you like to meet them?"

Glancing up at him, I set the last bite down. "They're all-um, *shifters*?"

"'Course." His eyebrow went up, asking the unanswered question.

I watched him for a long moment, still a little wary of him, and yet, he'd given me no reason *not* to trust him. I let out a loud sigh. "Fine. It's not like I have anything else planned."

"If you don't feel comfortable, just say the word. You're under no obligation to stay, but you should train with us. The change can be overwhelming at first and we can help."

I caught his eye again. Something compelled me to listen. His voice resonated with a tone not accustomed to being ignored. "Okay," I said in a small voice. "I'll meet them."

Kane stood and offered a hand, looking rather too pleased with himself. "Good. They're going to be thrilled to meet you."

Chapter 5

Only a month had elapsed since Danny arrived, and he was already prepared to bolt.

The pack was welcoming and friendly ad nauseam. They did everything together, not giving him a moment to breathe. Half-changed mutts tore up the house at all hours and it took every ounce of patience he had not to swipe at the brats.

Living on a farm was supposed to be quiet. How wrong he'd been. But then the news broke that they were expecting another shifter. A young woman showing signs of the change: Ryker's daughter.

Exactly as agent K had anticipated.

She was different from the others, though. Kane had bitten her after a near-fatal crash a year ago, saving her life. Most of the pack members were born, not made.

Serena, an unbred bitch, kept insisting he cook or clean up around the oversized farmhouse.

This is a joke, he thought, considering shagging her and getting it over with. The only thing stopping him was Greg, the big brute who'd taken an interest in her. He might not appreciate Danny stealing her matehood. Everyone else in the pack was hitched, and even the second in command was getting some.

If sex was water, he was a desert.

He waited until they settled into their evening routine, sneaking into the garage and pilfering the Audi for the evening. Without effort, he eased it onto the main road towards the city.

Getting out of the backwater was his first priority. After that, he'd see what the evening had to offer.

Once across the bridge, he slowed to a crawl and inspected the merchandise. The businesses were closed at this hour, but there were certainly things to buy. And to take.

Human bitches lined the buildings, leaning against the brick with their skirts hiked. Danny rolled the window down and waved at one of them. A sweet little trick pointed at herself and then sauntered over. "Hey, cutie. What you lookin' for tonight?"

He bit back the hunger. "I think I found it. Want a ride?"

She opened the door, settling into the seat and flashing her eyes at him. "Where we headed, darl?"

Danny grabbed her knee and explored upwards.

The bitch moaned. She was acting, of course, they all did, but she wouldn't be for long. "I know just the place."

Before agent K's Marines captured his old pack, they had a safe house. He was the only living creature that knew about it.

He sped through the streets, zipping around jaywalking drunks and parking behind one of the many apartment buildings on the riverfront.

As he got out, she draped herself over his shoulder.

Danny led them through a back alley to the entrance.

Though not necessarily handsome, he was amazed at what he could get away with before anyone questioned his judgment.

Danny blamed it on his boyish face.

Unlocking the door with a spare key, they plodded down the stairs, entangled in each other's limbs. She already had a hand in his pants, attempting to rouse him, which wasn't difficult after his involuntary celibacy.

Lifting her up by the hips, he tasted her neck.

She wrapped her legs around him and ran her hands through his tousled locks. The bitch planted a feverish kiss on his mouth, delicate flesh mingled with the chemical tang of drugs.

Danny grabbed her hair and pulled back, revealing her throat. She moaned, breath coming in ragged gasps as her eyes flashed with real desire. He flung her to the bed and twisted her hips to match his.

He plunged into her, losing more of himself than he cared to admit after so long without a bitch.

The farm was painstakingly without any decent tail to chase, nothing worth the string of problems that came with the mating part, at least.

The bitch beneath him gasped when he went too hard, but he didn't mind her frail protests. Her arms were spindly and weak, no challenge to him, of all creatures. If he'd bothered to pay attention, he might have thought she was cute, beneath all the makeup. But it wasn't his primary head he was thinking with, under the circumstances.

Danny tossed her to one side, so he could get better leverage. She shouted for him to stop, so he closed her throat with a firm grip. It wouldn't do to have the humans catching onto the hideout. He had enough dealings with them as it were, with agent K breathing down his neck.

Something the bitch said brought him back to the current moment as he finished inside her.

"Motherfucker!" She yanked away from him in tears, shoving a finger into his chest. "You owe me double. I don't do assplay, you piece of shit!"

Her volume grated against the bliss of his release.

Danny took hold of her neck and pushed her to the bed. "Shut the fuck up," he hissed in her ear, squeezing so the tender pink of her cheeks faded to blue. Fur bristled on his arms and a frightened gleam in her eye told him she finally realized what she'd gotten herself into.

He watched with delicious fascination as she mouthed one final plea, the crunch of her neck stealing the light from her eyes.

Danny left her lifeless form on the bed to finagle with his belt buckle. Glancing back at the corpse, he scoffed before stretching and pacing the tiny safe-house.

The lay would do. For a while, at least.

Chapter 6

After five miles of turbulent back roads, Kane parked the behemoth behind a mossy old shed.

We rounded a corner and a sprawling farmhouse came into view, teeming with life. From my vantage point, I could see a wide kitchen window, with strangers moving about within.

A group of kids sat in a circle on the lawn, chanting something in unison.

"...*doubled and bound. 'Neath Beltane's blooded moon...*" One of the children froze and glanced our way. "Kane!" he shrieked, causing the others to look as well.

They stopped their strange game and barreled at us, making me take a step back before pausing, realizing they weren't coming at me. Kane pretended to fall as the children swarmed him excitably.

He sat up from the pile and hoisted one onto his lap. The others gathered around close. A girl grabbed his ponytail with chubby, pink fingers. "Remember to be on your best behavior while we have guests," he chided. "Don't fight. Izzy, that means you. And keep out of the shed. It's dangerous."

The longer I watched, the less they appeared to be ordinary children. A tail poked from the seat of a young boy's overalls, wagging excitedly. One of the girls glanced up at me, flashing a toothy grin. The boy on Kane's lap even stared at me with curious, yellow eyes.

"…alright, go play!" He shooed them off so they bolted into the yard as one of the girls dragged the littlest one away. He crossed his arms contentedly and stood beside me. "They're a handful but it's amazing watching them grow up together. Not everyone is lucky enough to live around other shifters."

I eyed the farmhouse with anticipation, then him, but kept my reservations to myself. "You're good with them."

Kane led me up the stairs. "I have to be, it's my job." Putting his hand on the door, he paused. "Are you ready?"

At the restaurant, the prospect seemed so far away, but these were *werewolves*. Nothing would prepare me for this encounter. "As I'll ever be."

"Say the word, and I'll take you straight back to the apartment. No questions asked."

I nodded, uncertainty making my stomach hurt. "Okay."

He opened the door and a flood of very ordinary human chatter swallowed us up.

Kane led me to a woman with a solid build and mouse brown hair who was cutting slabs of meat, her hands covered in juices. His voice rose easily over the noise. "Amy, meet Serena. She keeps the food hot and the table set."

Serena flashed me a sincere smile. "Good to meet you, Amy." She dangled her hands over a cutting board. "I'd shake, but I don't think you'd appreciate it!"

I dipped my head and smiled back, caught off-guard by the unexpected warmth. "No worries. Nice to meet you."

A brawny man with a buzz-cut slid past with a plate of steaming food.

"That's Kyren, my second." Kane pointed. "You can meet him during lunch." A lean, older man with dark skin and graying curls nearly disappeared as well, but Kane caught his shoulder. "Gary, remember Amy? She decided to drop by and meet everyone."

Gary shifted a tray to one arm, offering his hand in welcome. "Good to have you."

I returned the shake firmly. "Thanks."

While the others were busy setting up lunch, Kane weaved through the house with experience. I followed, though not quite so gracefully as my host.

He stopped a stout woman with a child on her hip. "Crystal, this is Amy."

Crystal's eyes widened. "Amy!" She beamed up at me, her golden skin casting a beautiful contrast against her perfect teeth. She rubbed my arm with a free hand. "Welcome! I've been wondering if you'd take up his offer. How are you feeling?"

I had to be honest. "It's a lot but, um, not what I expected."

"Well, I'm so glad you could make it." She squeezed my shoulder. The child in her arms bucked impatiently and scrambled off her. Crystal chased after him. "Xander!"

Kane glanced at me with a wry smile as we exited the kitchen. "What do you think so far?"

"I don't know. Everyone's really nice." *Too nice.* "I figured it'd be strange, but it isn't. Other than the fact that kid had a tail."

He didn't answer right away, stroking his goatee thoughtfully. "They can't control the transition yet. It's attached to their emotions. Once they hit puberty, they'll change at-will, which is something you can learn when you're ready."

I considered it, following him down the hall towards the living room. A handful of people were lounging around, watching 'Storm of the Century' on a massive flat screen that hung over the fireplace.

Kane's mere presence tore their attention from the screen. "Johnny, stop the movie for a moment."

A gangly, dark haired teen hit pause, but continued typing on a laptop. The others glanced between me and Kane with curiosity; all but one man, who snored soundly on the couch.

"Jean," Kane said, "has second shift gone out?"

"Yeah," a tall, lean man answered. "They left a few hours ago, Greg's leading. They should be back soon."

"Good." He paused, turning to me. "Everyone, I'd like you to meet Amy. Why don't you introduce yourselves?"

A woman in her mid-sixties with cropped white hair answered first with a wave. "Moira."

An elegant blonde raised her hand. "Emily."

"Johnny." The dark-haired kid spoke, glancing up from his typing for only a second before continuing his work.

"Jean, obviously." He gave a sheepish nod. "And this useless lout here is Danny." He elbowed his sleeping companion, causing him to loll into the couch.

I acknowledged each with what I hoped was a pleasant smile. "Nice to meet you all."

They murmured a response.

Kane dipped his head. "Thanks, guys." The movie resumed as we departed. He led me back through the hall at a slower pace. "Now you've almost met everyone, except the scouting group – they'll be back after lunch – and Aurora, my sister. She's around somewhere."

"Why do you need a scouting group?"

He opened another door that led into a dining room, the table laden with food. He lounged in the end chair, offering the seat to his right. "Remember I said there are other species?"

I slid in next to him, waiting for him to continue.

"There have been abominations roaming the woods, 'parasites', is what the scientists called them. They're humans that'd been rounded up and injected with something that kills the person and leaves a bloodthirsty shell. Parasites deteriorate rapidly, but they're strong and fast during their first month. They'll attack anything living if given the chance. So, we patrol the perimeter to keep them away from the farm."

"Why haven't we heard about this on the news?"

"Parasites are new, and it's not widespread. But whoever's doing it I expect intends to use it as a bioweapon. We're just seeing the failed experiments."

"Do you know where they're coming from?"

Kane's eyes darkened as he looked away. "No."

"Oh," I mouthed.

The silence didn't last long as a young woman – no older than sixteen with chestnut hair and a slim build – swung into the room. She froze upon seeing me, her sharp blue eyes flashed with resentment. There was no doubt who her brother was.

Kane's sullen mood broke. "Aurora, there you are. I wondered where you ran off to. Meet Amy."

She stood beside Kane as he wrapped an arm around her. "*Another* mutt?"

"Don't be rude." He squeezed her in warning, then glanced to me. "Amy, I'm sorry. This is my sister. She's all bark."

Aurora yanked from his grasp. "Yeah *right*," she spat, glaring at me. "Keep away from me, bitch, or you'll find out exactly how hard I bite." She stormed into the hallway, slamming the door on the way out.

Kane looked as if he wanted to pursue, but didn't. Instead, he shook his head. "Don't mind her. She has trouble adjusting to change. I'll talk with her later."

I shrugged, not wanting to be a source of dissent. "You don't have to do that. I get it."

He looked at me with consideration before Gary and Crystal came in with heaping plates of food. A dinner bell rang in the distance, and, for the second time today, I was in front of a feast.

The group filed in. Emily entered with the yellow-eyed boy on her hip as two more children dodged around the adults' legs and dashed under the table.

Friendly chatter blossomed along with a medley of aromas. Despite having eaten more than my fill at Bob's, I was already growing peckish again.

They settled in and waited for Kane to give the go-ahead.

He leaned up and looked around the table as they hushed. "As always, we have Serena to thank for this amazing spread."

Serena smiled, then her face went rigid in horror. "I forgot the drinks!"

Throwing her chair back, she dashed out of the room as lighthearted laughter was shared around the table.

"While she's getting those, I want you to welcome Amy, who's been a sport through the last twenty-four hours. The first change isn't easy, and being introduced to this new life suddenly can be daunting, as some of you understand. But she decided to meet you, so it's up to you assholes not to scare her off before dessert."

He pointed a fork at them in a mock threat. As they laughed again, I noticed Aurora hadn't joined us yet.

"Second shift will be back after lunch with an updated report on the perimeter. In the meantime, let's not waste Serena's hard work, and eat!"

A hungry tension snapped and everyone flew into action, distributing heaps of food onto each other's' plates. Chairs squealed against the tile floor and plates chimed with the rush.

The bounty waned with each oversized serving. I swiped a couple of ribs and chewed on the tender meat.

Serena reemerged with a cooler full of drinks.

Gary helped with the distribution, tossing me a bottle of water. I plucked it from the air and tipped it at him.

Aurora snuck in, sliding into the seat next to Johnny and stealing one of his drumsticks. He called out for a beer, which sailed through the air. Johnny caught it and cracked the top open on the table, chugging half before refilling his plate.

I leaned closer to Kane. "What's he doing with a beer?"

He laughed, passing a bowl of broccoli to Moira. "I told you, we don't get drunk easily. One's not going to cut it. And besides, he's just trying to impress Aurora."

"You're fine with that?"

Confusion crossed his face, then realization. "Shifters mate for life. They'll never be with anyone else." At my blank stare, an amused smile formed. "Don't worry, you'll get the hang of how things are around the farm."

I tore a strip of meat off the bone, considering what he'd told me.

The children, well-fed and sleepy, crawled under the table. The littlest boy passed out in Crystal's arms, and a meditative quiet settled over the group.

My expectations were so far from the truth, I almost laughed out loud.

They'd only been friendly and inclusive, something I was unaccustomed to. *Remember what happens when you trust people.* The thought invaded my peace of mind, tearing that little shred of hope from me.

I stood from the table, squealing my chair by accident. "Where's your restroom?"

Kane and the others glanced up at me. "Down the hall on your left." His gaze followed me out the door as I left, trying in vain to settle my nerves.

Missing the bathroom, I opened the door to a bedroom and a closet. I found it on the third try and locked the door behind me. Sitting on the edge of the tub, I ran a hand through my hair and debated how the hell I'd gotten here.

I couldn't stay.

This simply wasn't my world. And even if I did, it always ended badly. As the spiraling thoughts cycled, I considered the next step. I could ask Kane to drive me home. They all knew I didn't belong, nice as they were.

I could sneak out before they thought to check on me, but unless I stole a car, I was too far from the city and the comfort of my apartment.

No. I'd own up to it and ask after lunch.

My heart performed backflips as I emerged from the bathroom. I'd never considered trying to escape paradise adjacent. But here I was.

Thankfully no one looked up from their plates when I returned. I attempted to look – if not ecstatic – then at least not completely miserable. If leaving was the right decision, then why did I feel so awful about it?

Soon enough, they began excusing themselves from the table, offering parting words of encouragement to me. They had no idea how much harder that was making my choice to leave.

Johnny and Aurora adjourned to the porch, hand-in-hand as Crystal and Emily put the little ones to bed. Moira offered to make Serena some tea as the men meandered into the living room. The man they called Danny snuck a lingering glance on the way out, a smile forming when our eyes met.

They left Kane and me to clean up the mess.

"What do you think?" he asked.

I stacked the plates, doing my best not to make them rattle. "They're nice. I'm surprised. I never had anything like this when I was, um- sorry, it's a lot to get used to."

He scraped leftovers into an empty bowl. "Sure. I can get Danny to help with the cleanup, if you'd prefer to explore the farm. You're my guest, after all."

"No, it's okay." Where had my spine gone? *Spit it out, girl.* "I just-"

As Kane was about to interject, something exploded through the sliding glass door. A bloody half-wolf landed on the shards, oozing blood from many lacerations. His face was almost sheared off as well, leaving a raw mask of exposed bone on the left side.

Kane bolted into action. "Moira!" he shouted, rolling the stranger over.

Moira barged into the room. "Oh, my goodness." She knelt by the injured man. Kane stood, smeared in black ooze, and bolted out the broken frame without a backwards glance.

The others elbowed into the room, Emily and Serena among them. Jean held Crystal as they watched Moira tend to the man. She touched his face and a gentle glow pulsed from her fingertips to the man's ruined flesh.

Before my eyes, the skin flapped back over the wound, healing in a matter of seconds. Kyren rushed in and eased the man into his arms, murmuring reassurances to his mate.

Then Kane returned, dragging a weathered old man inside. He was in worse condition than Kyren's mate. Moira finished her healing and helped ease the second victim against the wall. The old man murmured something to her, and she nodded with a stern frown. She healed his injuries with a touch.

Frozen to the spot, I was struck dumb by how quickly shit hit the fan.

I glanced at Kane, who'd stood to his full height.

Any humor or kindness vanished, replaced by a fierce scowl that left no room for negotiation.

And, without another word to anyone, he stepped outside.

When the men's injuries were tended, Moira stood as well. Her frame was heavy with an invisible burden as she pulled Emily into the hallway, out of sight.

A mournful wail shattered the stillness of the house.

Chapter 7

Gabriel Ryker struck a stick against the tent pole. "Again!"

Celeste and her sparring partner matched up. She readied herself to dodge the barrage of attacks. Her adversary was huge, and fast, despite his size. It took all of her focus not to be at the mercy of his claws. Her father never let them go easy.

That defeats the purpose, he'd said.

The brute came forward with a cocky grin. "What's wrong, little girl? Had enough?"

Celeste allowed her claws to slide out and dodged the obvious attack, propelling off his momentum. "Just getting started." It was a lucky miss, and he knew it.

Swinging back around, he clipped her shoulder, sending her face-first into the dirt.

Dust plumed up around her, obscuring the target.

"Again!" Ryker demanded. "Use your instincts, Celeste, not your brain."

She stood and brushed off, settling into a fighting stance. In truth, she couldn't concentrate since last night, when she found out the birthmark was gone. The only reason her father kept her in the first place, and it had disappeared.

Celeste was nothing without it.

Her sparring partner clawed up, ready for another go. If she botched this, her father would not give her another chance, 'chosen one' or not.

Fear gripped her as she let out a guttural scream, throwing the cretin off-guard. Flipping onto his shoulders, she clamped his fat head between her thighs and flung him to the ground. She landed and assessed her victory, but a leg swept her off her feet.

Then an elbow came down on her jaw, sending her reeling into the void.

*

Celeste woke in her own tent with a weathered medicine woman holding a bag of herbs to the throbbing face.

Ryker loomed over her and crossed his arms. "Your technique is sloppy."

Sitting up, her head throbbed, but she wouldn't let him know that. "I'm sorry, sir, I'll practice more." She'd learned from an early age not to acknowledge the pain.

He waved the medicine woman away, who gathered her supplies and left. When they were alone, Ryker stared down at her with utter scrutiny. "What aren't you telling me?"

"Nothing. I- it's just girl stuff. I'll feel better next week."

"There isn't much time, Celeste. Convergence is approaching and you need to be battle-ready." He opened the tent door. "Strategy in the war tent. One hour."

At least he hadn't asked to see the mark. She breathed a sigh of relief, but she couldn't keep this secret for long.

Chapter 8

When Kane disappeared, I was shown to the guest bedroom. I collapsed on the bed as Moira asked if I needed anything.

"I'm fine, thanks," I murmured into the pillow.

She lingered in the doorway. "Serena and I will be in the kitchen if you change your mind."

After their sudden loss, I thought it best not to bother them.

Get out while you can. I groaned and rolled onto my back. *How dare he leave you alone in a house full of strangers.* "How dare *you*." I shot back to the empty space, growing weary of the internal harassment. The pack had lost three of its members today, Emily's husband and Johnny's father among them.

My presence here only complicated matters, but I wasn't going to let my fear get the best of me, and decided to accept their hospitality. I stretched to relieve the tightness in my limbs and rolled out of bed, peering down the hallway.

Hopefully, they'd let me use their shower.

No one was in sight, but hushed voices resonated from the kitchen. "… is out there. I'm worried."

"Kyren thinks we should send a search party, but it's too dangerous. He's still upset about Max," Moira responded. "I convinced him to wait until morning."

It was Serena who answered. "How are they doing?"

"They'll survive. Max will be fine, but Solice- he's older. It will take a greater toll on him. After this, I won't permit him to go on another shift." A pause. "How are *you* doing?"

Another pause, followed by the clunk of a mug. "Greg has to be alive out there somewhere. I can't imagine him not coming back. He's always- always so strong-"

I eased into the hall, closer to the archway. One of the floorboards creaked, and both women stopped talking.

Moira spoke first. "Amy? Is that you?"

Busted, I stepped into the doorway, shrouded in guilt. "Sorry. Do you mind if I take a shower?"

Serena offered a weak smile. "Sure." She led me to a linen closet and handed me a towel. "There's a hamper and fresh clothes in your room. Help yourself to whatever you need."

"Thanks."

She nodded with a sniff and returned to the kitchen.

I slipped into the bathroom and set the water on high. The last twenty-four hours hadn't been kind and my body ached something awful.

The rhythmic tempo of the showerhead soothed the tension and washed away the bar grime. After sudsing and rinsing, I noticed a strange mark on my inner forearm. Scratching it only irritated the discolored skin. It looked like a birthmark, but I didn't have a birthmark.

Washing the area didn't cure the blemish either, only making it angrier. What looked like a mole was encircled by a splotch of dark skin that resembled a tapered hourglass. I'd have thought the worst if it weren't so symmetrical.

Giving up on the anomaly, I stepped out of the shower and dried off.

With the towel wrapped securely around me, I dashed to the spare bedroom and tossed the dirty clothes in the hamper. A dresser full of simple shirts and pants were already stocked, just like Serena said. I chose a pair at random and slid them on before the warmth evaporated from my core. Warm and clean, I nestled into the blankets, considering.

Maybe it wouldn't be so bad to stay *one* night.

Chapter 9

Ryker's piercing stare bore into Celeste. He'd confronted her after the lessons in the war tent, and she didn't figure he was in a talkative mood. "Is there something you wanted to tell me?"

Celeste shifted, keeping her gaze low, and her hopes lower. "What do you mean, sir?"

He stood and rounded the desk, his presence boring down on her. "Is there something I should know?" Ryker brushed a lock of her golden hair back. "You wouldn't lie to your old man, now, would you?"

Her lip trembled and she had to spill the secret to her father, her alpha. "I'm so sorry, father. I didn't mean to hide it. I- my birthmark disappeared, I thought you'd get rid of me! I just want to be useful to you."

Ryker placed a heavy hand on her shoulder, weighed down by the silence that followed her admission. When he finally spoke, she could breathe again. "You're still useful to me."

Tears sprang to her eyes and she looked up at him in surprise. "You're not upset?"

His features softened into something almost paternal. "I'm only upset you didn't trust me. I thought we were closer than that, my girl."

"We are, father!" she countered, then quieted her tone. She was an idiot to think he wouldn't find out. "I didn't mean to keep it to myself, I just- didn't know how to tell you."

He wiped an errant tear from her cheek. "My sweet girl, my sweet, *stupid* girl. Do you think me so callous?" He wrapped her in a tight embrace that smelled of pine and engine oil.

Celeste folded into the hug with a relieved sob.

"No," she whispered, almost believing it. "Of course not."

"Glad to hear it," The words radiated into her skull. Releasing her, he gripped her shoulders. "As of today, you must work twice as hard. If you are not the conduit, then your sister is, and we'll need you in prime shape."

"*Her?*" Celeste's nose wrinkled. "She's just a human!"

Ryker shook his head. "Not anymore. She changed for the first time last evening. We'll need her brought back in one piece, along with the bloodhound protecting her. You're the lucky one, Celeste."

"Why, father?"

"Because the conduit has to die."

Chapter 10

A baying howl woke me from sleep.

Through the window, the sky hung heavy with stars, no hint of dawn on the horizon. My dreams dissipated in the dim light as reality came rushing back.

Another howl echoed across the field. High-pitched yips joined in, but much closer. I jumped out of bed, bolted down the hall, and slid out the broken side door.

The moonlight illuminated the field as a huge figure ambled out of the gloom, dragging behind it a heavy burden. Two creatures blitzed past me and bounded off the porch, following several others who were already en-route.

Four stood on hind legs and relieved the burden, dragging several loads to the house. When they were close, I recognized Kyren, Gary, Jean, and Crystal, all brazenly nude. They laid three corpses on the lawn with care.

Moira ran by me and knelt by the bodies.

The huge bipedal wolf limped behind them, dropping four round objects to the ground. One rolled away from the others, revealing sunken eyes and needling teeth. Severed heads, I realized in my shock.

I glanced up the creature and fell into icy blue depths. "Kane," I said breathlessly. Disbelief and caution mingled as I eyed his hulking form. His long black ears flicked as he watched me with a curious scrutiny.

A blonde wolf collapsed onto one of the mangled corpses, its bones cracked and fur shed to reveal a naked, weeping Emily, who cradled her dead husband. She wailed and stroked the body's chestnut hair, curling over him defensively. Two pups snuggled beside her, yipping and whining.

Another wolf emerged from the house, thin and gangly with a shocking white stripe along its spine, in contrast with a midnight coat. It advanced upon one of the corpses and let out a shuddering chirrup from its throat. A caramel brown wolf nuzzled the jittery shifter's head.

The third body lay untouched.

Kane's voice resonated with regret. "I'm sorry for leaving so abruptly."

I tore my gaze from the scene and met his eyes. He was human again, spattered in a mixture of blood and black ooze. Without a shirt, his massive physique was intimidating, and more than a little distracting.

"But you came back." I couldn't blame him for taking care of his family. Though his second form was alarming, it didn't frighten me quite the way I expected it to. "What happened?"

"Parasites." He pointed at the heads. "They ambushed the scouting group. I killed a few, but there are still more in the woods. We'll discuss a raid team soon, to put the rest out of their misery." The next question came suddenly. "Did you want me to drive you home?"

Yesterday, I would have jumped at the offer. Now, it only served to compound my self-doubt. "I can go if it's easier. You have a lot to deal with, and I'll only get in the way."

Kane glanced down at me. "You're welcome here, Amy. Please don't think I'm trying to push you out."

My cheeks burned as I shot him a melancholy smile. "Are you sure about that?"

He offered a nod, the pain never leaving his eyes. "Training starts tomorrow, if you're staying."

Kane left to help Kyren and Jean dig graves for the fallen before I could give him an answer. I swallowed back a retort as I watched Moira console the grieving.

A clanging noise drew me to the kitchen, where Serena was digging leftovers out of the fridge. "Do you want help?"

She almost dropped the pan from her hands in surprise, eyes bloodshot from crying. "Amy." She took a breath and set down the tray, whisking a tear away. "Sure, would you take these outside?"

I obliged, carrying the food to the deck. She brought out the utensils and plates, setting them to the side. "Sorry they're cold, but help yourself." Serena ducked into the kitchen again, seeming to avoid further conversation.

The sky blushed with the coming sunrise and birds trilled their jubilant song. As the hazy glow eased over the horizon, a hand clamped over my shoulder, startling me.

"So, you're the fresh meat." An unfamiliar, husky voice spoke too close, the owner leaning in and inhaling. "You don't smell like a shifter."

I turned, tearing away from him. "What the *fuck* are you doing?" I hissed, facing the fair-haired Danny.

My arm's prickled, little hairs receding into my pores.

Had I come so close to changing?

"Sensitive much? Can't even take a joke. Mutts are so high strung, nowadays." His pale hazel eyes glanced to the field. "Not like the natural-born, at least *they* have some grace."

I kept my voice low. "Shove it up your ass." I refused to make a scene because of him. "Touch me again and I'll keep that hand."

His long-toothed smile set me on edge. "I'm only kidding, Amy." His looming figure fell into a submissive cower suddenly, as if I'd hit him. "Don't hurt me!"

"Danny, you skite." Gary appeared out of nowhere and grabbed him by the collar, pulling him close. "Is this how you treat our guests? Knock this shit off." Their noses almost touched, then he shoved him back. "I know what you're up to."

Running a hand through his tousled hair, Danny made for a quick exit, avoiding Moira's pointed stare.

She followed him into the house.

"He's a right git," Gary conceded. "Don't let him get away with anything, he needs to learn his place. Danny's only been here about a month."

"Thanks." I glanced over the field at the pre-dawn hustle. "But I can take care of myself."

He shrugged, helping himself to leftovers. "Never hurts to have allies. We're stronger as a pack."

I took a drumstick to ease my stomach, watching the men dig. They were almost finished with the plots.

A despondent Emily clung to her dead husband, refusing to part with him even as Crystal and Kyren tried reasoning with her. She fought until Kane intervened, pulling her lean frame away and wrapping her in a bedsheet. He whispered something to her until she collapsed against him, sobbing uncontrollably.

Kyren folded the body into a shroud, blood soaking the tan linen. The bodies were laid out next to their designated holes as the diggers finished.

Once Emily could stand on her own, Moira – who'd reemerged from the house – sat on the grass and simply held her. Emily clutched her pups close. The little girl changed back and sobbed with her mother.

Kane stood by the bodies as the pack gathered around. I sat up to hear what he had to say, feeling like an intruder in their very intimate moment of loss. "David, Gregory, and Mortimer were some of our best. They gave everything to defend us, and we will not let their sacrifice be in vain. Johnny, Serena, Emily, Izzy, Riley: you've suffered a great loss, but as they were your family, you are ours. We can protect you as fiercely as they did. However, we also know there is nothing that can replace a Father, a Husband, or a Mate."

Emily buried her face in Moira's shoulder, heaving with the effort of crying.

Kane nodded to Jean and Kyren, who lowered each body into the ground. The white-striped wolf lunged at one of the graves. Kane caught him midair and held him tight until the shifter rested its jaw on his shoulder and whimpered.

With all others accounted for, I realized it must be Johnny.

"What about the parasites?" someone asked.

A murmur of agreement went around the group.

"We have to attack them directly," Kane announced. "Even if the lab hasn't been found, we can destroy the rest that are stalking the woods. It's going to take most of the able-bodied fighters, and it will leave the farm vulnerable. But if we split up evenly, we'll risk a weak attack."

"What if the men go?" Danny said, speaking from the edge of the crowd. "Leave the women and children. They'll be fine for one night, don't you think?"

His sentiment left the others in a strained silence.

Moira whipped her head in his direction. "You mean to say we can't fight?"

Danny looked her up and down. "I *meant* to say that you wouldn't stand a chance against me, one-on-one."

Moira closed her eyes for a second, shaking her head slightly. "I may be an old shifter but I will lay you out if I have to prove a point."

He grinned, upper lip curling. "Bring it, bitch."

"*Danny.*" Kane growled, "quit it, or I'll let Moira keep your bits in a jar."

"Sorry, boss." His head dropped to his chest, making a point to say nothing more.

74

"Kane," Jean said solemnly. "The graves are ready."

He waved over Emily and Serena, Johnny already by his side. "Would you do the honors?"

Emily was held upright as she broke down again. Jean offered her a fistful of dirt, which she tossed onto the shrouded corpse. The brunette wolf stood, fur falling away to reveal Aurora. She comforted Johnny as he did the same to his father's grave. Serena was the last, sprinkling the soil and quickly walking away. She held a hand over her mouth and watched the sunrise from a distance.

Kane comforted them, sorrow wrinkling his brow.

My first encounter with him was less than ideal. I had been completely rude and misunderstood his intentions. But he'd taken it in stride and even welcomed me into his home, despite my bad attitude.

Weighing the risks, I gazed at their tight-knit group.

If I accepted his offer, my life would change forever, beyond anything I could imagine. Standing on the fringe of Kane's world was thrilling, and a little frightening. What could I become here on the farm?

I had to take the leap and find out.

Chapter 11

"Doctor Casey, the patient is suffering from blunt abdominal trauma of the peritoneal wall. There's not much time left," someone whispered next to agent Lazaro. "We've given him seven transfusions already and can't afford another one. Doctor Warren-"

"No one asked for your opinion. I'm waiting to hear back from headquarters." A disgruntled voice interrupted the nurse. "What's the point of performing surgery on a dead man? I will not waste my time or skill unless the director demands it."

"But, sir-"

"You're dismissed." The doctor ended the nurse's protest.

Silence filled the space. Lazaro couldn't see or move as if he'd been blindfolded. He knew Dr. Casey was in the room, maybe even watching him.

A ruffle of papers betrayed the man's location: ten feet to the left, likely perusing chart notes without a care in the world.

He's right, Lazaro thought, unable to feel his body. *I am a dead man.*

*

Cool air drifted across his skin. He was on the move, but still in bed, and still blind. A touch of cold metal against his chest brought his focus to the timid heartbeat beneath.

"85 over 57. We can't allow for a blood sample, doctor."

Someone rotated the bed and continued forward, disorienting Lazaro.

"I need to get one," a woman's melodic voice insisted. "I'm here on the director's orders. Everyone here is in danger if I don't get that sample."

A pause. "Is it a bloodborne pathogen?"

"Possibly."

The nurse sighed. "We'll ask the doctor in the operating room."

"Thank you."

He sat in silence the rest of the journey, but Lazaro sensed a warm presence to his right.

A set of doors clunked open, his bed turned one more time, and stopped. Lazaro was overwhelmed by a wave of seasickness.

"I need a sample, doctor. Five milliliters and I'll be out of your hair. I can call in the results once I get them. Should take about an hour."

"Get what you need, Samantha." Dr. Casey was as impatient with his colleagues as he was with his staff. "Until we know the results, take all safety precautions," he lectured to a hidden audience. "Caps, masks, gowns, gloves, booties. Take them off when you leave, put new ones on when you come in. This is basic undergrad shit. You don't want what this guy might have. And get the anesthesiologist."

"Agent," the woman's voice whispered. "I don't know if you can hear me, but I'm going to draw a blood sample from you. You're going to feel a little pinch on your inner right arm."

As promised, a bee sting pricked his skin.

"Very good," she said. "You're doing great. Dr. Casey is going to take care of you. He's the best in the state." Someone lifted the blinder off his face. Through his watery vision, he saw a set of intense green eyes, haloed in red fire.

"Morgan Lazaro." A droning male voice interrupted his thoughts, while a shiny bald head obscured his view. "I'm going to put you under so the doctor can fix you up. Take a deep breath as I count." The anesthesiologist counted down. "Ten, nine, eight-"

Seven...

Six...

Chapter 12

I'm behind the counter at the bar. Matt is yelling and I can't focus. He's furious at me, hates me, even, and I can't understand it. I push past him, stumbling out the back door. A forest grows where it shouldn't, overtaking the city.

And then darkness creeps in.

Cold rain patters my skin as the air grows frigid.

I am alone, searching for anyone in this gloom. A crack of thunder is a voice so low, I strain to understand the words.

I'm lost, groping for a familiar shape in the darkness.

A pulse of light appears, glowing gently at the edge of my vision. It grows brighter with each passing second, its radiance mesmerizing. As I peer into its brilliant fractals, I notice a figure begin to take shape.

Before I can reach for it, a stabbing pain erupts in my stomach. A blade of pure midnight is buried in my gut. I grab the hilt and pull…

The pain jolted me from sleep.

Gasping, I clutched at my belly: no knife, only the throb of hunger in my gut. Beads of sweat had condensed on my forehead. I wiped them away and sat up.

Back in the unfamiliar bed, I was safe. And starving.

The smell of bacon and eggs lingered in the air, possessing me to rise from the covers.

A clock on the nightstand read ten to three.

After the funeral, I must have passed out on a lawn chair. With growing suspicion, I realized someone had carried me back to bed. But as long as it wasn't Danny, I did my best not to brood over it too much.

Shaking the sleep from my brain, I navigated the farmhouse, narrowly avoiding a collision with the rowdy children. They giggled and chased each other down the hall.

In the dining room, Crystal implored her son to eat. "You know you like eggs! Just one more bite, then you can go play."

I ran a hand through my tangled, dark hair. "Morning."

"Afternoon." She hoisted the boy on her lap. "Help yourself. Everyone else has finished eating, except for Marty. They're so picky at this age."

Marty struggled until he slid under the table and bounded off, likely to find the other children.

She let out a sigh. "When you have kids, just have one. One's great, three's too many."

"*If* I have kids." I gave a snort, taking a seat and dishing up a plate. "My mom had two of us at the same time, I'm not going to risk it."

Her eyes went large with excitement. "Oh, you have a twin! That's neat! Do you keep in contact?"

I didn't want to talk about my sister, or any of my family, for that matter. "No, she's, um, not around anymore."

Crystal shot me a look of pity. "I'm so sorry."

"Don't worry about it. It was a long time ago." I offered a weak smile. "I'd rather forget." I used the silence as an opportunity to take a bite, balancing my hunger with the nausea that came with eating too quickly. The glass door hadn't been repaired, but was instead covered in a sheet of plastic. I pointed at the hole. "When is it going to be fixed?"

She craned her neck. "Hopefully tomorrow. They would've fixed it this morning, but the blueberries needed to be planted. How are you liking it here?"

"You're all so nice, I-" *don't deserve it.* "It was terrible, what happened."

Crystal's smile faded. "Everyone knows the risks. But still, I can't imagine what Emily's going through right now. If

I lost Jean, I don't know what I'd do." She touched her stomach, then shook her head, seeming at a loss for words.

"Good afternoon, Amy." Moira entered the room, rousing us from the sullen torpor. "How did you sleep?"

"Honestly?" Half a laugh escaped me. "I don't remember. I didn't realize I'd drifted off."

She nodded, taking a seat. "Not surprised. Your energy will be up and down for a while, until you get used to changing. You showed Danny a bit of fur last night, if I recall."

I blushed out of lingering embarrassment. "He knows how to get under your skin, doesn't he?"

"Danny rubs everyone the wrong way. He's still adjusting to this life." Moira sat next to me and patted my arm. "I wouldn't put too much thought to it. Let us know if he does it again."

I nodded, chewing on a strip of bacon.

She sat up straighter, as if she was about to say something important. "Oh, before I forget: Kane wanted you to meet him on the field when you're done eating. After yesterday, we decided it's best you train sooner rather than later."

I gulped involuntarily, the bacon clawing its way down my throat. "Right."

"Don't be worried, dear." Moira's lined face broke into a smile. "It's a simple thing to change. You'll be fine."

I lost my appetite suddenly, pushing away the last of my food. "Where is he?"

Without hesitation, both women pointed towards the field where, sure enough, Kane was uprooting a particularly large stump from the ground.

"Good luck," Crystal said.

"Thanks." I slid the broken frame open, and stood on the porch. I was wholly unprepared as I took a shallow breath and descended the porch steps.

Kane had his back to me, easing the troublesome root out with the tip of his shovel.

"Moira said to meet you after I ate."

He struck the sharp end into the ground and turned to me, looking wholly amused. "You're up early."

I glared at him.

He leaned against the handle. "I hope you got enough to eat. You're going to need the fuel." Kane strode to the garage and picked up a leaking bag, a handful of pikes, and a mallet. "C'mon. We'll kill two birds with one stone."

Following him, I pointed to the bag. "What's that?"

"They're parasite heads."

A black ooze leaked out of the bag, becoming sinister. I did my best to avoid the stray drops that hit the earth with each jostle. "What are you going to do with them?"

"We'll be piking them up around the territory, so the other parasites are less likely to cross into it. Then I'll teach you how to change."

Kane led me deep into the woods. He didn't acknowledge, but I couldn't help eyeing him. His mere size was enough to intimidate most men, standing at least a head taller than everyone in the house. *Don't let your guard down.*

After a good ten minutes of silence, I had to break it. "Is all of this your property?"

He pointed deeper into the woods. "I own most of this up to the National forest but we haven't been able to enjoy it since the parasites showed up a few months ago." Kane pointed again, but to the left. "Do you see that trail?"

I pretended to.

"That's the path we take during the shift runs. We've expanded the route recently to push the parasites further into the woods, but they're getting smarter." He trudged on.

"This is all your land?"

"It was my father's." He seemed to consider something. "After he died, I was the beneficiary. The land and all its rights are mine. We've owned this property for four generations." Finally arriving at some invisible edge, Kane tossed me a pike and hammer. "Nail that in a foot deep." He said, opening the bag and removing a head.

I drove the stake into the ground.

Kane crushed the head onto the end of the stake, fluid spilling from its puckered lips.

"That is disgusting."

He picked up the bag and trotted into the woods. "Suck it up, buttercup. We've got three more."

I followed, pressed to stay close.

After each pike, he jogged a little faster, nearly losing me twice. I blamed it on his long legs.

He stopped and tossed the last pike. "Here."

I hammered it in, breathing hard.

Kane jammed the final head onto the stick. "That wasn't so bad, was it?"

I groaned as my heart still hammered away. "Oh, shove it."

"Let's try something easier." He led us away from the morbid head, its sunken eyes seemed to follow us. "It'll give you time to catch your breath." In a small clearing surrounded by saplings he pointed to the ground. "Sit."

I did as he said, crossing my legs.

He did the same. "Take a deep breath and let all your assumptions go." I rolled my eyes, then closed them, focusing on my breathing. "Don't try to feel anything. Let your heart rate slow down on its own." Kane took a big breath, himself, exhaling through his nose.

We sat quietly for a moment, the woods around us resumed the hushed melody of wild things.

I peeked at Kane, who seemed to enjoy the ambiance more than I. My breathing had finally slowed so that I could inhale without waking the dead.

A warm tingle coiled in my chest. I breathed in, and something loosened, unfolding into my limbs. Prickling overwhelmed me and I opened my eyes to look: needling fur protruded from my arms.

I gasped and stood abruptly.

My stomach lurched as the hairs retreated into my pores, almost making me reject my meager breakfast.

Kane opened his eyes and stood as well. "It only hurts when you fight. Remember, this is completely natural. Keep that in mind while we train."

I regretted the words even before they flew out of my mouth. "Easy for you to say, I'm just a mutt."

Kane's face went blank for the briefest moment, then his eyes darkened. "Where did you hear that?"

"Sorry." I burned with guilt. "Nowhere."

He grabbed me by the shoulders, his gaze searing me. "Where did you hear that, Amy?"

I glanced away with my jaw clenched. "Danny." I looked up at him. "It's not a big deal, I shouldn't have said anything."

Kane's features softened as he released me. "If second shift returned as planned, he wouldn't have had the opportunity to say that to you."

"You're not going to take it out on him?"

"Why on earth would you think that?" Some grand realization dawned on him. "No, of course not. But it sounds like you and I need to talk."

This is it, my mind piped in, *you don't belong here. They all know it.* I prepared myself for the sting of rejection, already used to its bitter taste. "About what?"

"You were abused as a kid, weren't you?"

The simplicity of his statement hit me in the gut harder than I could have anticipated. "No-" I countered, "Everything was fine. I mean, my father left, but he never hit us."

"Not all abuse is physical." His voice dropped low. "I think you know better than that."

How dare he stick his nose into my business. "Who cares?" I snapped. "And why do you, for that matter?" I stormed off in a random direction.

Leaves crunched behind me. "You're a Ryker."

I froze. No one knew my real last name, it wasn't even on my ID. I spun around, my heart leaping into my mouth. "How the fuck do you know that?"

"You have your father's dark hair." He'd stopped several feet from me. "I met him once, when I was young. My father was trying to sign a truce and Ryker refused. We met his daughter, but she was blonde." He gave me a funny look.

Celeste? I thought. *It's not possible.* "My father was a human. You don't know anything about me."

"Actually, I do." Kane's eyes were heavy with regret. "Your father was a shifter, an alpha, like me. But he was notoriously cruel to his own pack, not to mention his enemies."

I scoffed at his remark. "I grew up in the suburbs. There are plenty of Rykers. It's just a coincidence that I have the same name as some random shifter."

"Where did you live when you were five?"

I threw up a hand in defeat. "I don't fucking know! Who remembers that far back, anyway?"

A shadow crossed Kane's face. "We all do. Soldiers came after us. They murdered my parents, captured the rest of us and took us to a lab. For seven years they conducted tests, trying to find out what could kill us in an attempt to *improve* us." He cleared his throat and continued. "Hardly any packs survived intact. Ryker's was not an exception. After we escaped, rumor had it that he was killed during the raids, as well as his mate and daughter."

"That proves it, then," I said quietly. "My father left when I was eight." I failed to mention my sister, or the recurring nightmares he left behind. "I'm- sorry that happened to you."

He spared a melancholy smile. "It was a long time ago, now. Should we get on with training?"

"Only if you don't bring up the past again."

"Agreed, but this time, we're running." Kane took off, daring me to follow. I heaved and did my best to keep up. It wasn't enough. Within a minute, he'd disappeared from sight.

"Oh, god damn it!" I shouted, startling a flock of birds into flight. After running, I was exhausted and hopelessly lost. The forest was a maze without landmarks.

I sat on a fallen log, refusing to play his stupid game.

Catching my breath, the thing in my chest uncoiled again. The same, roiling force spread a tingling sensation into my fingers and toes.

A warm pulse flowed with each heartbeat as it filled my senses, unraveling. A ringing deafened me, as my spine bent forward on its own accord and threw me to my hands and knees. I gasped as light sent a delicious ripple down my spine.

I lost focus, concerned only for the coursing rhythm within me as I curled into a ball. My clothes tightened against my skin before bursting open, unable to contain this new form.

As bones shifted and grew, the light eased my transition, making it bearable.

Soon, the ringing faded and my vision returned, but different. There were more colors than I could name.

The forest was raucous as I stood on four legs instead of two. What was once my fingers flexed into the silken soil, the air pungent with many odors. With this new vision, I saw fresh footprints retreating deeper into the woods.

I perked up and listened. There was a creature nearby, breathing loudly. Something watched me from behind, but as I turned around, it slipped away. It did, however, leave a trail.

Dashing through the trees, I pursued my quarry.

Running in this form was fluid and graceful. The wind parted to let me pass as I chased the source of the disturbance.

As the trees gave way, I zeroed in on my target and collided into his back. As he fell, he pivoted and shielded his vitals with an arm. I latched onto it. A growl escaped my throat as my quarry held a firm hand to my breastbone.

"Amy," Kane commanded, "stop."

Staring into those cold, blue eyes roused me from my instincts. I let go and scrambled off him, sitting several paces away on a grassy patch.

He sat up and brushed himself off, laughing at the indents I'd made in his arm. "That was incredible, especially for a first time!"

I let out a low whine in a futile attempt to speak.

"Changing back is easier." He crossed his legs. "The energy that stretched from your center needs to constrict again. It wants to return, like a rubber band."

My pores bristled as I inhaled, the glow contracting to a singular point in my chest. Thousands of needles pierced me as my bones cracked and reformed into something familiar.

Sitting on the forest floor, I was human again.

Modesty caught up with me. "Turn around!" I shrieked, covering myself.

Kane smirked as he did so, tugging his shirt off and tossing it to me.

"It's not fucking funny." I pulled the shirt over my head. It smelled like him. "You didn't tell me that would happen."

He turned back cautiously, peeking to make sure I was covered. "It's not magic. You lost your clothes the first time as well. Someone's always running around the farm naked. Just like last night. You'll get used to it."

My heightened senses were still picking up chatter all around us. "You were loud."

"Was I?" He stole a glance. "Well, *you* were amazing. Can you tell me where the farm is from here?"

Over a hill to our left, about a mile away, familiar voices drifted through the woods.

I pointed.

"Good. I expect you won't be lost after this?"

Standing, I shook my head and dragged his shirt down to my knees.

He held out a thick arm, his bare pecs flexing with the motion. "I'd say your training was a success. Lead the way."

Walking back in silence, I brewed over wearing his shirt, mortified at what the others might think. Shoving an errant strand of hair from my face, I set my jaw.

Despite everything, I already missed cutting through the wind, bending it to my will. Kane had showed me a new world, one I couldn't deny any longer. How could I live in my cramped little apartment, knowing *this* existed inside of me?

"Thank you." I hesitated at the edge of the woods. "For everything. And, I'm sorry."

He raised that damned eyebrow of his. "For what?"

"For being a bitch, and- for trying to hit you with the bat. I sort of have a hard time trusting people."

He shot me a strong smile. "I noticed. No need to apologize."

"So, we're good?"

"We're good."

"Oh, and thanks for the shirt," I added quickly.

"Course." Kane glanced at me with amusement. "But if anyone asks, it's you who attacked *me*." He grinned at my scowl.

I punched him lightly in the arm. "I might not have thought you were a wild animal if you showered once in a while."

We passed Jean and Gary in the field, who watched us with renewed curiosity. My cheeks reddened, though I refused to be embarrassed in front of virtual strangers.

My stomach growled again. "You've got to be kidding."

"Serena should have food ready soon. It's nearly five." We stepped onto the porch together. "Go and get dressed. I'll see you at dinner." Kane watched me as I slid into the house. An ambivalent look crossed his face.

What surprised me the most was how level-headed he was. Until all hell broke loose, then he was frightening. I saw the fire in his eyes when his packmates were killed, and again today when I revealed what Danny said. There was potential inside him that scared the living shit out of me.

And, if I dared to admit it, compelled me.

I brushed off the errant notion and grabbed another pair of clothes. How could I ever be alone with him if my thoughts strayed so easily?

Kane was just a friend.

Like Matt?

I didn't believe him to be as impulsive, but it bothered me. What if he expected more from me than I had to offer? Could I refuse him if it came to that?

Would I want to?

Chapter 13

Celeste had to make the most of the shadows.

She'd known for a while, but couldn't admit it: *father has gone insane.* Stuffing the last of her clothes into a knapsack, she went over the plan again.

For most her life, she'd fooled herself into thinking he actually loved her. Over the years, however, she realized it wasn't Celeste he saw, but the fruition of his plans. Ryker's eyes were blind to anything but his great cause.

She was only a means to an end.

After living her entire life in his shadow, she was finally done. The fact remained: She wasn't the conduit, and that freed her from obligation. She hoisted the sack over her shoulder and steadied herself. "No matter what he says."

Celeste peered through the tent entrance and proceeded around the corner. Father's men would already be drunk around a campfire by that time, leaving the perimeter mostly unguarded.

Two more tents, and she'd be home free. She wanted to go to the city first, and disappear into the throng of humans.

One more tent was pushed up against the woods. Celeste hung a left, then a quick right into the thicket. She pushed through the brambles and glanced up at the trail ahead.

Her heart skipped a beat.

Ryker stood in the shadows at the forest's edge, with Brody and Jeb flanking him. "My darling girl."

"Father." She took a shallow breath. "I was just-"

"Leaving, I see. But so soon?"

Rather than spouting some lame excuse, her throat closed up. So, she ran instead, as her instincts told her to.

"Jeb, collect my daughter, will you?" Her father's voice was calm, collected, as if he were merely asking Jeb to gather a parcel for him.

Celeste crashed through the trees, shedding the knapsack. Falling to all fours, she dodged trunks and fallen logs. A mass knocked her off-course, smashing her into a tree. As she fell, she lashed out, shredding Jeb's cheek to ribbons.

"Fuckin' bitch!" He shoved Celeste to the soil and sat on her chest. His weight bore down on her as he wrung her neck, causing her to gasp and claw at him. Her lungs burned with the lack of oxygen.

"That's enough," Ryker commanded. The hands fell away, and she gasped for air. "Bring her to my tent."

*

Within the war tent, Ryker, several mystics, and his second-in-command convened around Celeste. Jeb still had her around the waist, with a firm hand on her bruised throat. His crotch was pressed against her rear end. If Ryker noticed, he didn't say anything.

"I'm disappointed." Her father broke the silence first. "That you, my loyal daughter, felt the need to run away."

The mystics waited in their shadowy robes. They'd always struck fear in her. Their magic was dark and evil. Even though they were shifters, it was witches who sired them. Magic was infused in a mystic's blood, allowing them the benefits of both races. The ones father entertained were for the new recruits, to help them see things… differently.

Celeste struggled against Jeb in vain.

Ryker stepped closer. "Why did you leave?"

She looked into his unfeeling eyes and yanked against her captor's grip. "What am I to you, father? Am I not your child?! You never cared about me, only your precious fucking conduit!"

"Celeste, there's a larger plan at work, here. You're a Ryker, and as such, you're expected to rise above your uncertainty and fear." He held his hand out, palm up. "We must separate the wheat from the chaff in the short time we have left, and I still have to wonder if you are fit to join me, my girl." Ryker signaled the mystics.

A withered hand slipped from a robe. She pulled away, but Jeb shoved her head forward while the creature pressed a thumb to her forehead.

The searing pain lasted only a moment, but she recoiled at the assault. Their voices barraged her mind as she bucked in Jeb's grip. Celeste cried out as an invisible hand clamped over her brain and squeezed, crumbling her resolve.

A quiet calm settled over her as Jeb let go.

When she opened her eyes, her father held his arms out to her. "You understand now?"

She fell into his warm embrace with relief. "Yes, father." Celeste smiled into his shirt. "I understand."

Chapter 14

A pair of big blue eyes stared down at me, filled with hatred. For a split second, I thought it was Kane.

But my better senses kicked in and I jolted my hips forward, throwing the intruder off the bed. Their limbs tangled in the comforter on the way down.

The figure was lighter and faster than I expected.

Aurora's mess of chestnut hair emerged from the shredded blankets. Speckled in down feathers, she stood, glaring at me. "Who gave you the right to be out so long with my brother?!"

A growl escaped my throat. "Who gave *you* the right to invade my room?"

"This is *my* house, not yours!" Aurora's body shook as fur bristled on her forearms. She leaped back on the bed, hunkering over me with the promise of murder.

The energy in my core threatened to uncoil. "Back off, Aurora." I thwapped her with a pillow, sending her reeling off the bed once again.

Aurora rose, brushing feathers off her blouse. Down littered her hair. "I've got my eye on you." She used two fingers to accentuate the point. "Back off, *slut*." She stormed out of the room with her nose in the air, leaving the door wide open.

So much for sleeping in. I plucked stray feathers out of my clothes and hair, trying to make sense of what happened.

Serena appeared almost instantly in the doorway. "Did she- oh, dear Lord, are you alright?"

"Fine, I think." I assessed the damage. "What the hell was that about?"

She picked feathers off the floorboards one-by-one. "Honestly? I don't know what's gotten into that girl."

"It's okay, I'll take care of it." I refused to let her clean up a mess I helped make. She was too-kind.

Kane's frame was silhouetted by the hall light as an amused grin spread across his face. "What happened in here?"

"You might want to ask your sister that." I folded the blanket so no more feathers escaped while Serena rifled through the closet to find a replacement.

Kane's smile fell. "Aurora did this?"

"She didn't wake the whole house?" I glanced at the clock to see it wasn't quite five. When I turned back, Kane was gone.

Serena reemerged with another comforter.

"Thanks. Where should I put this one?"

She pointed to the window. "In the trash, outside next to the garage. Go ahead and put it on top. We'll be taking a load to the dump in a few days."

Hoisting the comforter into my arms, I rounded the house and found the dumpster. I set the load on top and almost went back inside when I heard a quiet conversation around the corner.

"… you don't understand," Aurora whispered. "I don't trust her. Why don't you listen to me?"

"I am listening, but it's not your decision to make," Kane's voice answered. "You've never liked change, I get it. But she's one of us, and she needs our help."

Her voice rose with her temper. "But why *you*? Let someone else train her, or send her home!"

"What's really going on, Aurora?"

Silence lingered a moment. "I'm scared she's going to take you away from me. After our parents, after Clara- I can't lose you, too."

I dared a peek around the side. Kane knelt and hugged his sister. "Oh, Goose. No matter what happens, you're still my little sister. I'll always love you. Don't forget that."

Guilt coursed through me. I slid back in the house before they noticed. Despite her rough edges, she was only a frightened girl reacting out of impulse.

The bed was already made when I returned. Searching the house for Serena, I found her in the living room with Moira, watching an early-morning rerun.

"Thanks for making the bed. You didn't have to."

"Don't worry about it." Serena paused the show. "Your phone was going off earlier. I thought it might be important. And I could use a hand with breakfast soon if you'd like to help."

"Sure, I'll be out in a bit." I padded back to my room and saw the flashing light on my phone. My boss called twice, leaving only a single message. I hadn't missed a shift and wondered if the till had been short when we clocked out last.

"Hey Amy, I know you're not scheduled for today, but I need you to cover. Matt is a no-show and I can't get ahold of him. Call me back." My boss's voice sounded strained.

Strange, that wasn't like Matt.

I dialed him. "Fuck it."

The clock read 4:57, much earlier than he usually got up, but I needed to make sure he was alright. It rang until going to voicemail. On the second attempt, it rang twice before Matt's prerecording started.

He's bitch-buttoning me.

No one could say I didn't try. I sighed and tossed my phone on the bed. If he wanted to act like a child, he could do it alone. I had better things to do.

Brushing my hair back, I joined Serena in the kitchen.

Someone had bought three boxes of donuts and she assigned me to organize them. Staggering the variety donuts in the center, I lined the outside with a ring of plain ones.

Serena folded a pastry box and put it in a recycling bin. "Fourth shift is coming back soon. I've got Max and Solice set up in the dining room. Could you bring it out to them?" She glanced at the spread. "Those look nice. You're definitely in charge of the donuts from now on."

I shifted the tray on my hip and brought it to the dining room, setting it in front of Max and Solice. I offering some to the old man, who I hadn't been introduced to yet. He was only just recovering from the attack and barely came out of his room during the day. "Will this help?"

His vision focused on the plate, then trailed to my face, his navy eyes brightening. "You're new." Solice smiled distantly and picked a donut. "Amy, right? Moira told me about you."

My cheeks burned. "What'd she say?"

As he laughed, I saw the man he might have been in his youth. He patted my hand endearingly. "That you're a goodun. You training went well?"

"I learned how to change, I guess."

The old man sucked in a breath, causing him to wheeze. "In one day?" When he'd collected himself, he bumped Max with a thin-skinned fist. "We've got ourselves a natural talent!"

Max lifted his head long enough to shoot me an unenthusiastic smile. His hazel eyes flickered back to the table. The scars on his face were improving, but he was still pretty pale under his mop of brown curls.

I pushed the plate forward. "Did you want one, too?"

He took one, nimbler than the old man. "Thanks."

Serena arrived with a platter of meats. A few of the pack members straggled in behind her, including Kyren and a few of the children. Kane hadn't arrived, and I wondered if he was still speaking with Aurora.

One of Crystal's kids zeroed in on my donut platter. "Ooooh, what's that one?" He pointed at a jelly-filled donut, his tail wagging excitedly.

"Raspberry, I think."

"And that one?" He pointed at another. "And that one?" He made a game of it, hardly giving me time to list them off as he pointed at each.

"Which one would you like?" I interrupted his endless questioning.

He tried touching several more. "Umm."

"How about this one?" I asked with enthusiasm, offering him a plain one.

"Yeah!" He grabbed the donut and scarfed it down. "And that one?" he asked again with his mouth full. I eyed Crystal, who just stepped in the room with her youngest.

"You can have *two*, Xander." She hoisted Marty onto her lap to choose a donut. "Don't bug miss Amy, bubba."

"Fiine." He sighed and put his face to the level of the plate. "Uhm, *that* one!" He pointed at the raspberry-filled donut. I plucked it out and put it on his plate. It only sat a moment before it, too, disappeared into the boy's stomach.

Johnny and Aurora took their seats, neither glancing my way. Apparently, I was being actively shunned by the couple. Luckily for me, though, Aurora didn't seem to have much sway with the adults.

Everyone present was seated and waiting to begin. Danny, Jean, Gary, Emily, and Kane's chairs were vacant.

Serena pulled in the cooler. "Don't let it get cold, guys." She waved the hungry onlookers to serve themselves. Kyren assisted his mate in dishing up the food as Moira did the same for Solice.

I snagged an omelet and sausage, considering the rude awakening Aurora choreographed before the crack of dawn.

Between that and Matt's rebuff, I was irked.

I considered speaking with Serena about it, but decided not to air my troubles. Some part of me needed to resolve this tension between Matt and me, so I could finally close the door to my mundane life.

Kyren reached out to see how I was adjusting.

I laughed. "It's different. I'm not used to living with so many people, but it's nice. I'm enjoying it here." My sentiment drew Aurora's attention. I caught her eye, and her gaze unfocused, sliding back to Johnny with a sour expression.

Kyren didn't seem to miss the silent exchange. "If you need anything, don't be afraid to ask."

"Actually," I said, "I was hoping to pick up some things from my apartment. I didn't bring anything with me."

He nodded. "Sure. Make a list, and one of us can pick it up for you. Unless you want to go, yourself?"

Kyren's offer was too kind.

"I just need my laptop and phone charger, really, and my purse and some clothes, I guess." I missed the few items that kept me connected to the outside world. "If it's no trouble."

"Not at all." His smile was warm. "Is this afternoon soon enough?"

"That's perfect." I didn't expect him to be quite so friendly. Kyren's severe buzz and sinewy bulk gave him an edge that might deter lesser beings from messing with him.

Except for Aurora and Danny's weirdness, the pack was exceptionally kind.

But something nagged at the back of my mind, refusing to go away: *You don't belong here. They all know that.* Pessimism rose in my gut, threatening to engulf me again.

Before it dug its claws in, Kane entered the room and my focus shifted. He was an impossible creature to ignore.

His brow was stuck in a permanent furrow. "We need to deal with the parasites tonight."

Maxwell spoke first, his voice strained and low. "We did everything, but it wasn't enough. Those *things* still got them. If it wasn't for Greg, we wouldn't have made it out."

Johnny shifted in his seat, shooting Aurora a worried glance. "What are we supposed to do?"

"They caught you by surprise, Max," Moira chimed in. "They're smarter. Don't expect them to die as easily, either."

Kane nodded in agreement. "Moira's right. Whoever created them has been making improvements to the virus. I figured out where they're being unloaded."

Moira tapped a long nail on the table. "Where?"

"The old lab," he said with some measure of gravity. That silenced the otherwise quiet group. "These parasites were

107

created for warfare. If I have to guess, they're getting close to the final version, that's why production has slowed. We've got to fight them off at the source."

Crystal shook her head. "But that will leave the farm defenseless. How many are left, do you suppose?"

Kane glanced in her direction. "Two dozen, maybe more. We'll need at least six able-bodies. Max, you took a major hit. Do you think you can fight?"

"Of course." He straightened. "I'll give it all I got."

Kyren rubbed his mate's shoulder and shook his head. "Maxie, you need more time."

Max shot him a defiant look. "The others are dead because of them. I won't sit around while you risk your *life* out there." He stared at his mate until Kyren's scarred forearms flexed.

"Fine. But if you're going, you'll stay by my side." He wrapped an arm around Max, squeezing tightly. Max murmured an agreement and Kyren looked up at Kane wearily. "He's not getting hurt again."

Kane's jaw twitched. "We won't go in blind this time. Nothing bad will happen."

"Fourth shift is back," Crystal said as three wolves, brown, blonde, and gray, climbed the porch, stood on two legs and shed their fur.

Serena let them in. Danny was the first to enter, shooting her a coy smirk before taking his place at the table in the nude, loading up a plate.

Gary and Jean followed.

"Hey, buddy!" Jean lifted Marty high in the air. The boy shrieked with excitement at getting his father back. They both sat next to Crystal and Jean planted a kiss on her brow.

Kane greeted the by name. "Jean, Gary, Kyren, Max. Danny and Johnny, you'll all come on the raid tonight. It'll leave the farm vulnerable, but only for a few hours. Moira, Emily, Serena, and Crystal will stay here."

Crystal gaped. "Don't bring Johnny. He's just a kid!"

He didn't answer immediately, when he did, his response had an edge to it. "Johnny's almost grown, Crystal." He turned to the teen. "What do you say, brother? Ready for a scrap?"

Johnny stiffened as he nodded.

Aurora buried her face in his shoulder and hugged tightly.

"You be careful with him." Crystals motherly instincts seemed to be in full swing. "Mortimer wouldn't have wanted him out there."

"Mort isn't around to say." Pain laced Kane's words. "I wouldn't consider it if I thought for a second that we'd lose. Anyone else disagree with the plan?"

"Yeah," a voice from the hall interrupted. "I'm going too, *alpha*." Emily stood in the doorway, leaning against the frame.

"Not if you refuse to take orders." Kane watched her. "Can you control yourself tonight?" He seemed to allude to a moment I'd not been privy to.

Her hand tightened on the doorframe. "Fine, but don't hold me back. I won't suffer any of them to get away. Not after they killed my David."

Kane gave her a concerned look. "I'm worried about you, Emily. Think of your kids. They need their mother."

"I *have* to go," she whispered.

Kane considered it, then relinquished. "Alright. Then it's just Moira, Serena, and Crystal staying behind. Once this is over, everything will go back to normal and we can put this mess behind us." They'd buried their dead but were haunted by them. I saw it in the kids' eyes, the way couples consoled each other as if it were the last time. Offhandedly, I wondered what 'normal' looked like. "Moira, you're in charge while we're gone. We'll leave this evening. At dusk."

Moira raised her mug with a sigh. "Yes, sir."

My presence was largely ignored as breakfast continued. The pack murmured to each other about the oncoming fight. Kane was deep in conversation with his second, planning the attack out down to the letter.

The room had grown stuffy, and I needed fresh air.

I excused myself from the table and slipped into the garden. The hum of insects droned from the field and a crow cawed high above me, dropping into the trees.

"Lovely day, isn't it?" A grizzled voice cut through the quiet. It came from a hunched form, sitting on a log at the edge of the garden. I might have missed them completely if they hadn't spoken.

I stood in surprise. "Who are you?"

The old woman rose off the log, standing all of five-nothing as she waved the question away. "That's irrelevant." A mess of gray hair was pulled into a haphazard bun that framed her wrinkled features. The skirts she wore were a quilt of vibrant color that draped over her wide hips.

Is she a parasite?

She grimaced, as if she'd heard my thoughts. "What a terrible notion! No, dear, I'm a witch."

A witch, who could read my mind, apparently. *What else is she capable of?*

"Much more than that, Amy. It's good to see you." She hoisted her skirts and stepping over the grass. "It must be nice to live with your own kind again."

My own kind? "What? I don't understand."

She approached, and I backed away. "You're right to be wary, in any other circumstance. But I don't mean you any harm. Events are in motion, I'm afraid there's not much time

111

to prepare you." She closed the gap between us and snatched my hand faster than I could blink. "Keep this until I return." Her fist balled into mine, dropping a cold, round object into it.

"What is it?" I opened my hand to reveal a crystalline marble on a leather string. It captured the sunlight and sparkled, every color refracting through its delicate veins. "It's beautiful."

"When you're ready, you'll know what to do. Your father won't succeed."

I looked back up. "My father...?"

The witch was gone.

Serena slid the back door open, breaking me from my paralysis. "Amy, you alright?" She leaned out the door and glanced around the lush garden. "Who were you talking to?"

I slid the necklace in my pocket, doubting she'd believe me if I told her the truth. "Sorry, thinking out loud." I followed her back in the dining room and helped with the cleanup, pushing the encounter to the back of my mind.

The anticipation of the raid crept up on me. I trusted Kane's judgment but worried nonetheless. At least Moira, Crystal, and Serena would stay behind.

Kane strode into the kitchen as I was elbow-deep in dishwater. "Have you got a second?"

"Um." I looked at the pile of dishes, and then Serena, who nodded. "Sure." I dried my hands and he led me to a sparse office with a mahogany desk, two chairs, and a closed laptop.

Kane reclined in his chair behind the desk. "How are you doing so far?"

"Well, it's terrible, what happened." I sat and traced the woodwork of the armrest with a finger. "I mean, everyone's so nice, I don't know-" *that I deserve it.*

His smile was weary, likely from all the planning. "What happened the other night was a tragedy. Pack members come and go, but usually by choice. We haven't lost anyone in a long time. I thought we had the parasites under control. It was my fault they died. But it won't happen again." He seemed resolute. "You aren't obligated to stay. I've made advanced payments on your apartment if you decide to go back."

"You *are* trying to get rid of me." It made sense, in a way. He'd never once acknowledged me at breakfast. I was only in the way. For a second, I was eight once more, watching my father pack his things. *Not again.*

"No." He shook his head. "That's not what I meant. We love having you, but with the parasites, it's becoming more dangerous and I don't want you to feel trapped." He waited for me to speak, his eyes level to mine.

They were too kind to accommodate me as long as they had. No need to make it harder. "I told you, I can go."

113

Kane stood without a word, rounding the desk and leaning against it. "Do you *want* to leave?"

An irrational sob escaped my lips. "No."

He brought his hand to my face gingerly, stroking his thumb over my cheekbone. I lost count of the dark strands sprouting from his chin. "I don't want you to leave, either."

I held his gaze as his thumb traced a path of fire across my jaw. "I-" Kane cut me off with a passionate kiss, gathering me into his arms.

I melted against his solid chest, letting him lead. A fire had blossomed since he'd first appeared in my apartment. No one had ever roused such a fire in me.

When he left, I wondered after him. When he was near, I wanted to close the gap. Only now did I realize he felt the same.

I broke our kiss. "What does this mean?"

"That I am yours, if you'll have me," Kane supplicated, his hand finding a home on the small of my back. He leaned down for another kiss.

I put a finger to his warm lips. "How do I know this isn't just some freaky shifter thing?"

Taking the hand that stopped him, he held it to his heart. "One thing about us: loyalty runs in our veins. I don't *want* anyone else, now or ever." My hand stroked the dense muscle beneath his shirt, a fiery heat pulsed from his core.

His musk made me weak at the knees. "I want to stay."

"Then stay."

I allowed him to pull me in for another kiss.

The future hung over us all like an anvil waiting to drop, but for a moment, life could hold its fucking horses.

Chapter 15

Between chasms of endless blackness, Morgan Lazaro could barely make out his surroundings. The doctor was long gone, leaving his care in the hands of sour-faced monsters, who buzzed about with little regard for him.

Witches cackled over him. Devils determined his fate. If he tried to focus, the walls melted into the floor, dripping into a great, black canyon. He did his best not to fall in, but clarity evaded him. He garbled at the creatures, trying to get their attention to fill his basic needs. If they did see him, they shoved splinters into his arms, severing him from his broken body.

In sleep, he dreamed of fiery locks and emerald eyes, the only reprieve in the troubled storm. At one point, he saw a brilliant light, intense yet familiar.

"Don't go in," the Valkyrie whispered, "you won't come back."

Lazaro turned from the light gladly, slogging through a gray mist that surrounded him on all sides. The beautiful luminosity was waiting for him. He had eternity to explore it but there was still work to do here.

He wasn't done yet.

Chapter 16

Moira and I watched the raid team take off in the evening light. "Things will work out," she said, not sounding entirely convinced, herself.

With the sky outside a bruised purple, Kane's pitch-black fur was the first to disappear into the woods.

"It's best you get some rest. They'll return by morning." Moira shooed me off with a conspiratorial smile, and I had a feeling she knew what transpired between Kane and I in the privacy of his office. The others hadn't been told yet, especially not Aurora, who would take it the hardest. Kane wanted to tell her, himself, after the raid was a success.

Not that we'd sealed the deal, but we were *together*, in a sense, something I'd done well to avoid in my adult life.

Until today, apparently.

Laying atop the covers, I was somewhere between justifying it and reasoning myself out of it. I'd known him for all of two days, *two days*. Perhaps Aurora's spiteful words weren't off their mark if I was so gung-ho about jumping into bed with her brother.

Even she caught on before I did.

Sleep evaded me as time dragged on. I tossed and turned, checking my phone and getting up to readjust the curtains for the umpteenth time.

All was silent, save for the chirping cicadas, then, even they fell silent.

Something was wrong. I cracked the window, glad to have left the light off when I'd risen. The gloom was pervasive, but a rank, familiar smell assaulted my nose. Urgency caused me to close the window and cross to the bedroom door.

Two things happened simultaneously: a splintering explosion rocked the house, and Moira swung my bedroom door wide, ushering two of the boys into my room. They dashed to the closet, and Moira urged me towards the door. Her tone was deadly serious. "Get in, Amy."

"I can help."

"There's no time. Get your ass in the closet." Her pale blue eyes hardened as she grabbed me by the arm. With more strength than I expected, she led me to the door. "Don't make a *sound*," she said with a hiss, locking us in.

Only a sliver of dim light kept us company. Xander and Riley curled up to me as we cowered in the darkness. I draped an arm over each of them, little Riley buried his face in the crook of my neck with a whimper.

The house erupted into chaos.

Serena screamed in the distance, doors slammed open and shut, a menacing growl was cut off by a yelp. Somewhere close to the house, a motor started up, shaking the foundations. Boots pounded the hall, searching for the pack.

Searching for *us*.

We waited until the house fell silent, and then an eternity longer before trying the door. Dawn was coming soon, and I had to find out what the raid team would be returning to.

The closet was secured, no way to unlock it from the inside.

"Stand back." The children crouched behind a set of shelves as I kicked the door, using all the strength I could muster. My foot glanced off painfully.

Backing up, I tried again without result.

I screwed my eyes shut and let all my anger flow, strengthening my resolve and nearly bringing on the change. My foot snapped through the door, splintering the wood panel. I found the lock and unlatched it, letting the door swing open.

Turning back to the kids, I put a finger to my lips. They slipped back into the closet silently, wide-eyed and trembling.

Muddy footprints were everywhere, smears of red-brown mud trailed the walls, as if someone had purposefully marked them. The house was empty, save for the living room. Solice lay on the ground, wheezing. Blood was spattered on his chest and face, some of it looked like his own.

"What happened?" I leaned over, brushing tangled white hair off his forehead. He didn't respond, instead he pointed at the gaping hole that had been the front door. I helped him rise slowly to the couch, making sure he was comfortable before navigating the debris to the porch.

Moira was on the ground outside, sprawled in the lawn. She was in her second form, belly down with her head rested on a forearm. Her face was spattered in blood.

"Moira!" I knelt by her, the grass in front of her face flitting with each shallow breath. Looking for signs of the intruders, tire marks in the sod evidenced they were long gone. "Can you get up?" I stroked her gray coat. Whining, she rolled over and lost her second form.

She let me hoist her up and lead her into the house, where she collapsed into a chair. When she spoke, it was barely a whisper, "They're gone. It was- Vorrin."

"Vorrin?" I asked.

The old woman laid her head back and breathed peacefully. She'd expended all her energy trying to protect us. Me and the boys were safe because of her.

Whoever violated the farmhouse had taken everyone but the elders, Xander, Riley, and myself. Crystal, Serena, Aurora, and the rest of the kids had vanished, the signs of their struggle everywhere.

A predawn light lit the sky.

I paced the porch and waited for the raid team to return. I feared the worse until jubilant howls rose above the cicadas, who'd resumed their early morning celebration.

Familiar shifters dashed from the woods, one-by-one. The last to emerge was Kane in his hulking form. They were smiling, or as best they could in their current form. Johnny's tongue lolled as he dashed towards the house. Only a dusty blonde wolf appeared injured, limping slightly.

All seven bolted towards the house, celebrating a likely well-earned victory.

Kane's eyes zeroed in on me and dashed forward, pounding up the steps and shed his fur.

Emily, who hadn't lost her coat, ran past me into the yawning entrance. Johnny followed suit along with Jean and Kyren, each a different shade of panic.

Kane's cold eyes darkened beneath his brow. "What happened?"

Whatever resolve had held me up to this point let go, and I collapsed against the post and trembled, though no tears came. He caught me and stroked my hair, whispering reassurances until I could breathe again.

Kyren helped Max up the steps and assessed the damage. "Whoever did this knew exactly what they were doing. They disabled the elders and took everyone else. There's not enough blood to think they're dead. Not yet," he told Kane. "But it wasn't the military. Too messy. There was enough time for Crystal and Serena to put up a struggle."

Moira had told me the last piece of the puzzle before passing out. "Vorrin." I found my strength again. "Moira said it was Vorrin."

Kane's arms flexed around me. "That *sorry* bastard."

Kyren looked aghast. "He promised to keep his lackeys off our land."

Kane's growl reverberated into me. "That he did. Get the truck and bring it around."

Kyren nodded, escorting his mate inside.

He glanced down at me. "Amy, you should stay here. Vorrin is dangerous. It's not safe for you to be near his pack if you're unmated."

"I'm not staying behind. I don't want to be locked in a closet again."

"You were- locked in a closet?"

I groaned. "Yes, I can't stand being this useless."

Despite everything, or, perhaps because of it, he chuckled. "Okay. But under no circumstance can you tell them your real name. For *any* reason."

"Easy." I shrugged, not as if my name mattered. Because of the attack, no one had mentioned the raid yet. "What happened out there?"

Kane glanced at the woods. "Kyren's plan worked perfectly. Parasites don't sleep, but they hibernate, and their eyesight isn't too sharp in the dark, so we used it against them."

A truck engine came to life around the house. Kyren rolled the behemoth to the front. He parked the monstrosity and got out. "It's all set. I'll take care of the damage, who's going?"

"Jean, Amy, and I. Get me some clothes, too."

"I'm coming with you." Emily's eyes were bloodshot. "They've got Izzy."

Johnny jogged out. "And Aurora!"

Kane froze, his voice barely a whisper, "no." No one seemed to hear it but me. A little louder, he said, "get in the truck, kid." He let me go and pounded down the steps. "Jean!"

Jean bolted from the house. "Yes?" His brown hair tousled over his tormented face. Vorrin's raiders had taken everyone but his son.

"We're leaving *now.*"

124

I slipped into the back seat as Johnny and Emily rode in the bed. Kane got in next to me and stretched out in the cabin, pulling me close.

Before Jean changed gears, Kane leaned out the window. "Kyren, take care of them, we'll be back soon. And fix those doors; make them *fucking* impermeable."

"Yes, sir." Kyren tipped an imaginary hat and tossed Kane his clothes, then gave a few extra pairs to Emily in the back.

Kane shook the pants on and tossed the shirt over his head, then turned to me. "You have to understand something: Vorrin is a slaver. Don't talk to him unless he asks you a question, don't be rude, and do *not* piss him off, understand?"

"Sure, but- why did he attack?"

Kane sighed heavily, kicking on his pants. "I wish I knew. Luckily, the bastard owes me a life debt. He'll give them back but he's fickle. It won't be a good idea to linger."

I leaned against him and nestled into the safety of his arms, wishing it would all fade away like a bad dream.

Chapter 17

Danny paced the halls out of boredom.

Amy brought no end of trouble with her; already quick to snap at him that first day, making *him* look like the bad guy. She was a sensitive bitch in heat, and too high maintenance for his taste.

Since the funeral, Kane didn't let him near her. Though nothing had been said, the murderous looks were clear enough: he'd already claimed her.

Danny sighed and retreated to his bedroom, picking up the landline and dialing. "Ryker."

"What's the situation?"

Danny murmured into the phone, cupping a hand between his face and the mouthpiece. "She turned again, yesterday. They're headed to Vorrin's camp now."

"Why?"

"Slavers raided the farm, kidnapped some of the pack."

"*Have you seen an old woman around?*" So like Ryker to ignore him.

"We've got an elder bitch. That count?"

"*Don't fuck with me, Danny. She's not a shifter, she's a backstabbing witch.*"

A witch? "Nah, there haven't been any visitors."

Ryker paused, then said, "*keep me posted.*" The line went dead abruptly.

Danny cursed into the phone before dialing another number.

K picked up on the third ring. "*Daniel,*" the velvet voice cooed. "*It's good to hear from you. Have you planted the microphones?*"

Danny had stuffed the box of bugs under his bed. "Fuck, I'll get on that. Just calling to tell you she changed again, and she has the mark. Amy's definitely your target."

"*Fantastic! I'll expect the security devices to be emitting a signal by this evening.*" The agent's silky voice irritated Danny.

"Yeah." He wasn't looking forward to it. But today might be the only opportunity, what with the unexpected assault on the farmhouse keeping everyone occupied.

"*Very good. And expect Amy to be getting a call soon. We've got something she'll want to see. Give her an hour lead,*"

I don't want our test to be… interrupted." He emphasized the last word before hanging up.

Did no one say goodbye anymore?

Rude, Danny grumbled, slamming the phone down. His work for today had barely begun, he realized, considering how to set up the equipment without being noticed. He wasn't even getting paid for this shit.

Chapter 18

The truck heaved over rough terrain, jarring everyone in the vehicle. More than once, Kane had to catch and pull me close, grabbing the roof rack for stability.

I snaked an arm through his and held tight to his thick shoulder.

Jean had to make several awkward turns, narrowly missing a patch of trees. Finally, after the insufferably bumpy drive, he made a right turn and parked behind a steep ridge covered in foliage. "We'll walk from here."

Emily and Johnny leaped out of the vehicle in their second forms as we filed out, flanking us. Over the ridge lay an expanse of populated territory. Even from this distance, it was clear the inhabitants lived an unfortunate life.

Tasting the air, I recognized the scent from the farmhouse. It was the same odor that wafted through my window, and something older. A strange memory evaded me.

Emily whined, her ears flattening against her head. Izzy and the others were somewhere, lost in the mad cacophony that bustled below us. The territory appeared largely undefended, and perhaps it was, but I soon realized why: it sat beyond a huge ravine that cut through the hills, traveling as far as they eye could see in each direction.

The inhabitants had built a rickety bridge that could be easily cut to deter entry. It was shoddy, but seemed functional, guarded by two men who straightened at our approach.

I chanced a peek into the ravine, regretting it instantly.

An awful, necrotic smell drifted out of the blackness. The bottom wasn't visible even in the morning light.

One of the men put his hand up, looking tensed for a fight. "No visitors allowed."

Kane advanced towards the guard, who was dwarfed by his sheer size. "Get me Vorrin. *Now*."

The guard peered up at Kane defiantly. "Name?"

"Blackmoor, and I suggest you get to it quickly."

He huffed and stiffened, marching over the bridge in no rush to make good time.

"Jean." Kane eyed him, lowering his voice. "Get the truck ready when I tell you to. We'll need to make a quick exit after the others are recovered."

Jean inclined his head. "Yes, sir."

Every minute we lost weighed heavily on our group. The guard was gone for quite some time and I was beginning to wonder if he'd come back at all.

Johnny grew restless, changing back and sitting on the grass, fiddling with a leaf. "That bridge isn't going to last the winter," he mumbled, glancing at the structure, his tail brushing the grass flat. "I could build a better one in my sleep."

Kane chuckled. "I wouldn't doubt it, kid."

The guard's eyes swiveled before ignoring us again, donning a look of irritation.

After several more minutes, the first guard returned. Someone seemed to have lit a fire under his ass, and he invited us over the bridge impatiently. "Vorrin will see you, now."

Our weight rocked the construction perilously as the stench of death oozed from the crevice. I was not keen on joining their unfortunate victims.

Once we made it across, the territory sprang to grungy life.

Filthy children bolted through the shanty structures, rolling in the dirt and snarling at one another. They stared up at us with hungry eyes as we passed, stomachs bloated from malnutrition.

I must have stalled because Kane took my hand in his and murmured, "remember why we're here."

131

The other inhabitants roused less compassion. Women watched us with a mixture of disgust and resentment. A man sharpened a cruel blade, smiling with glittering hate. Several males leered at me, baring blackened teeth.

The guard pushed through the crowd, parting the way, though Kane's size garnered unwanted attention from the shifters of Vorrin's overpopulated pack.

Maybe they recognized him as the alpha he was.

Jean brought up the rear and kept them from trailing us.

Gradually, the low construction gave way to tin rooftops and wood slats. These children weren't desperately chasing rats for lunch, and the men wore nicer clothes, the colors only slightly bleached by the sun. A young woman noticed us and disappeared into one of the shanty structures.

Down the way, a fight broke out.

One shifter, infuriated at another, screamed obscenities in his face. The other reacted out of instinct, leaping at his throat mid-change. They hit the ground with a thud and tore at each other's coats. The darker wolf clamped down on his enemy's neck and squeezed, cutting off his protests.

Our guard intercepted, yanking the offender off his victim and tossing him back to the rough circle of shifters.

The fighter on the ground rolled to one side. Two women picked him up and dragged him away, eyeing the gathering crowd defensively.

With the entertainment concluded, they dispersed and allowed us through.

At the end of the road, a real house came into view.

It was the only well-built structure we'd seen so far, albeit old and covered in moss. Our guard ascended the creaky porch steps and opened the door for us.

The stench of unvented sweat and drugs blasted my senses. I almost threw up. Jean, Johnny, and Emily reacted accordingly, but Kane didn't seem to notice.

Repurposed maroon bedsheets lined the walls, rudely imitating wall curtains while pillows and long-haired carpets covered the hardwood floor in a cheap attempt at grandeur.

The guard brought us to a bedroom and opened the door. "Kane is here."

Kane blocked my view of the room. I peeked around him to see a gilded, dark space. The air quality was worse here than in the rest of the house.

A heavyset man leaned against a cherrywood bedframe, ignoring the guard. Three women draped themselves over his bulk, including a bony brunette with whom he was shamelessly engaged. Kane took a breath and bellowed, "*VORRIN!*"

The fat man tore his lips free from the brunette's teeth. "*What*?!" Vorrin turned his attention to us, completely naked and unashamed. The woman glanced at us with disdain; the two blondes began toying with each other, trying to distract him. He ignored their banter and heaved off the bed, hobbling over with his beady eyes twinkling. "Oh, it's just you, Kane! It's been a long time, hasn't it?"

"Eight years." Kane's features were unreadable. "I could have spent the rest of my life without seeing you again."

"Good to see you, too." He peered around Kane's bulk to look at me. "Who is this? Aren't you going to introduce us?"

Kane stiffened, then drew me to his side. "This is Amy. My mate."

"Oh-ho!" Vorrin grinned at the both of us. "So, the bachelor of Blackmoor decided to get hitched, huh?" He shot me a lecherous sneer as the brunette helped him shrug on a robe. "It's a pleasure, Amy- what is your last name?"

"Johnson," I lied.

The tension in the room was ready to snap. Despite Kane's presence, I was utterly exposed to Vorrin's searing gaze. "Amy *Johnson*." He toyed with the syllables, snatching my hand before I could pull away. "It's a delight to meet you." He planted a thick wet kiss on my knuckles.

I considered cutting off the hand to spare the rest.

"I'm not here for introductions, Vorrin." Kane's anger rose to the surface. "Not after you kidnapped my pack."

Vorrin's glittering eyes dulled to coals. "We pick up slaves where we can. I don't ask questions." He shrugged, stealing a kiss from one of his girls. "What do you want me to do about it?" He pulled the giggling blonde towards him and smacked her ass hard enough to make her squeal.

Kane flexed involuntarily. "You're in charge, here. I saved your life, if you remember. A decision I already regret."

Vorrin let out a boisterous laugh. "You're so dramatic!" He shoved a fleshy fist into Kane's solid chest, then sighed. "*Fine*, I'll release their contracts. Your pack members are no good to me, anyway. Too feisty." His gaze lingered in my direction a little too long.

Kane's lip curled, his arm becoming a vice around my shoulder. "You swear to never poach on my lands?"

Vorrin waved the threat away. "Oh, quit it. I'll let the trappers know." He waddled over to a low desk and scribbled on a sheet of parchment, then handed it to Kane. "Give this to the market clerk. They'll sort it out for you."

Kane snatched the paper and stuffed it into his front pocket. "I don't want to see you – or any of your pack – on my lands. *Ever* again."

"Nor I, you," Vorrin retorted. "Jake will see you out." Losing interest in us, he returned to the women, whose peals of laughter followed us out.

The moment we were outside, I could breathe again.

Kane patted his pocket. "Well," he said with a sigh, "we'd best get started."

135

Chapter 19

Our guard was exchanged for a young shifter named Faron, whose brown eyes sparkled with a kindness that seemed scarce everywhere else in this hellhole. "I've been briefed on your situation. We'll get this mess cleared right up."

He led us back through the encampment to an open building made of scrapped wood slats. The inside reeked of rusted iron and misery.

A few of Vorrin's pack members gathered around the building, seeming to be waiting for something to happen. Faron ushered us past the patrons and into a stuffy office, where a woman in her mid-fifties sorted paperwork. "Macy, we have a neighboring alpha here to reclaim his pack members. With Vorrin's permission."

Kane proffered the document. "Their names are Crystal, Serena, Aurora, Martin, Jessica, and Isabella." Emily, who'd followed silently behind, whined when Izzy's name was spoken.

Johnny and Jean looked equally restless.

The woman stared at us with disinterest. "They won't be under their names but we can find the lot number if we know when they were checked in."

Like luggage, I thought, disgusted.

Kane's jaw set. "This morning."

"There were seven shipments this morning, and one in transition." Macy sighed with terminal boredom.

This conversation was going nowhere. "Hey." I slammed my fist on the table, rousing the woman from her comfortable stupor. "We need to find them, *now*. Vorrin gave us written permission to reclaim our pack, in a *timely* manner." I stole her gaze and held it until she shifted uncomfortably in her seat.

She swallowed and glanced to the papers in front of her. "What time this morning?"

"Early." Kane slid an impressed glance at me. "Around sunrise, probably."

Macy snatched a winner. "Here. Trapper 32 brought in ten parcels at 6:43. All but one is in the rear quarters."

Faron took the papers and a set of keys. "Thank you, we'll be in and out."

The 'rear quarters' were nothing more than low cages filled to the brim with a diverse group of prisoners. Some were only human, scared and crying.

Emily ran towards one of the cages and I saw Izzy wrap her chubby arms around her mother's neck, tears streaming down her dirty face.

Jean found Crystal and his two little ones.

Faron unlocked the cages and let them out.

Aurora stood and ran to Kane and Johnny, her hair tangled and blouse ripped, but she was intact. They shared a tight embrace.

Jean assisted his wife out of the cage and picked both Martin and Jessica up, swinging them around joyously.

Emily got her daughter back and cried, stroking Izzy's hair.

In Izzy's cage, I saw three other shifters eyeing us. Before Faron could lock it up, I stopped him. "They're ours, too."

Faron shrugged and released them. A young woman – no older than Aurora – and two small children exited and lingered next to our group, watching uncertainly.

"Jean." Kane interrupted their tearful reunion. "Bring them back to the truck and get it started. I'll meet you there, soon."

Jean nodded.

Everyone but Kane and I left. "You should follow them, Amy. It's too dangerous right now."

"No way. You won't get rid of me that easily. Serena is the closest thing I have to a friend on the farm, and I won't let *you* get lost trying to find her."

Kane chuckled and squeezed my hand, most of the tension in his features had abated. "Fair enough. But if anything happens, don't disobey me." He glanced at me in earnest. "I'm not going to lose you, either."

"You won't." I leaned against him and slipped my hand into his. Glancing at the cages one last time, I wished I could steal them all away. Kane's head shook minutely.

There was nothing we could do.

He looked to our guide. "Faron, does your sheet say anything about where Serena is being held?"

"It doesn't say a name, but I do have a location. It's down the way, I'll show you to the property." Faron led us through the side streets, avoiding the main road.

"So, what's up with you?" Kane asked Faron. "Why do you care about some rival pack?"

He looked up at Kane a moment, seeming to consider his question. "For the most part, it's my job. I was turned later in life, but that doesn't change who you are. I've always enjoyed doing good work. Also, I see how close you are, willing to risk Vorrin to protect your own. It's admirable. We rarely get visited by other alphas." Faron shrugged, checking the paper again. "I don't think anyone denies that Vorrin is an unstable alpha. But he's better than Ryker."

I winced, then glanced away.

Kane didn't seem surprised. "The old man is alive, then."

Faron nodded and said, "Vorrin's been butting head with him regarding territory, but he won't give. Rumor is Ryker's planning something big."

"What do you mean?" I asked, curious about the ruthless alpha that shared my name.

"He's building a structure in the middle of nowhere. No one knows why. His pack members don't talk, Ryker makes sure of it. We've all heard the stories of those who do."

Kane readjusted my hand in his. "Where?"

"One of our scouts spotted a vehicle trailing the Johnson river north, but she couldn't pursue without being compromised. The area is heavily guarded, but- I probably shouldn't be telling you all this, I suppose."

Kane gave Faron a faint smile. "I appreciate it. Vorrin is no friend of mine. Not after this."

Faron's voice dropped low. "Vorrin doesn't have any friends. We all hate him but there isn't an alpha willing to challenge him. This place is a mess."

"Then why do you stay?"

"Because Vorrin doesn't let his property go. If we leave,

he'll send others after us. I have a daughter, Adara, who's only seven. I don't want to see anything happen to her." Faron gave a grimace as we arrived at a ramshackle building, little more than wood slats being held up by a shanty metal frame. He waved at the shanty structure. "Soreno's house."

The prospect of Serena being in there gave me chills.

Kane approached the door, knocking hard.

A crash emanated from the inside, followed with a string of expletives in a cracked voice. The door opened to reveal a wiry old man with a balding scalp. "What do you want?" The numerous stains on his closed expressed a sincere disregard for laundering.

Kane shoved past the man. "Serena is here."

Faron and I followed in after.

The man's protests followed us down the hall. "Hey! Get out of my house. This is *my* property!"

Faron tried reasoning with Soreno while I chased after Kane. "Vorrin has issued a recall of the slaves from lot forty-three. You'll be reimbursed at auction."

Kane disappeared down the hall.

I followed after as the man's shouts filled the house.

"It's too late for that!" He escaped Faron and followed us, crossing his arms as if waiting for us to find her with a blackened grin. "She belongs to my boy, now."

I could barely detect her scent above the buildup of filth and grime. But Kane's nose was apparently sharper, and he found a door that had been locked tight.

It was a small effort for him to yank it off. The door creaked open and we peered into the gloom.

"Serena?"

"Amy? Is that you?" It was her voice, clear as a bell.

I stepped inside. "Serena, we have to go."

A low growl echoed from the gloom as my eyes adjusted. Serena was shackled to a wall, next to a large shifter equally restrained, staring at us with hungry eyes.

"I can't go." Her voice was weak. "I'm mated."

Chapter 20

"There's nothing you can do." Soreno seemed all too pleased with himself. "She belongs to him, and he belongs to me. Now, get yer asses out of my house."

Kane whipped around and hooked the man's jaw with a fist. The old man spun impossibly, careening face first into the wall.

He crumpled to the ground, knocked out cold.

Faron didn't bat an eye, and nor did I.

I wouldn't leave Serena in the hands of Soreno or Vorrin. "We're getting you out of here, Serena. You *and* your mate."

Kane put a hand on my shoulder. "Amy, the man's son is rabid. There's no coming back from that."

"But what about Serena?" I couldn't release her if the son attacked me. "We can't leave her here."

"And we won't." Kane closed in on the rabid shifter.

It growled and fought against its restraints to get at him, blind to the dangers of facing an alpha. Kane avoided the creature's jaw and clamped his forearm around its neck, holding firm until his writhing form slowly lost its strength and slid to the ground, unconscious.

I dashed to Serena, checking the locks that held her. "Kane, I can't get them undone. I need your help." He released the shifter and yanked the chain, snapping the cheap links. Serena still had cuffs around her wrists, but she was free.

Her face contorted with misery as she fell to her knees and stroked the beast's fur. "I can't leave him behind."

Kane looked down at her for a long moment before groaning in defeat. "Fine, but your mate is going in a *cage* when we get back to the farm. He's too dangerous to let loose." He picked up the unconscious wolf, threw him over his shoulder, and followed us out the exit.

Serena limped out of the house with my help, looking man-handled, but physically intact. "Thank you," she said under her breath. So much about her had changed in a few short hours, I wondered if it was the kidnapping or the mating. I worried that they had damaged her gentle demeanor irreparably.

Faron stopped us before the main road, glancing around for onlookers. "You need to get out of here."

"Come with us." Kane readjusted the unconscious shifter, waving a hand at the territory. "You're better than all this."

"I can't. If you think you have problems with Vorrin now, imagine what he'd do if I left with you. He's as jealous as they come. Maybe one day I'll take you up on it, Blackmoor," he said, shaking his head. "-but not today."

Kane gripped Faron's shoulder. "Thank you for your help. I look forward to seeing you again."

"Same. Now get out of here. Use the back road so you don't draw attention. I'll call in a false report so you have some lead time. And try to watch out for projectiles." Faron turned and jogged off before we clarified the meaning of 'projectiles'.

Kane took off in the other direction. "Let's go."

Serena and I followed close behind.

He turned right on a vaguely familiar path, passing the auction house where slaves stood on the stage. Bidders raised cues and shouted numbers, a few of the patrons glanced at us with suspicious scrutiny.

We ran through the poor side of the territory at breakneck speed, ignoring the hateful glares.

Another right turn revealed the bridge dead ahead, a hundred paces away. The guards, seeming to have heard nothing of our theft, watched us blitz over the bridge.

"Hey!" One of them shouted with a delayed sense of duty. "Come back here! Where the hell is your guard?!"

They gave chase, but we were almost home free. Jean and Johnny stood waiting for us around the hill, the godawful territory nearly out of sight.

A hail of bullets scattered around us, piercing into the ground in little bursts. One nearly hit me as I ran, adrenaline coursing through my veins.

Behind me, the air heaved from Kane's chest as he fell, a bullet buried into his shoulder. "No!" I screamed and doubled back. Jean was quick to follow.

Emily and Johnny picked Serena's unconscious mate off Kane, while Jean assisted in getting him on his feet.

Another skittering barrage of bullets missed us. "We have to go!" I picked up Kane's other side with as much strength as I could muster, as Jean caught hold of his other side. We dragged him onto the truck bed with much struggle.

Behind the sharp hill, we were safe from further assault, at least from the bullets. Crystal was already in the driver's seat with the engine roaring. "Ready?!"

Jean and I laid Kane down on his stomach.

"Go!" Jean shouted back to Crystal, who, despite her short stature, managed to reach the gas pedal and spirit us away from Vorrin's shit-hole camp.

Kane panted short, rattling breaths, each bump jarring him.

Frantically, I assessed the wound. From the look of it, the bullet was buried deep in his right lung, between the ribs. He coughed and spit up flecks of blood. "Is it bad?" His cheek was pressed against the embossed steel bed, but I could tell he was teasing me, despite everything.

I held back bitter tears, trying not to let him see. "You'll be okay. Moira will make sure of it."

He caught my hand and squeezed. "You did good back there."

My laugh melted into a sob. I curled up next to him, ignoring glances from the pack and brushed his hair back. "You stay alive, okay?"

"Sure." He inhaled too hard and spit up more blood. The bloody grin that followed was not at all reassuring. "No problem," he said, "I've been through worse."

I scrubbed a tear away before it rolled down my cheek. "Is that supposed to make me feel better?"

A rumbling laugh caused Kane to go into a coughing fit. When he recovered, he whispered. "Don't cry." Then his eyes closed. My heart skipped a beat. For a split second, I thought I'd lost him. The terror abated only slightly as I watched him take one shallow breath after another.

Jean held tight to his kids. "He'll be okay."

I looked over, seeing that everyone was accounted for. The girl who I'd claimed was curled up in a corner with her eyes averted. The children clung to her and watched us fearfully. I could only imagine what they'd been through.

We saw firsthand what Vorrin's men did to the farmhouse. Would those children even have a home to return to?

Finally, after an ocean of trees and so many miles behind us, the clearing lay ahead, and with it, the farm.

Kyren and Moira stood waiting to meet us, looking nervous. They must have smelled blood on the wind. Crystal parked in front and everyone but Kane and I unloaded.

Moira heaved onto the tailgate, looking much improved since we left. "Let me see him." She touched the bullet's entry point with kneading fingers.

He hissed. "Ow."

"Get over it. I'll have it out in a jiffy." She grew her nails long and eased it out. The shiny pellet finally emerged, blood gushing from the wound as Moira placed her hands over it. Light accumulated between her fingers and Kane's breathing improved. "I'm healing your lung and the skin, so you don't drown or bleed out. I don't have the strength to heal the entire wound, so take it easy, boy."

He gave a great sigh, his eyes fluttering closed. "Thanks."

I overheard Serena talking with Kyren behind us about the rabid shifter. "Do we have a cage?"

"There's one in the garage, do you need help?"

"Please." Serena's voice was thick with despair. "I don't want him to hurt anyone." The shifter was beginning to rouse in the truck bed. She ran to him and whispered into his long ears, comforting him until Kyren could carry him into the garage and lock him away.

Crystal took it upon herself to corral the young woman and her siblings into the house. I saw the little girl's shocking red hair disappear through the entrance.

Gary assisted Kane into the house, with me trailing after, and laid him on the couch where he fell asleep. He snored deeply, breathing normally again.

Confident that the world wouldn't end if I stepped away, I retreated to my room and lay on the freshly made bed. Relief washed over me as I let my muscles relax into the soft mattress. *Maybe*, I thought, *it can all fade like a bad dream.* Things would improve, with Vorrin off our asses, and maybe, just maybe, I'd be able to appreciate paradise adjacent.

An uncomfortable bulge in my pocket made me explore the sensation. I drew out the white stone, lashed to a leather string. *The witch in the garden.* I had forgotten, until now.

Through the haze of relief, I could only marvel at the pebble, watching its opalescence glitter in the light, and

149

wondered why she meant for me to have it. "*Keep this, until I return.*" I pulled the cord over my head, fitting it around my neck. The stone was cool against my chest.

My phone buzzed twice, rousing me from my exhaustion.

One new message and thirteen missed phone calls. Matt had called me a dozen time, leaving me a single voicemail.

Work called once.

The voicemail played after a short delay. "*Amy,*" an unfamiliar man's voice came through. "*if you want to see your friend again, you'll come to the waterfront warehouse on First and Everglade by five o'clock tonight. You tell your friends and no one will find the body.*"

My eyes shot to the clock, realizing it was almost four fifteen. I leaped off the bed, forgoing a new pair of clothes.

I considered who might help that wouldn't also ask questions. *Serena?* No, she was wrapped up in her own problems. *Gary?* He might help, but he'd want to know why and would probably alert Kane.

Danny? I gritted my teeth – douche of the century – but he was the least likely to ask questions. I caught him in the hallway retreating back to his room. "Can I talk to you for a second?"

He looked surprised and a little pleased that I was searching him out. He gave a conspiratorial nod, leaning too far into my personal space. "What's up?"

"I need a car or something, like, *now*. No questions asked. Can you figure it out for me?"

"Sure, I got you, babe. Come on." The way he said it made me cringe but I followed him to the side of the garage where a slick black motorbike was hidden beneath a tarp. "Will this work?"

"Perfect."

He handed me a set of keys. I donned the helmet and started the engine. "Please don't tell anyone I'm leaving. I'll be back soon." Not checking to see if he agreed, I rolled out of the driveway and onto the gravel path.

I hadn't driven a motorcycle since the accident. But I couldn't care. I didn't have the luxury.

The engine between my legs thrummed smoothly as I accelerated, silently praying that it wasn't too late.

Chapter 21

I peeled down the two-way street, passing tractors and cars on the shoulder. It was after four when I left the farmhouse, and it would take another thirty minutes to get into the city.

Time was running out.

Even if Matt and I parted on questionable terms, I couldn't live with myself if he died because of me. He was still my friend and I owed him this much.

Flying down the road at breakneck speed reminded me of the crash. Time had slowed to a stop as I'd vaulted through the air. Sparks from the crash scattered, so that I might have been watching the birth of stars. I'd reached out to touch one, but a heavy dark force knocked me from the sky. I remembered hearing my Ducati explode, miraculously sparing me from the shrapnel. As I'd passed out, a chill overtook me, but not before I saw a pair of cold blue eyes. *Kane* was *there*. The paramedics had found me sprawled out on the side of the road, unharmed besides a few minor abrasions, and Kane's bite.

I gripped the handlebars and drove faster.

Not today.

Speeding around another utility truck, I took a left onto the highway. Farmland turned into suburbia as houses sprang up around me. I followed signs for the freeway and merged.

Luckily the river wasn't far now, and traffic was moving.

The off-ramp for First street approached. I used the shoulder to exit and sped through, watching for a sign that read 'Everglade'.

A faded green warehouse loomed over the intersection. I slowed to a stop and killed the engine, jogging to the front of the building. The windows were barred shut with weathered wood slats, so I checked around back for another entrance. A broken lock lay scattered on the concrete in front of an open door.

I pushed it further despite its rusty protest.

A single, glaring light illuminated the space beyond, casting a long shadow on the floor. The light enveloped a single figure, strapped to a wooden frame. His head lolled to one side, but unconscious or dead, it was impossible to tell.

I gasped when I recognized his lanky frame. "Matt."

He groaned, troubled even in sleep.

I stepped inside for a closer look, avoiding broken bits of glass. Whoever did this hadn't gone far, their scent still lingered.

I took a tentative step forward. "Matt, I'm here-"

"Amy Ryker." A familiar voice announced behind me. That same, sickly sweet droll from the message.

I spun around to face Matt's kidnapper. He was short with lean features and beady dark eyes. The black suit he wore accentuated his pale skin.

I held out my arms to shield Matt from the suit, assessing him with utter scrutiny. "Leave him out of this, I'm here now."

"That's not how this works, Ryker." He smiled, exposing a set of perfectly straight, white teeth. "Doctor, if you would be so kind?" He proffered a hand to the entrance as a perfumed presence stepped through.

She was a tall, classic blonde in a lab coat. The doctor strode past me and sniffed with distate, assaulting my nostrils with her suffocating fragrance.

I grabbed her arm in a vice grip.

The man raised a gun to my face. "I wouldn't do that if I were you. Your kind doesn't recover from a bullet to the head. I've tested it."

Grudgingly, I let her arm go. Disgust roiled in my stomach as I watched her grab Matt by the hair and insert a long needle into his neck. She depressed the lever, sending a dark fluid rushing into his veins.

The room started to reek of cloying sweetness and rot. With her job finished, the doctor backed away with smug satisfaction and returned to the man holding us hostage.

He aimed the gun low and shot me in the leg.

I dropped to the ground in agony, biting back a scream. Blood rushed from the wound, and I clamped my hands over it to stem the bleeding.

"Help your friend, Ryker." His parting words echoed. I looked up through my blurry vision, but they were gone.

Tearing off a piece of my pants leg, I wrapped the cloth around the injury, slowing the flow.

He'd clipped my wings; I wouldn't be able to drive the motorcycle back in this state.

Remembering why I'd come, I glanced up at Matt's limp form. "Matt." I winced and stood. "You have to wake up! We need to go to the hospital." I put my weight gingerly on my right leg, and limped towards him, slapping his face in a desperate attempt to rouse him. "Wake up!"

Matt groaned again but didn't respond.

At first, it started as a twitch in his cheek, then the convulsing developed into a full-blown seizure that rocked the wooden frame. Matt's eyes bulged as his whole body tensed against the restraints.

I stumbled over my bad leg, watching helplessly as my friend's eyes glazed over, his mouth opened wide: a frothing, black void. His scream, laced with agony, made me cover my ears. I couldn't look away as Matt became something else, a nightmarish caricature of the man I knew.

His skin blackened as if burned by invisible heat, darkening with each pump of his heart. Matt's long fingers shriveling into stiff claws. White bones protruded from the tips as I witnessed the last of his humanity burn away.

I choked back tears. "Matt…"

Its eyes focused on me, bloodshot and withered in their sockets. Jagged teeth gnashed, still spitting foam. What had once been my friend lurched against its confines, snapping one of the restraints and swiping in my direction.

I scrambled back, ignoring the pain in my leg. "Matt, please, it's- it's me, Amy."

It lurched again, tearing the other restraint with ease, and falling with a crunch onto its knees. The creature lingered there a moment, hunched over itself, then stood to its full height. Another deafening scream tore through its ruined throat and it charged directly at me.

Using my good leg, I twisted out of the way, but not fast enough. A raking claw caught my arm as it passed, pain searing through my flesh.

The change began to take hold, fur sprouting from my pores and my knees buckled. The bullet wound twisted unnaturally as my legs changed. I cried out through sharp teeth.

It turned and charged towards me again, shrieking in frustration. This time I was faster, lunging and slicing open its stomach before rolling to one side.

The thing paused and stared down at its stomach.

A guttural growl filled the warehouse as it looked up with pure rage. The only option was to put him out of his misery as quickly as possible, and then maybe someone would put me out of mine.

It lurched towards me on unsteady legs and caught my shoulder, throwing me to the floor. I extended my arms as it landed on top of me, trying to take a chunk out of my face. The creature swiped lines through my flesh as I thrust my hips upwards, knocking it off balance and rolling it over. The change fully took hold of my jaw and it crunched into a new shape.

Remove the head, remove the head, remove the head. I tore at its neck, its claws gouged deep into the skin on my arms and face.

As I ripped, black ichor flooded into my mouth. I bit down hard until my teeth connected with bone. A sickening crunch echo in my skull and the creature stopped fighting.

157

Matt's body shuddered once, twice, then went still.

I spat a mouthful of congealed putrescence onto the dirt floor, trembling from more than the taste.

My face was covered in sticky black ooze, my skin unrecognizable and burning with noxious fire. I collapsed, fully changed, onto Matt's corpse.

I couldn't even move. It was too much effort just to stay conscious. I lay that way forever. The surrounding air cooled my skin as I balanced on the verge of oblivion.

Bobbing lights glared through my eyelids, I tried to squeeze them shut. *Go away and let me die*, I thought miserably. A man's voice shouted unfamiliar words. Someone touched my ravaged skin. Pain lanced through me. I yelped and pulled away, which caused my other injuries to flare up.

The string of words began to make sense. "What happened? Why didn't she say anything?"

Was it Danny or Gary?

"Amy." Kane's baritone voice cut through the pain. "We need to move you. Let us help."

I sighed heavily through my nose, conceding.

Several pairs of hands lifted me off Matt's cold body. The pain lessened if I allowed my limbs to stay limp. A wet cloth was scrubbed over my uninjured snout. "Let's get her to the farm. Moira needs to see to her wounds as soon as possible."

A huge engine rumbled to life beneath me and rolled onto the street. Kane's hand braced me gently. "Amy, what happened? Can you turn back for me?"

I let a whine escape and turned my head away from his questions as Kane continued wiping away the remnants of Matt's gore with a cloth.

He made the mistake of rubbing my shredded skin the wrong way. I yelped and shot my head up, opening my eyes.

Kane held my face in his hands and scrubbed my undamaged ear. "I'm sorry. We'll have you back to the farm soon enough." I lay my head in his lap for the rest of the trip, each bump jarring my tender flesh. I peeked out a slitted eye. Kane appeared fully recovered from the bullet wound, almost entirely back to his old self.

The truck turned onto a gravel road and stopped, the engine falling silent. But searing pain coursed through me again as they hoisted me into the house.

Moira made a sound of surprise and disgust, chiding the men for their handling of me.

"Don't move her like that! Lay her on the floor. Carefully! Oy vey!" Her cold hands brushed the fur on my forehead. "Amy, you'll have to hold still."

I scoffed in response.

"Just while I clean your wounds. It's definitely going to hurt, but it'll be worse if you move."

159

I gritted my teeth together, anticipating more searing pain. Instead, ice cascaded over my front. I screamed in agony, the freezing liquid finding Matt's tainted blood and obliterating it. Firm arms held me down while the stuff burned away the infection, encompassing me in cold fire.

Moira offered a cup full of clear liquid. "Amy, I need you to change back so you can swish this. Can you do that for me?"

It took all my effort to allow the energy to return to my center, releasing my limbs. Bones shrank and reformed, my bullet wound protested, but exhaustion left me too weak to react.

"Very good. Now swish and spit." I took a mouthful, the bitter liquid fizzing violently. Peroxide. Moira held an empty cup for me to spit into.

Kane gingerly wrapped a towel around my undamaged flesh. "Can't you do anything for her?"

"I can mend the entry point, but too much parasite blood got in the lacerations. There's nothing more I can do." Moira pressed her hands over my leg, crawling relief soothing the damaged tissue even as it throbbed.

Moving without poison infecting me was only slightly less painful. I shivered beneath the towel, the peroxide still bubbling in the new folds of my skin.

Kane hoisted me up into his arms, towel and all. I vaguely noticed that my clothes were gone, but since my skin had been turned into confetti, it was the least of my worries. "Where are we going?"

"I'm going to treat your injuries. What happened in there?"

I breathed shallow breaths to avoid stretching my skin. "Matt. They injected him with something- I don't know what."

"Who did?"

"A doctor. And- some kind of agent, I think." Tears welled in my eyes. "They threatened to kill him if I told anyone." *He never had a chance.* "How did you find me?"

Kane pushed open a bedroom door and laid me on the bed. "Johnny's father had been testing GPS trackers before he passed. We put them on all the vehicles, just in case something like this happened." He touched my uninjured nose. "Now hold still, I'm going to wrap your wounds."

He opened a bedside drawer and pulled out a first aid kit. I realized I wasn't in my own room near the kitchen. Sitting next to me, he moved my left arm onto his lap, pulling out a roll of gauze and weaving it over and under my arm. "You took on a newly made parasite without any battle training." I cringed at his words. It hurt to realize that when I destroyed the creature, there wasn't anything left of Matt. "I know he was your friend and we'll find out what happened, I promise.

161

But you're not going anywhere for a while. Not until you're all healed up. Bed rest for at least a month, and no more half-cocked adventures, okay?" The mirth didn't reach his eyes.

"What about work?" I asked groggily.

His smile was muted. "Do you really want to go back?"

"No, not particularly."

"Then don't. I'll take care of your notice. I'm sure they'll understand." Kane wrapped the other arm and shoulders, pulling me forward to bind my back and chest.

The bullet wound had since stopped bleeding because of Moira's efforts, but he wrapped it anyway. He stopped to admire my necklace, which had survived the abuse my flesh did not.

"I must look like a mummy." The cuts throbbed, but the wrappings allowed the skin to stay where it belonged.

He smiled and kissed my undressed forehead. "A cute mummy." He wagged a thick finger at me. "But take it easy, I mean it. If I need to get someone to sit on you, I will."

My injuries might heal, but it would take longer to forget Matt's face contorting into something out of a nightmare. "Yeah, yeah. I don't want to move, anyway."

"I'll bring dinner, soon." He stood and turned on a television across the room. I finally noticed the bedroom he brought me to was painted a burgundy red, with vanilla sheets that smelled like him.

162

The local news streamed on the TV. He changed the channel and placed the remote in my bandaged hand.

"Channel 59 is good too, there are some re-runs of old shows." He glanced at me one last time before leaving, shutting the door behind him.

I settled into the sheets miserably and bunkered down for a long, uneventful recovery.

Chapter 22

Secret Agent Morgan Lazaro groaned out of boredom.

It had been over a month since he was admitted into the critical care unit and not a word from headquarters. His belly itched with a fiery passion, but Lazaro's broken wrists were suspended above the bed in a vice they called an 'external fixator', making it impossible to quell the burn.

The doctor had successfully restored his insides to their proper locations, leaving his peritoneum to fuse together with the help of the stitches. Dr. Casey said there was minimal damage to the internal organs; however, he warned that if Lazaro were to stand at this point in the healing phase, his work would be compromised and he could find himself back under the knife.

No one he spoke to had heard from central.

It was all much too quiet.

The director had either written him off as a lost cause or was waiting until he recovered to take corrective action.

Either way, it only deepened his uneasiness.

Word might come any day, and so could an assassin with a needle or a knife. Lazaro, himself, was given the task of neutralizing his mentor, Agent Bell, under the previous director. No one questioned a direct order, and even Bell had taken his death in stride.

Lazaro, on the other hand, had to watch his teacher die at his own hand without being given any explanation. Bell's face, frozen in agony from the neurotoxin, would stay with Lazaro for the rest of his life, which might be shorter than he had assumed.

A cheerful nurse he'd nicknamed 'Pink' leaned into the room. "How are you doing? Did you want me to change the channel or turn up the volume?" She was sweet, like the hundredth piece of candy corn. He called her Pink because she didn't go a day without wearing her hot pink scrubs and feathery earrings of the same, sickening hue. Her demeanor, also, was one of perpetual sprightliness, far too intense for the dismal clinical setting he was forced to exist in.

He didn't like how her eyes flashed when she spoke either, or the way she leaned over the bed too far to adjust the settings on his monitor.

Lazaro figured Pink should still be in high school, but since he'd turned forty-three, he couldn't tell the difference anymore.

"I'm good, thanks." He feigned interest in another terrible episode of M*A*S*H. Within the first five minutes, they'd already managed to make several tasteless jokes.

Pink hesitated at the door. "Alright, I'll be back in an hour with breakfast. Don't go anywhere!" she warned as if he could have left, leaving the door wide open.

Lazaro glanced at the clock.

It was barely past eight in the morning.

He threw his head back and sighed, settling back into the barbed cocoon to wait for a sentencing that might never come.

Chapter 23

Since ripping Matt's throat out on that cold dirt floor my dreams became twisted and dark, preventing me from truly appreciating my new place in Kane's bed. More nights than not, I awoke, sweating and crying as the guilt-riddled nightmares slipped away, only to return again the next evening with a vengeance.

The scars still burned like hell, but if he caught me itching, he'd smear calamine lotion all over me.

And I didn't look good in pink.

Kane had taken it upon himself to care for me as I healed, and it gave us ample time to discover each other all over again.

We spoke long into the night, asking each other questions about childhood, where we grew up, what our parents did. Certain memories evaded my recollection, and I admitted it was hard to remember much of anything before I turned eight.

We abandoned the quandary for more pleasurable pursuits. Kane loved to tease me with deep kisses but held himself back when our passions rose. He dismissed it with a different excuse each time until I finally confronted him.

I pinned him to the bed. "Why won't you have sex with me? Don't tell me being alpha forces you to stay celibate. And you can't *possibly* be a eunuch." I pressed my hips into his defiantly.

Kane ran his fingers through my hair and sighed. "I don't want you to rush into mating. You should know what you're getting into, and you're sort of new to this life."

In the last handful of weeks, I grew accustomed to the minute fluctuations in his mood that the rest of the pack never seemed to see. "What are you afraid of?"

He *was* scared of something.

"This job is going to kill me, sooner or later." Kane readjusted my hips so our faces almost touched. "I don't want to leave you without a mate. You deserve more than that," he said, planting a sweet kiss on my nose.

"Screw the future, we'll deal with it when it comes. We have right now, and I don't want to waste it. Love me, damn it." I pressed my lips to his fiercely.

Kane grinned between kisses. "I do," he relinquished with a murmur, "always and forever."

We mated once, twice, thrice.

Our scents mingled in the heat of desire, so I couldn't tell where my flesh ended and his began.

After one last mounting release, we sighed and fell into each other's arms, drifting in and out of sleep.

Since that morning, there was a pronounced change. We orbited each other, dancing an intricate pirouette that only we seemed to know the tempo to.

When he left, his absence with a yearning that dwarfed anything I'd ever felt. It was easy to see why he waited so long. No one would ever own my heart the way he did. I felt a renewed sense of empathy for Emily and Serena.

They both kept busy, but the pain of their losses was tangible, though they could not be compared.

Emily no longer let her children out of sight. Her body and soul waited for a mate that would never return. Sometimes Moira would comfort her, but Emily had since closed herself off to compassion. She spent days locked in her room with Riley and Izzy sometimes, refusing to emerge.

Serena did the best she could to care for her mate, who never left the new cage Gary welded for him. Though she was considerate as ever, the openness disappeared after her rescue. She still cooked and cleaned, but it seemed mechanical, as if she were on autopilot. I hoped she'd come back to us one day.

As far as anyone recalled, no one came back from what Serena's mate was afflicted with. Danny and Jean were

169

adamant about putting him down. They assumed the creature would eventually escape its confines and kill someone.

Kane refused to consider it, commissioning Gary to check the cage regularly and make absolutely certain of the integrity of the structure. He seemed to have a soft spot for Serena and wouldn't make a move against the rabid shifter she protected.

Elder Solice had, since the attack, remained in bed most days. He emerged less and less, eventually needing someone to bring in food for him at every meal. Moira gave him half a year. Through his poor health, it became apparent how close they really were.

Evvy – the girl I'd claimed in Vorrin's camp – fit in seamlessly here, working alongside Serena in the kitchen and becoming best friends with Aurora. Johnny now had to vie for Aurora's attention, and the dynamic made for interesting gossip with Crystal. Evvy's siblings, Scarlet and Quil, lost no time warming up to the horde of children, Scarlet becoming the unofficial leader of the group. Whether it was due to her distinct vermillion coloring or her age, I couldn't tell.

Everything was quiet from Vorrin's camp. There was no retaliation for our grand egress several weeks before, and Kane wondered aloud if he should pursue a peace conference with the fickle alpha. I warned him against it, unable to forget his most recent injury-by-projectile.

As soon as I was well enough to leave the house, they invited me to go on their nightly runs. Since the parasite infestation had been stemmed, we were free to roam the woods in our second forms without fear of lurking danger.

We dashed through the forest on all fours, throwing ourselves into our wild nature. Even Emily joined us for the hunt sometimes, the untamed freedom irresistible. By the end of each evening, I was winded and ecstatic. This was truly what it meant to be a shifter: existing, moment by moment, in a place of endless beauty and hidden secrets far away from the stifling city. I could see why shifters avoided living among humans. We just couldn't live up to our full potential beside them.

Spring hit suddenly in mid-April and flowers took over every inch of the farm, making my nose itch. Everyone enjoyed the spring weather, except for Danny, who remained scarce and avoided helping around the house. Serena didn't have the willpower to argue anymore, so Moira took it upon herself to box his ears now and again until he got off his ass.

Kane wasn't pleased but dismissed the idea of evicting him, despite mounting evidence.

"I'm not going to be exclusive. Danny is one of us," he said, stroking back my hair one day in bed.

"He's a dick." I couldn't believe Kane didn't see it. "He barely tolerates the kids, doesn't have any interest in helping

171

out *at all*, and he disappears with the car, doing who-knows-what?!"

He sat me on his knee. "Amy. You're new to this life. I understand it doesn't make sense the way he's acting. But everyone learns to cope differently. You seem born to it, but he isn't, and we can't change that. Give him a year, you'll see." He left a lingering kiss on my neck.

"I don't like the way he looks at Serena." *Or me, for that matter,* I thought, but kept my mouth shut.

If Danny crossed a line, I'd whip him back into it. Kane was teaching me combat training since I had mastered the various transformations and I was getting pretty good at laying a beast like him out, if I did say so, myself.

I left him to lounge on the porch by himself, irritated that he couldn't see what was right in front of him.

My stomach grumbled and I padded into the kitchen for a bite to eat, waving at Moira and Serena. "Morning." They sat at the kitchen table, nursing what smelled like Earl Grey.

Moira smiled at me. "Morning."

Serena gave a half nod, known better for her few words, as of late. I noticed something strange about her midsection.

Was it just me, or was she gaining weight?

Moira shook her head, pleading silently for me not to ask. I cleared my throat and averted my eyes. "So, um, how are things going with-"

172

"Owen," Serena finished, dejected. "That's what his father called him. He doesn't understand anything I say. His condition won't ever improve." Her mood was bitter, and rightly so.

From what I could glean, her love interest died in the parasite attack. Greg was supposed to be her mate, then their choice was taken from her. Serena had been dealt a bad hand that would affect the whole of her life.

Moira patted her arm. "You have us. It doesn't make up for a mate but we'll support you, through all of it." A thought seemed to go unspoken, hanging in the air for a moment before the children rushed through, shattering the tension.

Johnny moped into the kitchen and sat down next to Moira, dropping his head into his hands.

Moira scrutinized him. "What's gotten into you?"

He gave an irritable sigh. "*Nothing.*" I noticed his thin shoulders were thickening with muscle, soon he wouldn't be considered a kid anymore.

She smiled at the teen. "Aurora, right?"

I laughed under my breath, grabbing a cup of coffee and a muffin, and sat down beside Serena.

"Well, yeah, of course." He folded his arms. "I just don't get why she spends so much time with Evvy. I'm her mate. I want time with her, too."

I took a sip of tea. "Have you told her that?"

173

"Sure, but Evvy ripped on me, and now Aurora won't take me seriously."

Moira rolled her eyes. "Go out on a run with Aurora, just you and her. I'll keep Evvy busy tonight. And don't forget to remind her why she loves you. She'll come around."

"Yeah, I guess you're right." Johnny perked up a bit, swiping the dark hair from his eyes. "Thanks Moira."

As he left, we shared an amused look. "That poor kid. I hope he gets a break."

She dismissed my sentiment with a wave. "They'll be fine. They're mated, after all. Aurora and Evvy are the same age and Aurora's never had that since her sister died." Moira hesitated; Kane and Aurora's sister was a taboo subject in the house. Even though I knew, no one dared mention it. I didn't even know the girl's name. "They'll get over the honeymoon phase and Johnny will have her back soon enough."

"I hope so." Serena's bitter mood had abated slightly. "No reason for all of us to be miserable." She shot us a small grin, trying to make light of her own tragedy. "Ready to make breakfast?"

I smiled. "Sure." Kitchen work was the physical therapy I'd needed to heal. Now it was just habit to join in. I even enjoyed helping plan the next big feast. I set my coffee down and we began the momentous task of feeding the horde.

Chapter 24

"*Code Gray. Repeat, Code Gray*," the loudspeaker crackled overhead. "*Personnel be on alert for any suspicious behavior. Repeat, Code Gray*."

Lazaro cupped the sensitive flesh of his stomach as he pushed off the wall, forcing his legs to obey. He hissed at the pain, doing his best to ignore it. "Just move it, fucker."

A team of nurses turned down the hallway forty feet to his right. It took all his strength to roll into a corner and hide behind a linen cart. They marched past, looking for the missing patient.

P-3056 was plastered on his front. It would be pertinent to replace it if he wanted to escape. After the surgery, a black car had driven him straight to the military hospital with the claim that his health was being monitored. Lazaro's injuries were merely twisted pink scars that ran along the flesh of his belly.

No, they weren't keeping him for his best interest.

He was a prisoner here.

And he was getting out today.

"*Code Gray. Repeat, Code Gray.*" The announcement grated on his nerves.

A doctor emerged from a nearby room, ignoring the alarm. Lazaro slid in before it shut, finding himself in a locker room for hospital staff.

Perfect. He could dress as personnel and walk right out of this place. Gingerly stealing a pair of scrubs, he shook them on, careful not to jar his mangled wrists. In a few moments he was in blue shirt and pants, donning a white lab coat. The last thing he required was identification. Lazaro dumped his patient garment in the hamper. If anyone noticed, he was merely another official in scrubs.

He took one last look around the room. Lockers lined the walls, but one hung ajar. He rifled through its contents and pulled out a lanyard. *Dr. Maurice Casey.* What were the odds?

"Thank you, *Maurice.*" He put on the lanyard and checked himself in the mirror, deciding to wear a hair net to cover his spiky, graying locks.

Down the hallway, more personnel dashed around, the alarm still sounding repeatedly. He strode towards the exit, calmly and confidently so as not to arouse suspicion. Unless the staff knew Dr. Casey by name, he was unlikely to be questioned, but he turned the lanyard around just in case.

Lazaro took another right turn, realizing the entrance was directly ahead. The few people that crossed his path hadn't contested his status. *Thirty feet, twenty, ten-*

"Stop right there," a guard called. Lazaro paused and turned slowly as if he couldn't be bothered with the man.

He tried mimicking the doctor's priggishness. "What's the meaning of this?"

"I need your name and registration number, doctor."

Oh shit. "My name is doctor Maurice Casey, unit 4830 post-surgical care." He heard it a million times in the hallways over the last few weeks.

The guard approached, one hand resting casually on his gun. "Registration number?"

It was on the badge, but if he looked, it might give him away. "I-" He feigned a sneeze, racking his scars and sending a spike of pain up his spine. But he caught sight of the number as the badge turned slightly. "Excuse me. It's 4850-23."

The guard mumbled something into a headset, waited for a response and then turned to him. "Apologies, doctor. We have an AWOL situation and we can't take any risks. Have a good day." He left Lazaro standing there, astonished.

He wasted absolutely no time, marching out of the building and into the parking lot where he purloined a car to take him to headquarters.

The director owed him an explanation.

The stolen '97 Chevy Blazer rumbled to a stop.

The front gate guard, Marty, strode towards the vehicle without a care in the world. "This is private government property, what's your-" Marty finally peered through the open window and his eyes widened. "*Morgan*? Morgan Lazaro? What the hell are you doing here?! Why are you dressed like that?"

"I had to sneak out of the hospital. I'm going to see the director and figure out what the hell is going on."

"So, *you're* that AWOL everyone's been talking about-" He returned to his booth and released the gate. As it opened, he shouted, "good luck! I ain't coming to your funeral!"

Lazaro dipped his head to Marty, whose gaze passed over him as if he was driving a hearse. His forehead tightened as he entered the lion's den.

Lazaro had broken protocol today, and the director could very well order his head in a box before the end of it. But he had nothing to worry about.

He was already a dead man.

*

"What the fuck, Lazaro?" Director Aldridge slammed a thick fist on the desk and a vintage green desk lamp shuddered in response. Aldridge may have gone gray in the last few years but it did not diminish his intimidating presence.

"Sir, let me expl-"

"No excuses. You failed. Then, despite direct orders to remain in the hospital, you went AWOL and stole a lieutenant's vehicle to come here, of all places! Give me one good reason I shouldn't put a bullet in your head right now." Aldridge's brow furrowed with supreme irritation.

"If I may be candid?" His words garnered no response from the director, so Lazaro continued anyway. "You sent me on a bullshit mission and withheld important intel regarding the nature of my subject and the potential dangers. You can't hold this against my otherwise flawless record."

He straightened his tie with thick fingers. "I gave you a mission, *Lazaro*. It seemed to me that you worked on your toes."

"You don't deny it, then," Lazaro pushed back. "That man wasn't normal, nor was my target. You knew, and you kept it from me."

Aldridge sighed, looking disgusted. "Honestly, we didn't know about the third party until after. But part of your job is to assess each facet of the situation and take the correct steps in protecting government property. That's *you*." He weaved his hands together, his fingers barely closing. "We've known for a while that there are other... species, that live alongside us. They blend in, for the most part. But sometimes they become a problem and we have to make sure they don't endanger the general population or risk exposure. The country could fall into chaos if civilians knew half of what we do."

Species? Though he rehearsed this confrontation in the hospital, this was the last thing he expected. "What the hell does that mean?"

Director Aldridge's intensity waned into an uncharacteristic unease. "Monsters- creatures, whatever you want to call them." He looked incredibly uncomfortable even mentioning it. "You know what? I'll have Dr. Warren fill you in."

Lazaro felt deceived. He'd gladly give his life for his country, but not without a damn good reason. "Did you even *need* intel on Amy Ryker? Or were you trying to get me killed?"

"My intention was to have you witness her, ah, changing." Aldridge waved his hand flippantly. "There was another agent tailing you, making sure you didn't go AWOL on the field. I had no intention for you to come into contact with one of them."

"Who was the other agent?"

"Classified. Any other questions?"

"Are you going to fire me?" They both knew what that would entail.

"No. You're a great field agent." Aldridge hesitated again. "I'm putting Dr. Warren in charge of you. Temporarily. Then we'll see where it goes."

Relief bloomed in Lazaro's chest. "When will I meet him?"

Aldridge shot him a secretive smile, picking up the phone. "Have Dr. Warren meet in my office immediately." He hung up. "Lazaro, I do want to make one thing crystal clear: if you ever disobey an order again, I will personally see to it that you're terminated on site. That being said, you handled your first experience with the- um, *supernatural* quite well, even if your first mission wasn't a success."

Before he could follow up with another question, a timid knock interrupted the tentative resolution.

A gentle woman's voice spoke through the door. "You wanted to see me director?"

"Come in, doctor."

The first thing Lazaro noticed was the fiery red locks that had haunted his dreams at the hospital. *You.*

Her green eyes flashed in recognition before quickly sliding to the director. "Good afternoon."

"Afternoon." Aldridge nodded to her. "Doctor, this is agent Lazaro. Agent Lazaro, doctor Warren. He needs orientation to the work you do. Show him around, introduce him to your team. Lazaro, when you're finished, you'll meet with a physical therapist in conference room B."

Lazaro nodded and turned to the short doctor, offering his hand out to her. She smelled of lavender this time, and on her hand was not a ring, but the indent of one. "Nice to meet you."

"Likewise." Dr. Warren took his hand and shook it firmly, her skin warm in his grip. For a larger woman, she was adorable in her softness, her features kind and open by nature.

The director plucked a radio from his desk and turned it on. "Attention personnel, the AWOL is secured. Repeat, the AWOL is secured." When the button released, he nodded towards the door. "Out of my office, and don't come back without an appointment, Lazaro."

He dipped his head and followed Dr. Warren out of the stuffy room.

As they walked down the corridor, the silence between them intensified until he couldn't stand it any longer. "Where exactly are we going?"

"My lab." She spoke curtly, mashing the elevator button.

Lazaro eyed her. Perhaps she didn't think he remembered her from the hospital. He had been on heavy painkillers at the time but he still recalled her soothing voice and those intense, verdant eyes that saved him from countless nightmares.

They reached the basement, and she turned left into a long, whitewash hall. Fatigue was building up in his muscles already. They'd atrophied slightly in the hospital, remaining unused for so long, and his breathing was harder than he should have been. "Are we almost there?"

She glanced back at him, a flash of pity sparkled in her eyes before she turned away again. "Almost."

An unobtrusive white door sat to their left. She ran her key card over the reader and the door clicked. The doctor shoved inside with a firm push. Lazaro followed through, the muted hum of mechanisms and voices greeted them.

Men and women in lab coats set up machinery jotted notes onto yellow pads and stared into microscopes.

A young, peppy woman strode towards Dr. Warren, her face flush. "Samantha, I figured it out!"

"Hang on a minute, Gabby," Dr. Warren hushed the excited girl. "Everyone, can I have your attention, please?" Those who could pulled away from their work and waited for her to speak. Those who couldn't disappeared behind the gathering crowd of scrubs and gowns. "This is agent Morgan Lazaro. He'll soon be out on the field collecting samples and gathering intel on our local creepy crawlies." The last phrase garnered a small laugh from the group. "Make him feel welcome. He'll meet you one-on-one as necessary to his missions."

The group dissipated. A few half-hearted waves and introductions were offered until it was just him, Dr. Warren, and the girl Gabby, itching to tell her something.

Dr. Warren looked up at the lanky girl. "Alright, what were your findings?"

"I think I found a cure to the V-32405 strain!" Gabby held out a stack of papers, unable to wipe the grin off her face. Lazaro couldn't help but judge her front tooth, which nestled behind the other like a shy twin. The air in the lab was as stuffy as the director's office, and he needed to rest.

Dr. Warren turned to him first. "My personal office is in the back, brown panel door. I'll be there in a minute." She pointed towards a door at the rear of the lab.

He left, happy to be away from the exuberant intern.

Papers ruffled. "What evidence do you have?"

"Subject 4D is showing marked improvements in cognitive functioning since yesterday's dose. It's in the results, I'll have more later when…"

Lazaro opened the door and slid through, thanking the powers-that-be he didn't gain weight in the hospital, despite Pink's best efforts.

The dark office was completely black. He turned and passed a hand over the wall to find a switch, flipping it on. The fluorescent lights hummed to life and revealed a huge display case directly in front of him with a figure inside so strange, it took a moment for him to adjust.

A bipedal wolf, frozen in mid-swipe stood inside the display, towering above him. Glassy eyes unfocused inserted above a permanent snarl.

It irritated Lazaro that it gave him a shock, but he soon amused himself at the quality of the work. Whatever artist created this piece had an eye for detail. He couldn't see the seams between the patches of fur.

These things were a novelty in southern bars. The most popular was the Jackalope, which a taxidermist would fuse deer horns to a rabbit's skull.

For this piece, there was no placard to indicate the year it was made or the artist. If he stood at the right angle, he could believe, for a moment, that it was one complete figure, the way they intended it to look.

There were other cases in the room, he distracted himself from the most obvious one and perused the far wall. A single claw was framed, with the first finger bone still attached. The frame offered no description, like the one before it. A huge jar contained some sort of jellyfish, preserved in a yellow fluid. The skin had since turned a sickly green where once it might have been a deep purple.

Nearing the doctor's desk, he noticed a cage fit for a lizard. Upon inspection the container was noticeably absent of any reptile, empty save for green slime dripping off of a small log. An eyeball plopped out of the goo and regarded him with intense boredom. Lazaro almost threw himself onto the desk, disturbing a very ordinary stuffed raccoon.

The doctor stood in the doorway. "Having fun?"

"What the *hell* is that?" He pointed at the aquarium with an accusatory finger.

"It's a Gelantine. His name is Leonidas." Dr. Warren rounded her desk, touching display cases on her way. "I'm surprised you weren't more interested in the rest of my collection." She plopped down in her chair and scooched forward, indicating Lazaro to sit as well.

He did, boxed in by the stuffed bear-dog that greeted him at the door. Lazaro indicated the display case. "Very impressive."

"Oh, it's quite real. That's a werewolf."

"A *werewolf*," he said in his disbelief.

"Yep! There's also an exotic shapeshifter claw over there." She pointed at the claw. "A collection of little people's artifacts in the corner." Across from Leonidas' cage lay tiny pick-hammers and equipment. "And vampire hands, paired with the skull. That's my favorite."

Lazaro's mind reeled. *Vampires, werewolves?*

Dr. Warren must have seen the look on his face. "Yes, they're real." She tucked a stray curl behind her ear. "Everything you think you know is wrong. While you're here, don't assume anything. The world is much bigger than we like to imagine."

"... they're *all* real?" He turned to the werewolf with renewed astonishment. It had to be at least seven feet, almost two feet taller than himself. Panning back around the room with awe, he saw the Gelantine motor its way over to a water bowl. The creature's slimy bulk rippled to accommodate a lack of appendages.

"You, agent, were attacked by a werewolf." The doctor leaned over the table, waiting for his response.

"You're not kidding." He realized, touching his stomach. The memory of his organs exiting his body was still fresh. "Then- my target was one as well." The director had told him she was supposed to change. Was that what he meant?

"Bingo." Dr. Warren grinned triumphantly. "She was just about to turn for the first time. Aldridge briefed me on your case after you were admitted. He needed my expertise to see if you'd become one."

"And if I had?"

"We'd have met on, ah- different terms." She fiddled with a pen. "I was able to get a sample of your blood to make sure

187

you weren't susceptible to the change. After the results came in, you were allowed to heal in the hospital."

He didn't want to admit that he remembered everything. Not yet. "I'm safe, then?"

"You won't turn into one, but that doesn't mean they're all bad. There's plenty of them coexisting among civilians as we speak. You've probably met a few in your life and didn't even know it." She gave a weak shrug. "In this field, it's best to scrap the idea of 'good' or 'evil'. The things we deal with don't fit neatly into those categories."

"What's my job, then?" Lazaro wanted to wrap his head around something simple.

"You'll do what you do best: fieldwork. The only difference is you'll have a new set of targets. Keep your distance and report back to me. Collect samples if it applies. We'll show you how."

His eyes narrowed. "That sounds too easy."

"Trust me, it isn't." Dr. Warren smiled, amused at his assumption. "That's why we need you. But you won't go unprepared, we've got a few tricks up our sleeves when it comes to the supernatural." She stood and rounded the desk. "Let me show you what we're dealing with." Samantha proffered a hand.

Lazaro took it, cautiously putting weight on his wrists. He was surprised at the doctor's strength as she hoisted him up.

She led him into the lab and took a right.

"The lab techs work long hours to find solutions to unorthodox problems. We had an infestation of Gelantines in Capitol's water pipes. One of my interns discovered a salt residue that dissolves their protective outer layer. We ran a few treatments through the water supply and within a week the threat was gone. Leonidas is sort of a living relic. I'm keeping him to test their lifespan. And he's cute."

They passed a lab tech dropping a bluish liquid onto fresh slides and collecting them in a wooden case.

"That's Mitchell. You'll meet him later." She waved him towards a big metal door. "Fair warning, it's going to get loud." Dr. Warren ran her card again, and the metal door hissed open. Hot air and an explosion of sound blasted them both. Hideous shrieks and hoots echoed through the room, big metal cages were inserted wall-to-wall, filled with a menagerie of true nightmares.

Dr. Warren shut the door behind her after ushering him in. "Stay away from the bars!" she shouted over the raucous, walking him through the madness.

To their left, a group of amorphous gray balls of fur rolled around on their own accord, screeching out of four orifices with no eyes that he could see.

The next held what appeared to be a writhing snake, floating around in a huge aquarium. He realized that the 'snake' had not one, but four tails and a tentacled head that bobbed with the water, watching them intensely.

Another held a single black vial, stoppered with a silver top.

"That's a wraith!" she explained. "No one wants that thing to break! It would be the end of our studies here!" Dr. Warren kept walking. "And this one, we think is a shapeshifter!" She indicated a huge silverback gorilla, roaring and shaking the bars. "He's in his secondary form! Sometimes they don't turn back for years! This one has a unique set of horns, too, but we can't figure out exactly why!"

Lazaro was stopped by the next cage.

A little girl was curled up on the floor, sobbing quietly. He saw the rise and fall of her tiny frame and wanted so badly to free her. Lazaro hunkered down for a better look. Her body tensed. The doctor tapped him on the shoulder and said something, but he couldn't quite hear. The little girl's head lifted, and she pulled herself off the ground, her back to him.

He waited for her to turn around.

She did slowly, her face wet with tears. Golden hair fell over her thin shoulders.

'Help me,' the girl whispered clearly, despite the noise. 'Help me.' The sweet voice carried through the air.

A firm grip yanked him back into reality and he saw the girl for what she was. Her eyes were empty sockets and her mouth a gaping, screaming coal chute.

She reached out to grab him with bony hands, missing him by an inch, thanks to the doctor.

"I told you to stay back! Once she touches you, that's it!" Samantha let go of him. "I have one more thing to show you and we'll get out of here, alright?!"

Lazaro's nerves were shot, and he wasn't sure he could survive another 'revelation'. But he followed her in a daze. They passed the rest of the cages without introduction, coming to a final door. Dr. Warren punched in a passcode and he entered a quiet living room straight from the '60's.

The hum of an old television came into focus. It was a room out of time. The furniture was all painted tacky yellows and oranges. A singular couch upholstered in an ugly green cloth sat across from the television. There was, perhaps, a kitchen around the corner and an adjoining bedroom.

The space had the basic comforts of a home, as if he'd stepped back into a grandmother's living room.

"Clara?" Dr. Warren called into the quiet space. "There's nothing to be afraid of. I want you to meet a friend of mine."

A young face peered out from around a corner, her intense, blue eyes wide with worry.

"This is agent Lazaro. Can you introduce yourself?"

191

Clara stepped out from her hiding place. She was in a plain, white sundress that contrasted nicely against her almond skin.

The girl was tall and lanky, about an inch taller than Lazaro himself. What shocked him the most was that she appeared entirely ordinary. The faint hint of roses wafted as she curtsied. "My name's Clara. It's nice to meet you."

"Likewise." He smiled up at her, perplexed.

The doctor looked all too pleased with herself. "Can you tell him why you're here, Clara?"

She nodded. "I'm a werewolf."

"Good girl." Samantha patted her back. "Go ahead and watch your show. Lunch will be here soon and then we'll work on evaluations, okay?"

"Okay." Clara's face broke into a grin as she plopped on the sofa, picking up the remote to turn up the volume.

As Lazaro glanced between the two of them, Dr. Warren stepped towards the door. "She was found in the wreckage of a hidden lab. It was set up by a covert section of the security department several years back. They were doing horrible tests on the subjects there. Then something happened and most of the subjects escaped, except for her. She barely survived the gunshot wounds. Since then, I haven't allowed anyone to handle her but myself and a few of the assistants. She's too delicate." Samantha glanced at the girl fleetingly. "Ready to get out of here?"

"Absolutely." He took a breath, bracing himself for the barrage of noise.

Dr. Warren unlocked the door again, and the sounds hit him, hot and loud. She ushered them through the narrow hall through the next door and slammed it shut with finality. "Sorry about that. They're louder with new people. What do you think?"

Unable to admit that his hands still quaked, he shook his head. "It's a lot to take in. Do you have any coffee?"

"We've got a lounge. I'll show you."

Past her office was a small nook dedicated to beverages.

"Milk? Sugar?"

"Black is fine." He took the cup gratefully and blew on the liquid's surface. Warmth flooded his core as he took a sip, settling his nerves. "Talk about a fucking crash course."

"Yeah, sorry. I know it's quick, but the important thing is how you handle it. This was test number two, and you passed."

Lazaro rolled his eyes. "Should I expect another?"

Dr. Warren grimaced, as much an apology as he would probably get. "Not that I'm aware. The first encounter is the worst because you're not expecting it, after that it gets easier to process. We all survived something. I went to school for biochemistry, not cryptozoology. But, here I am."

193

Lazaro took another draw of coffee. "Why *are* you in this business? It can't be the money."

Dr. Warren shifted in her chair and blushed, her cheeks reddening pleasantly. "Me?"

She's cute flustered, he thought, watching her over the rim of his cup as he took another sip.

"Well, it started when I was taking a course for my doctorate and there was a class called 'field biology'. They sent us to Manaus, Brazil so we could study phylogenetic mutations – the evolutionary history of organisms – of the Lantern Fly. It was supposed to be a fun, *engaging* class. Instead, we encountered something- horrible." Her eyes glazed over and she was no longer seeing Lazaro. "It murdered most of my classmates and the teacher before we escaped." She seemed to shiver at the memory. "We found a way to drive it off with what supplies we had, and it eventually retreated into the rainforest. When we returned to the US, director Aldridge debriefed us and offered me a position here, after I completed my doctorate." She glanced back at Lazaro, the red in her face returning.

"It must have been terrifying."

Dr. Warren took a sip of her own coffee.

The silence lingered, but this time he didn't feel obligated to disrupt it. Not after the unearthly howling in the holding room.

Samantha was the first to break it. "So, um, do you have any other questions?"

Lazaro's nerves had settled enough for him to think again. "Why don't we see more on the field?"

Her eyes lit up, as if the distraction were a blessing. "Good question. Some people go their entire lives without ever crossing their path. One, they're good at hiding in plain sight as they've been doing it a *long* time. Two, when a case does come in with a possibility of supernatural elements, we review the data before taking it or leave it with the director to assign a regular agent. If there's even a chance, we'll keep the mission and turn it over to one of our own agents, like you." She stirred her coffee slowly.

"How many agents do you have?"

"Two? Three, now that you're here. But you probably won't meet the others. Unless you have any more questions, you can go to your physical therapy. We'll contact you in a few days. Here's my card." She pulled out a crisp white business card and handed it to Lazaro. "If you need anything."

Lazaro stood, pocketed the card, and offered his hand again. "Thanks for your time, doctor."

Samantha took it, her hand just as warm and gentle as he remembered. "Absolutely. Do you want me to show you out of the basement?"

"Yes, please. I don't have the faintest idea."

195

Lazaro entered his cold, dark apartment. He didn't have a family to return to. It was easier, in his line of work, not having any ties to civilian life. No pictures lined the walls, no decorations, or silly accents to distract from the missions. There was nothing to incriminate him, nor to identify him.

Perfectly anonymous.

He flung the lab coat and lanyard onto a bland coffee table and sank into the leather couch. The knotted scars protested as he relinquished control of his body, allowing the plush seats to carry his weight. Lazaro's wrists ached from the physical therapy. He'd have to return the Chevy in the morning and get his own car towed back to the apartment.

Maybe he'd keep the lanyard to remember his near-miss.

The idea of sleeping in a bed was appealing, but sheer exhaustion weighed down on him, refusing to abate.

He could worry about everything else tomorrow.

Chapter 25

Things were going splendidly. Danny called in weekly updates and tried not to draw attention to himself.

Until he got the phone call.

Agent K informed him that he now had to enter some decrepit rich fucker's manor and steal an artifact from a vault. The code, along with the tools he needed, were all provided by airdrop for his convenience.

Danny wondered how much shit he would have to put up with until his servitude was complete. Being everyone's lapdog was exhausting. To top it off, Kane had been riding him for a week because he was 'too lazy' and needed to be 'part of the pack'. Fun.

Danny trudged through the brambles, dragging the utility sack behind him. If the agent was correct, he'd be arriving at the property in about a thousand feet.

All he knew was the inhabitants were supposed to blame Kane for the theft, but he didn't understand why. If the agent was upfront about his schemes, maybe they could have collaborated.

Either way, once he finished breaking in, Danny would plant the evidence and get the hell out. He'd wait for the world to end with his feet up.

Before he even crested the final hillock, a cloud of roiling death wafted over him. It set his hairs on end. *Vampires, of course*. He groaned and checked his watch: three minutes left.

The agent had set up a decoy to distract the residents, giving him exactly twenty minutes to get in, snag an object, and get out. He'd plant it in Amy's bedroom, a final touch of his own.

Danny's heart skipped a beat as he checked the time again: two minutes.

Something stirred within the manor. A light flickered and he could see figures moving around; talking, arguing? One vampire dashed out the front door, into the night, then several more followed until the house sat quiet as a tomb. He was lucky to have seen them at all.

The watch flashed twice more, and it was time.

Danny hoisted the pack over his shoulder and jogged towards the building. He checked every angle before advancing.

They left the doors wide open, just for him.

Provided was a layout of the building, Danny knew the vault was in one of the sub-basements, beyond a storage room.

Stepping into the stale building, the floorboards whined in protest. He ignored the sounds of the old manor and found a door that matched a mark on the blueprints.

Danny dashed down the narrow steps until he arrived at a huge metal door. As he gripped the lever, a chill ran up his spine.

There was bad vampire juju in there.

The door opened easily on well-oiled hinges. In the dim light, there was a table laden with shiny metal tools. The sour air blasted Danny in the face and he almost vomited. So much blood had been spilled here, it was impossible for him to breathe.

As his eyes grew accustomed to the dimness and the constant sting every time he blinked, he saw restraints bolted to the wall and more tools that appeared recently used in a rusted bucket. Danny wasn't a saint, but *this* was pure evil.

He plugged his nose and entered, avoiding dark stains on the ground. The pack would definitely smell it if he tracked that shit back to the farm.

The layout indicated there should be a lever somewhere to release a false wall, allowing him access to the inner vault. Checking the watch, he cursed, having already wasted six minutes. Agent K was stringent about the time limit. His safety 'couldn't be guaranteed' after the twenty-minute window.

Danny approached the table, picking a few of the tools up and regretted it instantly. The tools were still wet with some unfortunate sucker's blood. Leaning down, he grabbed a handful of dirt and rubbed it around his fingers. He noticed a switch against the wall, concealed by the table.

Danny grinned at his own dumb luck.

Once his hand was clean enough, he flipped the lever. The concrete wall rumbled to life and slid apart.

Behind them was a narrow hallway with snuffed-out torches lining the wall. Following them back he found another door made of old wood.

No lock barred his passage.

Within lay a huge collection of riches; gems, jewelry, boxes filled with gold bars, and a solitary safe near the back. Danny stuffed a handful of diamond necklaces into his pocket before trying the code.

It accepted it and sprang open.

Inside were just four items: two heavy coins that might have been Greek pressed flat with a design and made of copper. A large emblem which bore Egyptian hieroglyphs, weighing several pounds and made of pure gold. The last item was a simple vial, filled with a reddish liquid. Danny refused to touch it, knowing it was some creepy vampire thing he wanted absolutely nothing to do with.

Deciding to take the emblem, he stuffed it in the pack. If nothing else, it was the most valuable item there, which was always a plus. Danny backed out of the vault and checked his watch, three minutes remained of his twenty-minute allowance.

He readjusted the backpack and closed the secret entrance. The wall rumbled again, closing off the hallway. Satisfied, Danny dashed through the heavy metal door and up the stairs.

When he was finally at the edge of the woods, he glanced at the manor one last time, smiling to himself. He'd just pulled off a rather profitable heist.

Now, he just had to get back before they began to wonder.

Chapter 26

As the pack cleaned up after dinner, I stole away for some fresh air and a moment to myself.

I still wore the necklace and hadn't taken it off since the day Matt died. It was comforting when I healed, now it was simply habit to keep it on.

I stepped off the patio and into the garden, realizing spring was already in full force.

With the chill of winter gone, buds erupted from the earth into a magnificent blanket of greenery. The strawberries would be ready soon as well as rhubarb and asparagus. Kane expected deliver a shipment of produce to Bob's in a week or two, as well as a few other venues he had connections with.

Deep in the woods, third shift was returning from a run. We still hadn't heard a word from Vorrin's pack, so we thought it best that they patrol the perimeter regularly, just in case. No one allowed me to go on a shift run just yet. They wanted me to hone my fighting skills, first, before I went with them.

Danny, Emily, and Kane came into view, sprinting back to the farmhouse. I waved at them and Kane changed trajectory, bolting towards me and shedding his second form. He closed the gap and grabbed me around the waist. I stood on my toes to return his kiss. From the corner of my eye I saw Emily retreat into the house, but not before she shot me a bitter glance.

"How did it go?" I asked, sobered by Emily's resentment.

He reclined in a lawn chair, pulling me on top of him and inhaled my scent with a sigh. "No sign of trespassers." Kane captured my mouth again, making me squeak. A rumbling chuckle escaped his throat.

When we finally pulled away, I could feel a set of eyes on us. Danny stood awkwardly, shifting from one foot to the next. Kane noticed and sat up, readjusting me on his lap with an unamused look on his face.

"Kane, can I speak with you?"

I still had mixed feelings about him. Though he'd been a complete asshole the first time I met him, he also helped me get to Matt, even though his death was a miserable failure on my part. And Danny hadn't pulled any shit since.

"What is it?" Kane's irritation shifted into stern disapproval. Danny had been given a firm talking-to already, which didn't seem to change his behavior in the least.

He eyed me. "Alone, please?"

I moved to stand, but Kane stopped me with a forearm. "Anything you have to say in front of me, you can say in front of Amy."

Danny squirmed under the searing glare.

"It's alright." I moved his arm with a gentle shove. "You two should talk. I'll be in the bedroom when you're done." I winked and withdrew into the house.

Kane wanted me to be included in all pack matters, but in this instance, it was important for he and Danny to reconcile their differences alone.

My presence shouldn't have been a hinderance to the trust he'd built with them. It was a big move for Danny to approach him directly like this.

I dashed to the bedroom and peeked out the window to watch their exchange. Danny's back was to me as he expressed whatever concerns he had. Kane retorted with what looked like a grunt, which Danny responded to in great length.

The words 'big responsibility' crossed Kane's lips and his face softened slightly. Danny agreed enthusiastically, reciprocating with animation.

He pointed to the woods and spoke again.

Kane nodded, stroking his goatee in consideration. Their unabashed nudity was still hilarious to me, though I was already used to it by now.

Kane agreed to something, and they parted ways.

A moment later, he shuffled into the bedroom, seeming exhausted from the shift. I pulled him to the bed, impatient to hear about their exchange. "What did he want?"

"Danny asked to be in charge of the shift runs." Kane sounded astonished. "He's going to lead third shift tonight."

I pursed my lips. "Why the hell would Danny want more responsibility than he already has?"

"I don't know, but I'll give him this chance, and if he does well, he can lead another. Maybe he's finally starting to come around."

I pushed him onto his back. "It's still Danny, he's still the laziest clod on this farm. But forget everyone else, I need time with my mate."

"Yes ma'am," he growled, hoisting me up and running his nails along my thighs. Kane unbuckled my belt as I threw my shirt off. I moved to unlatch my bra when he stopped my hands, pulling me close. "That's my job." He found the latch, and pulling it apart, letting the bra drop. My heart fluttered as he ran his hands up my ribs and rolled my breasts in his palms.

"Quit your teasing," I rubbed the firm muscle of his hips and pressing myself against him. "Don't make me beg."

"I prefer you do." Kane rolled me on my back and finished tearing my pants off. He leaned down and trailed a path up my stomach with his tongue, kissing my shoulders and throat. He buried his face in my hair as we tasted each other.

Our scents mingled until there was no difference between him and I, and I was home.

*

When we finally tore away from our passionate reunion, the sun hung low in the window. I lay next to Kane as we caught our breath, cooling from the exertion.

I rolled a lock of his hair around my finger and tugged gently. "Third shift should be heading out soon. Should we see them off?"

Kane curled around me, locking me to him in a steely embrace, his breath in my ear. "Not yet. Five more minutes."

I giggled and stroked his tangled dark hair into place. "Fine." I planted a kiss on his forehead. "Five more minutes."

A knock on the door interrupted us well before time was up. "Sorry to bother." Kyren's voice was muffled but urgent. "Third shift needs instructions."

Kane didn't move an inch, still curled around me. "Then give them instructions! It's just a normal run."

Kyren hesitated at the door. "Yeah, but Danny isn't listening to anything we have to say. I think it's better if you tell him, yourself."

"Alright." Kane released me and sat up to find his jeans, grumbling to himself. "Be there in a sec."

I found my clothes, one at a time, strewn about the room. My bra hung off the bedside lamp; I snatched it and shifted it back on before anyone else happened to see it.

As I tugged on my pants, Kane slipped a shirt on, barely containing his rippling muscle. "Take your time." He caressed my lower back, planting a kiss on my head before leaving.

When I arrived in the living room, Danny appeared antsy.

Most of the pack was present, except for Solice and Serena.

"You've done the same run with us so many times, and you asked for this responsibility. Don't forget that." Kane shot Danny an incredulous look. "Should Kyren lead the run?"

"No!" Danny choked back a yell. "No, I mean, I can do it." He bowed his head. He appeared frightened. Maybe it was the pack members scrutinizing him.

"Then don't waste our time, show me you can." Kane peered down at Danny through narrow eyes. "Gary will be your second, and Jean, do you mind going as well?"

Jean's smile faded as he glanced at Danny and pulled his wife close. "Sure."

Kane's order was cold. "You're losing daylight. Move out."

Danny changed without hesitation and dashed out the open doorway, with Gary and Jean chasing after.

"Do you think he'll be alright?" Moira asked Kane, putting a hand on his forearm where I'd very recently bitten him during sex. I reddened, wondering if she noticed.

"Gary and Jean are with him. They can take over if Danny isn't able to lead. But I'm surprised he's acting that way, there isn't much to leading the run."

Maxwell, folded in Kyren's embrace, watched an old black-and-white classic. Johnny and Aurora also meandered to the couch, followed shortly after by Evvy. The young couple seemed to be making amends.

Crystal sat next to them, cuddled with Xander, and read him a storybook. Her eyes slid occasionally to the window, anticipating her mate's return.

Emily had already stormed off onto the porch, her mood yet to improve, but she was no longer stricken with immobility and often made appearances around the house.

"I've got an idea." Kane nudged me and strode to the kitchen. I followed as he grabbed a bottle of wine and some glasses. We went out back and found Emily and Serena watching the sunset together, a nearly inseparable pair as of late.

"Let's celebrate." Kane set down the glasses and uncorked the wine with a flourish.

Emily's mouth turned down. "There's nothing *to* celebrate."

"Of course, there is." Kane poured the rouge liquid. "We're alive. The children are safe. Things around here have been terminally boring, which I could get used to. We'll be sending a shipment of produce out soon. And we haven't seen any parasites in over a month. That's quite a lot to celebrate." He handed out the glasses, one to each of us.

Crystal found her way over with a ginger ale in hand, rubbing her stomach indicatively. "Jean and I have a bit of news, ourselves."

Only I seemed to notice Serena's look of dejection.

Emily groaned at the revelation. "Are you *trying* to overrun the farm with little mutant brats?"

Kane shot her an incredulous look. "Emily."

I took a swig, ignoring their banter and enjoying the bitter tingle on my tongue. The merlot reminded me of when Matt was alive and human, long before I'd ever made my first transformation. Kane reclined next to me and caressed my knee, taking a swig of his own drink.

Since our mating, he was more aware of my emotions, as I was to his.

He responded to something Serena had said while I zoned out, wondering if this was what being part of a family felt like. Serena's mood had improved mildly, despite no new development in her mate's condition. She'd taken the whole thing in stride and we were all proud of her for staying strong despite losing her choice.

A sudden sense of weightlessness encompassed me with a whoosh of air as I was whisked out of my seat. I could still feel the warmth of Kane's hand on my knee, the cold rushing in to take its place.

My vision departed rapidly from Kane and the others. Ice-cold hands gripped my stomach and neck, holding me securely against a bony frame.

I unleashed my claws and tried to tear the grip away to no avail, the arms around me constricting to the point of crushing.

"Kane Blackmoor."

Kane was already standing, his glass of wine shattered on the porch. I craned my neck to see my captor; he was rancid, like death and old blood. My nose shriveled in defense. The creature had a wisp of peppered hair streaked back, with a prominent nose and pitch-black eyes. Though he appeared to be a man in his forties, I could tell he was much, much older.

Kane took a step forward, his eyes wide with shock and desperation. "Let her go."

"She is mine until you return what you stole. But you better hurry, if you want her back in one piece." He took a step backwards, into the evening, yanking me back with him. "You have until sunrise." The cool palate of the night swirled into darkness, too fast for me to comprehend.

Chapter 27

Kyren caught a glimpse of Amy being whisked away into the darkness through the kitchen window. He ran outside, finding Kane in the garden crouched on the edge of change. But this time, roiling energy steamed off his skin.

Kyren jogged to his side, more than a little wary of the unstable alpha. It had been a long time since Kane lost control over his blood-wolf. "Hey, man. It's okay. Amy will be alright."

Kane stared up at him, his eyes burning a coal red.

He'd been able to calm him in the past, but now that he was mated, it might be impossible to quell the beast. Kane was the only one of his kind. And, as far as anyone could tell, the blood-wolf's passions ran deep. Kyren kept his voice gentle and low. "Listen to me, Kane. *Don't change*. If you do, we won't be able to help Amy. It will be *okay*."

Kane struggled with control, but eventually he took a deep breath and the heat simmering off him dissipated. The last of the fury ebbed into the surrounding air and he shook himself, his eyes returning to their usual pale blue hue. "I'm-sorry."

The danger had passed.

Kyren gripped Kane's shoulder. "It's alright. We'll get her back, I promise."

Kane's chuckle was dry. "What would I do without you?"

Kyren led him to the porch so he could recuperate. Moira and Maxwell joined them, looking distressed. "The first thing we need to do is withdraw third shift. We'll need every battle-ready shifter to get Amy away from that old bat."

Emily pointed to the edge of the forest. "Speaking of-"

Only two wolves had returned, several hours early.

Gary changed back as he ran, breathing hard. "Danny's gone! He bolted when we rounded the west edge of the property. Took off like a rocket. We couldn't keep up."

Maxwell's glance slid to Kyren. "What do you bet it's got something to do with the vampire problem?"

He nodded, considering their next move. "Obviously, Danny knows something, but we need to rescue Amy first."

Serena stepped down from the porch, wringing her hands. "The vampire said we stole something. If we find what he wants, he'll give her back without a fight. We can't go up against an ancient. He probably has a dozen offspring ready to ambush us. And even if we do manage to fight them off-" She looked at Kane before finishing. "I don't know that he'll let her live. It's too dangerous to try and fight."

Kane stared at each of them, no lingering fire in his eyes. "Then we find it. And I'll deliver it to him, myself. Kyren, if I don't come back, you're in charge."

Kyren's heart dropped. The pack would never follow him the way they did Kane, he couldn't fool himself into thinking otherwise. "But you will come back. You always do."

Kane shook his head. "Those are my orders. Find whatever it is Danny took, one way or another. I'm ending this tonight."

The group scattered through the house, tearing open the cabinets, checking under furniture, bedframes, mattresses, cabinets, anything that might conceal a mysterious vampire relic.

Within a few minutes, Johnny emerged from one of the first-floor bedrooms. "I found something." He held a tiny shard of glass between his thumb and finger. "It was in Danny's bed."

Gary inspected it closely. "It's a diamond, I think. It must have fallen off some jewelry, and I don't think he's the diamond type."

"So, we're looking for- what, a ring?" Evvy piped in.

Maxwell's face puckered in consideration. "Maybe. Either way, it's got a scent on it. We can track it down." He took a whiff and passed it around.

Kyren sniffed the diamond and searched the first floor until he came to Amy's old room. It had been repurposed into a study. Her laptop, purse, and singular picture of her family sat upon a smaller version of Kane's huge desk.

He felt bad opening a lady's purse without her permission, but when a pungent reek of death billowed out, he knew he was on the right track. Kyren grimaced, searching until, at the very bottom, he found a thick bar of gold with hieroglyphs pressed into its front and back. "I found it!" *This has to be it.* Danny was a fool if he didn't think they'd figure it out, but how had he snuck it into the house smelling like a tomb?

The pack stopped rummaging and filed into the study.

He revealed the gold piece. "It was in Amy's purse. The bag's got his scent all over it."

Aurora plugged her nose as she entered.

Evvy cringed at the smell, as well. "God, what is that?!"

Kane put his hand out. "Give it here. The diamond too."

Kyren handed them over. "Let someone come with you. It never hurts to have backup."

The way Kane looked at him made him realize the blood-wolf was just beneath the surface, clawing its way back out. "I've given the order. Follow me, and I'll kill you, myself."

No one doubted his words for a moment, the newer pack members had never seen Kane this way, but Kyren, Aurora, and the elders had.

Twice.

They moved aside to allow him passage out of the house. Kyren followed only long enough to watch him vanish into the woods. He crossed his arms as his Alpha and one of his dearest friends left to save the conduit.

All of their lives hinged on Amy's safe return.

Chapter 28

When Lazaro awoke nearly sixteen hours later, he had three messages waiting for him.

Director Aldridge wanted to meet with him again to discuss paperwork. A bizarre message left from an agent welcoming him to 'the team'. And his property manager expecting the last two months of rent, threatening an eviction notice.

A fantastic start.

One stray thought always returned no matter what he was doing, though, distracting from his obligations: when could he see doctor Warren again?

He wasn't sure why she stole his focus.

Lazaro called the other agent back on a secure line. He was given an initial, 'K', and a conference room at headquarters, arranging a meeting at midnight.

He cooked up a frozen dinner, found it to be unsavory, and promptly dumped it in the trash.

As he shrugged a jacket on, Lazaro's wrists ached and he had to monitor his ingrained habits to avoid putting too much pressure on them like he would normally do.

The drive back to headquarters on an empty road was a nice change. He pulled up to the security box and waved at the new night guard, who checked his ID and allowed him access.

But Lazaro still couldn't keep his mind off the doctor and her lab that sat just below them, teeming with unnatural life.

He looked forward to assisting in her research and wanted to be available to her the following day. She was honest in her pursuit for knowledge and seemed to genuinely give a shit about her work. He saw how well she'd taken care of the werewolf girl and even that little infestation, Leonidas.

After having his badge checked a second time, he found the conference room down the hall from the director's office. Lazaro entered cautiously, finding a slight man, roughly ten years his senior already waiting for him. "Agent K, I assume?"

"That I am." His smile was warm and inviting. "Come in. *You* are the infamous Lazaro I've heard so much about." Agent K slicked back his steel-gray hair. "Shut the door, please. We don't want any moonlighters satisfying their curiosity."

Lazaro did so and took a seat across the table from K. They watched each other, both with curious and apprehensive eyes.

Agent K was the first to speak, breaking the heavy quiet. "I have footage and information for you as we have a new development in the Ryker case. I figured you'd want to be kept in the loop, especially since it's your baby, after all." He pushed a thick file forward and used a remote to turn on a projector.

"Yes, very much." Lazaro pulled the file towards himself and opened it. It looked similar to the copies he'd been given on her before, but this one also had pictures with timestamps up to a few days prior.

"A lot has changed since you were admitted into the hospital. She's living with her own kind now." K tapped a picture of Amy. It was recently taken, with Amy surrounded by several other people he'd never seen before. "We have a mole in their group. He's kept an eye on her and collected evidence for us. We also have hours of recordings if you're interested. I consolidated the most intriguing tidbits."

"You have a mole? I mean, are they a werewolf?"

Agent K scoffed at his question. "Of course! I wouldn't send a *human* to do the job. I've implanted a tracking chip in him, so he doesn't go anywhere without my knowledge. We'll take him out when the mission's complete." He nodded resolutely. "He didn't have much of a life before this, anyway."

Lazaro didn't respond, waiting for the agent to continue.

Agent K plugged a cord into his computer, and his desktop appeared on the projector. He pulled up an icon which filled the screen with a grainy, black-and-white still-shot. Lazaro saw a man, strung up and unconscious under stark white light. Everything else was cloaked in darkness. "Do understand two things before I show you this. One: werewolves are heartless, *soul*-less creatures, no matter who they were in their human life, nothing remains once they've change. Two: this is in the name of science. We have to understand what can and cannot destroy them if we are to be their superiors." When the agent seemed satisfied with his point, the video began to play without sound.

A crude beam of light slid across a floor, illuminating the dark space. Amy stepped cautiously into view, spotting the unconscious man. She seemed to recognize him, but was interrupted by someone behind her, outside the camera's scope.

Amy mouthed something as a tall blonde in a lab coat strode past her. She grabbed the woman's arm, then released her.

Lazaro's gut clenched in anticipation.

The blonde approached the unconscious man and depressed a needle deep into his neck. Once the woman left, Amy was struck by an invisible force, *a gunshot?* After leaning down and wrapping the wound, she limped to the figure and slapped him across the face, trying to rouse him. *Matthew Pierce.* His head moved just right for Lazaro to see his features.

Pierce almost immediately began to seize.

Amy retreated a step back, watching in horror as Pierce became something unrecognizable, his skin paled and thinned, eyes sinking into his head. He screamed at Amy and tore free from the restraints.

She continued to back away, appealing to the creature from what Lazaro could guess. In a flash, Pierce dashed at her, missing by only a small margin. As he charged her again, Amy used her hand to slice a line through its stomach.

Her features, though the camera made it difficult to see, changed too. Lazaro noticed her teeth lengthen, her legs changed shape, and her hand, dripping with black liquid, had grown.

The two of them fumbled into a flurry of action, rolling until Amy was on top. But it wasn't Amy anymore. Lazaro clearly made out a wolf's head, tearing at Pierce's throat until he no longer moved. The wolf, torn to ribbons by the creature's claws, collapsed onto the corpse. Then the recording froze.

K turned to him deliberately. "So, what do you think?"

Agent Lazaro stared at the scene intently, quietly asking, "what did you *do*?" The changes he saw were shocking, but the orchestration was positively criminal.

"We simply isolated her with a newly made parasite to gauge her strengths and weaknesses."

Lazaro smashed his fist against the table. "But WHY? *You* murdered Pierce. Amy was only defending herself!"

Agent K shook his head. "It's for the greater good. You don't understand the danger this creature poses to our world as we know it."

"That's not an answer," Lazaro jammed a finger at the screen. "*When* did this happen?"

"Two days after you were admitted to the hospital-"

Lazaro cut him off. "Where is she now? Is she still alive?"

Agent K stared at him a long while before responding. "Perhaps I have made a mistake. I believed you to be a man of fact. Of evidence and proof. Was I wrong?"

"I believe in proof, and I have yet to see anything that indicates Amy Ryker is a danger unless provoked." Lazaro felt the urge to strangle the agent, but if he wanted to know any more of his plans, he had to slow his roll.

"Please allow me to explain before jumping to conclusions, will you?" K eyed him. "Are you willing to hear me out?"

Lazaro mastered himself, clearing his face of all expression, a necessary skill in his line of work. "Fine. What am I missing?"

K's smile returned to taunt him. "Maybe it's best you hear it from the beginning. Before we humans crawled from our caves, monstrous creatures roamed the earth. You've seen Dr. Warren's *zoo*. I'm sure you can imagine it well enough."

Lazaro kept himself from cringing in disgust. He didn't like the way K said her name.

"But as our culture sprang up, we were in opposition to those creatures. They drew their power from wells that run deep into the earth, all across the globe. Our ancestors learned of a way to close the currents off, sapping them of their primal energy. They soon faded into myth, and we were allowed to finally thrive as a species."

"What does this have to do with Amy?"

"I'm getting to that, Lazaro, be patient." K shuffled the papers in front of him. "Though we couldn't destroy them all, by the seventeenth century most of them were eradicated by various means. Some still live among us, but they're well-hidden and hard to detect."

Lazaro wondered if the doctor shared the same delusion. From what he'd seen, it was doubtful.

"A hundred years ago, one old witch—and before you ask, yes, *real* witches exist—claimed a conduit of great power would be born and unlock the wells, undoing thousands of years of human history in a single moment. Creatures long asleep would awaken. Those that hide among our ranks will crawl out and threaten our very existence.

"Our estimates are that within a week of the wells opening, thirty percent of the population will be killed. Two weeks, and humans will become an endangered species. In a month, the entire human race will be enslaved or extinct.

"Knowing all of this, and knowing that a single person, their *messiah* of sorts, will destroy everything we've fought for, can you allow that creature to continue living? I cannot, and I don't think a single beast's life is worth more than every man, woman, and child on earth."

"You're telling me Amy is that conduit?"

"You catch on fast, Lazaro." K's voice was cold, a blow but not delivered as such. "No matter how fond you are of her, I ask that you reserve your judgment here, for the sake of *your* species."

Lazaro puzzled over K's words. "If this was true, why isn't it in any of our history books?"

K's eyebrow rose. "Are you sure it isn't? We tend to call it 'mythology', but it's there. The Greeks wrote about it, as well as many other cultures, if you pay close attention."

"Does the director know?"

"Aldridge in charge of seeing Project Ryker through; however, he doesn't appreciate hearing the nitty gritty. I believe he's one of the superstitious types." Agent K leafed through the file in front of Lazaro and opened it on a specific page.

Lazaro stared down at the documents, concealing his frown. It contained dozens of photos, maps, and mission logs.

Reading over them, he found an image that was too familiar and reached for the knotted scar on his stomach. *Daniel Crichton, 26-year-old male, werewolf.* "That's him. That's the fucker that almost killed me."

"He's our mole. his tactics are somewhat brutal, and he has little regard for humans. But we got the son-of-a-bitch by the balls, and if the mission doesn't kill him, we will. Just last evening, he framed Amy Ryker for the theft of an artifact. We anticipate the owner will be taking swift justice. Danny's first attempt-" K's quick glance at Lazaro's stomach betrayed him. "-didn't exactly work out as planned."

He did his best to hide his dreaded realization. Lazaro looked down at the file one last time, committing the farm's address to memory. "She has to die, then."

225

"Exactly." K said with equal parts sympathy and regret. "It is for the best. I understand your attachment to the girl but I hope it doesn't impede on your commitment to the mission?"

"Of course, not. But-" he said, almost convincing himself, "-I don't understand, why haven't you killed her, yet? Surely it's not that difficult."

"She's being guarded by a hellhound and I do prefer to *live*. Normal humans don't stand a chance against a werewolf, not even in riot gear. But Daniel, he's a rabid wolf we captured. They're the easiest to snag, really, once they taste human flesh. They lose their last scrap of humanity, and we can force them into their human shape once they're in captivity."

"What do you mean?"

K averted his eyes and snagged the folder, seeming unwilling to answer any more of his prying questions. "This has been a lot of information. Let's meet tomorrow afternoon, when you're better rested. Bring any questions you may have then."

Lazaro nodded mechanically, knowing the real enemy was shaking his hand. Whatever possessed him to pursue Amy's demise was steeped in subjective anecdotes. "What time?"

"Same place, eight o'clock tomorrow night?" K pulled out his phone to punch in the meeting.

"I'll be here," Lazaro said, and he meant it. He had twelve hours to figure out a way to stop the agent from committing cold-blooded murder.

Agent K patted him on the shoulder in a gesture of comradery. "Welcome to the team, agent Lazaro."

He dipped his head in a final farewell, pacing into the hall and out the building. Lazaro counted his steps deliberately in case the agent was watching, refusing to give away the rising agitation that coursed through his limbs.

The video footage of Amy and Pierce got under his skin, and the agent's answers were equally disturbing. Not only that, but he admitted some responsibility in arranging Lazaro's 'accidental' encounter with the mole.

He finally realized he'd stepped on a hornet's nest with this one, but his only real concern was figuring out how to warn Amy before it was too late.

If she were still alive, that was.

Chapter 29

I was dumped onto a cold floor irreverently, my hip glancing painfully off the hardwood as I caught myself. My captor leaned against the doorway with his arms crossed, wearing a long, disapproving frown.

Stale air choked me as I stood to confront him, donning a defiant glare despite his murderous aura. "What the hell is your problem?"

His face contorted into a scowl, marring his smooth, pale features before he turned away. "I don't know how you dogs managed it without being noticed. None of my children would have allowed *this* to happen."

"Allowed *what*?" I looked around the sparse, dusty room with intense irritation. "I have no fucking idea what you're talking about!"

He turned to face me, his voice deadly serious. "Do *not* swear under my roof."

I laughed in disbelief, irritation threatening to bubble over into rage. "Who the *hell* do you think you are? Kidnapping me and-"

"Tempt me, child-" The tall figure towered over me, his eyes dark voids that dissuaded any further argument. "- and you will learn the extent of my wrath," he hissed between gritted teeth. The door slammed abruptly, and my captor was gone without a trace, faster than I could blink.

I glanced around the room, sparse save for a lit candelabra and a singular stuffed chair. Groaning, I plopped onto it and a plume of dust rose from the cushion. I sat there for a long while, clutching my knees to my chest. If I tried to leave, I'd only be met with the same, violent hand that had spirited me here. There was nothing to do but wait.

A slow clap shot me bolt upright, my skin flaring with shock. "Very nice work." A lanky young man, who looked about Johnny's age, took shape in the shadows. He wore the latest punk fashion, complete with a poison green mohawk that spiked skywards. "It only took you twelve and a half seconds to piss off Ezekiel. That's an all-time record, I'd say." His smile was wide, revealing two sharp canines. "The name's Garrett."

"Amy," I said warily, deflated from my previous handling. "What am I doing here?"

The kid seemed slightly more reasonable than my host. And even his face was softer, almost empathetic. "One of you stole something from the vault. Not an easy thing to do. I wonder how you managed to get ahold of the blueprints?" His eyes were disarmingly gentle, but curiosity flashed in them, exposing the eagerness he was doing well to conceal.

I stood as Garrett strode towards me, catching another whiff of death. "We haven't stolen anything." My nose wrinkled on its own accord and the inner wolf writhed to get out. "Stay the hell away from me."

He shot me an accusatory stare, all compassion gone from his features as his eyes filtered to blackness. "There's a reason we're natural enemies, you know. Your kind has been a thorn in our sides since the beginning."

There it is, I thought, *there's the monster.*

The coil in my chest loosened, threatening the change. I fought the urge. It was ill advised to transform in such small quarters with an untested enemy. Kane had taught me that much in my training.

He looked right through me and laughed at my pain. "What's wrong, little wolf? Can't you change?"

I doubled over with fur protruded from my pores. *Not yet*, I thought, bracing myself against the transition.

"Garrett!" A feminine voice shattered through the pain, making even my wolf pause. A young woman materialized behind him. Her doll-like features were marred by a scowl. "Stop it. Can't you see she's telling the truth?"

Garrett and his midnight eyes disappeared entirely, as if he never existed at all.

My stomach released some tension, but the change rippled impatiently beneath the skin. "Are you here to fuck with me, too? I already told them everything I know, which is nothing."

She offered a pleasant smile, her scowl gone. "Not in the least. You're a guest in our home, I wanted to be sure you weren't improperly handled. They mean well, but they're not used to company." She held out a hand for me to shake. "My name is Jane." When I didn't reciprocate, she dropped it to the side, swishing her yellow sundress with the motion.

"Funny way of showing it. When can I leave?"

"Not yet, I'm afraid." Jane watched me apologetically. "It's a matter of property. Once your pack delivers the cartouche, you'll be free to go. Not before."

"And what if they don't have it?"

"Then it will be a shame. You seem nice." She flipped her golden locks out of her face. A waft of the same decrepit air filled my nose. "It's rather important to my master, and I hope that, for all our sakes, your pack returns it promptly."

"What is it you think we stole?"

"An Egyptian cartouche," she said without hesitation. "A one-of-a-kind relic from the reign of Akhenaten. It has more sentimental meaning than even its monetary value, as it was a gift from his own master." Jane paused, looking to the door. "Though the others may not see it this way, we should be thanking you. Since the theft, we've secured a new location for the treasure so it'll never be at risk of theft again." She tilted her head. "Did you get outside help?"

I scoffed at her threadbare antics. "What is this, good cop, bad cop? *I* didn't do anything. If someone else in the pack did, I don't know about it! I can't think of anyone who might-" I trailed off. *Could* he *have?*

Her navy-blue eyes watched me intently. "Who?"

"It couldn't be. He doesn't lift a finger for anyone." But he was the only possible suspect, the only one that vanished far too often. "...Danny?"

"The bachelor with the dark brown hair?" she asked, then backtracked. If she wasn't a dead thing, she might have blushed. "Sorry, we like to keep an eye on our neighbors."

"If you had, you wouldn't have gotten your shit stolen." Irritation rose up again so strong that I could kick Danny in the teeth. "Are you going to kill me if we don't have it?"

Jane turned towards the door and cocked her head. "Let's hope not. Your mate is here." She was out of the room in an instant, holding the door for me. "After you."

232

I stepped into the hallway and Jane led me down a flight of stairs that curved into a main foyer. The thought of Kane being so near picked up my steps, and relief washed over me.

He would make things right.

As we descended, Ezekiel and an elegant young woman waited by the door. She was dressed in a floor-length, lavender gown and appeared extremely bored with the whole charade.

I couldn't agree more.

The front door opened to reveal a furious Kane. He flung a golden, glimmering rock at Ezekiel, who plucked it from the air effortlessly. "Beautiful work, Blackmoor. I knew you'd come through." Ezekiel studied it for a moment before tucking it into a coat pocket with a satisfactory pat.

Kane's eyes never strayed from Ezekiel. "Give my mate back. *Now.*"

My captor waved at Jane, who inclined her head, welcoming me to go with a secret smile. I jogged to Kane's side and he wrapped an arm around me. "Are you okay?"

"Fine."

As we turned to leave, Ezekiel put a skeletal hand up. "One matter more, if you'd be so kind to oblige me."

How *dare* he be amicable after ruining our evening.

Kane's rage was building. I could feel it through the thin fabric of his shirt. "What do you want, vampire?"

"Who did it? And where are the diamonds? Your thief stole more than just the artifact."

"A rogue shifter named Danny. He abandoned his duties before sunset, no doubt anticipating your retaliation. As for your diamonds-" He threw a tiny shard at Ezekiel. "He must have taken them with him. That was found in his bed."

The ancient vampire smiled wide, but it never reached his eyes. "If we happen upon this '*rogue*' shifter, might it be an inconvenience to you if he were to stop breathing?"

Kane's voice rumbled low with a growl. "You'd be doing me a favor, though it doesn't even the score. Stay away from my property and my pack, bloodsucker."

"The feeling is mutual." Ezekiel bowed deeply. "May we never cross paths again, Blackmoor."

Kane ushered me out of the building with haste as the door slammed firmly behind us. I snaked my hand through his and we walked briskly until we were deep in the forest.

When we were in the darkest part of the woods, he stopped suddenly, pulling me in for a kiss. I could taste the relief on his hot exhale. "They didn't hurt you, did they?"

A tear rolled down my cheek, and I couldn't hold back my exhaustion any longer. "No. They were fucking *weird*, but no one hurt me."

Kane gathered me up in his arms and walked us in the general direction of the farm. "You were right not to trust

Danny on the shift run. I was an idiot for giving him an inch. He tried to frame you for the theft by hiding the gold bar in your purse." He shook his head. "I can account for your whereabouts. It's him I should have kept a closer eye on."

I let out a blubbering laugh, half-way to a breakdown already. "I haven't touched my purse since-" *since Matt.* Unable to finish, I buried my face in his shoulder and cried, heaving with the weight of my own relief.

He kissed me on the head gently, a smile in his voice. "Let me know if this is going to be a regular occurrence."

"Oh, quit it," I mumbled into his shirt as he carried me home, back to the safety of the farm.

Chapter 30

Secret Agent Kipling held the phone close to his ear. "I anticipated the vampires would shed blood over the theft. They handled it with surprising cordiality, for *abominations*. And that puts us in a desperate situation. Gabriel can't be allowed to have her, or he'll use her to open the energy wells." He paused, listening to the voice on the other end. "Yes." Kipling clicked the end of his pen with nervous fingers. "No, the director doesn't know a thing." Another pause. "Yes, I understand. Thank you, Dame." He set the phone on its holder with shaking hands.

Danny had deserted Kane's pack, and Amy was recovered without harm. This was a terminal outcome to Kipling's plans. He did, however, have one final card to play before outright slaughter, and he needed Lazaro's cooperation.

The obstinate agent was still on the fence, which threatened the mission. Kipling believed that, when Lazaro saw the footage, he'd understand the danger they posed to humans, and join him freely in his attempt to wipe them off the face of the planet.

Instead, it may have backfired.

Is he blind? Agent Kipling's brow furrowed. Lazaro witnessed the hideous creature's transformation, but it failed to rally him. They were biological mistakes that needed to be scrubbed out of existence, one nest at a time.

Kipling picked up the phone again and punched in a number, drawing a breath. "Dr. Gray." He let the smile ring in his words. "It's always *so* good to hear your voice. I do need another favor from you, if you'd be so kind…"

Chapter 31

Unable to sleep in what remained of the evening, Kane and I curled up on the couch and watched a horror movie, escaping into another person's made-up problems, just for a little while.

Johnny, Aurora, and Gary joined us in the living room. There was no point in pursuing Danny. Everyone knew he was long gone by now.

With the betrayal weighing heavily over us, we decided it was best to maintain the perimeter check indefinitely. Between the turncoat, the vampires, and potential retaliation from Vorrin's camp still looming, we couldn't assume anything.

Kane insisted on going at first light to negotiate an agreement with the backstabbing alpha, no more waiting around.

I opposed it with every fiber of my being.

As dawn broke, he prepared himself for the journey.

"I'm going with you."

He pulled me closer on the couch with a sigh. "I almost lost you last night. That won't happen again. I'll be back before you know it."

The memory of Moira removing the bullet was still fresh in my mind, and it caused me to tremble as he disengaged and stood. "Don't do this to me. I can't stand the thought of you walking in there again!"

Kane offered me a smile, his rugged features heavy with remorse. "I told you this job was going to kill me, one day. This is my responsibility." He dropped to his knee so we were face to face. "I love you." Our noses touched and he kissed my forehead, inhaling my scent.

I threw my arms around him and mumbled, "I don't want to be like Emily, waiting for someone who's never coming back."

"Trust me, love, I've dealt with Vorrin before." He stood and signaled to Jean and Max. "You have to stay here, Amy. It's far too risky for you to tag along this time."

I learned all too quickly that Kane had unquestionable authority over his pack, which included me.

I writhed and bucked, trying to escape Jean and Max's hold without success. We watched Kane hunker down and dash into the woods together, my skin burning for the change.

The uncertainty of ever seeing him again was the worst, after everything that had happened to us.

As soon as Jean and Max felt I wouldn't jump ship, they released me from their iron grips. I returned grudgingly to the living room and sank into the couch, which still had a Kane-sized impression in it.

Johnny had occupied the living room and was tapping away at the keys of his laptop, peering over the screen at me. "Want to watch another movie?"

I ignored him and turned over, clutching a bolster pillow and scrunching my eyes shut, hoping for the best, but dreading the worst. I hadn't slept all night, and eventually exhaustion crept up on me, lulling me into a troubled state of unconsciousness.

Someone woke me abruptly, tossing a pillow at my head.

"You're not going to mope around." Moira leaned over me with an irritated expression. "Get up. Breakfast is ready."

Apparently, I would get no sympathy from her, either.

I must have slept longer than I'd thought, because as the dreams abated and I roused from the couch, the front door creaked open on its hinges. Kane entered smeared in soot with his eyes downcast, but he was intact.

Leaping off the couch, I collided into him, hugging tightly.

His arm circled me, but it was a cold gesture. The weight of whatever burden he bore weighed heavily on his shoulders. "There was nothing."

"Nothing wrong?" I asked hopefully as the other pack members gathered in the living room, awaiting the news from our neighbors.

"Nothing left," he corrected miserably. "It must have happened weeks ago. Hundreds of bodies were burned in the auction house, even the children." Kane paused, rubbing soot off his face with a sleeve. "The buildings were leveled, too, including Vorrin's. I couldn't find his body in the mess."

Kyren glanced around at the others. "Does anyone else feel we're being swept into a corner? After the vampire attack, the parasites, Vorrin, *Danny*. What the hell is going on?"

"A pertinent question," A voice I'd only heard once crackled behind Kane.

We turned as a unit to stare at the witch.

She hadn't changed one bit, still wearing a bright patched skirt and bangles that chimed when she moved. Her unkempt bun sprouted long strands of gray hair. A doughy smile spread across her face.

She's real, I thought.

She looked to me. "You had any doubt?"

Moira didn't hesitate, wrapping the woman in a friendly hug. "I thought I smelled a witch! How've you been keeping?"

"Same as usual." She caught my eye and winked, then looked around our quiet group. "Seems we're in need of introductions. These young'uns are so tense!"

Moira turned to us with a broad smile plastered on her face. "It's alright, everyone. She's a friend."

Kane waved us into the living room, his tense shoulders relaxing a little. "What should we call you?"

"Just 'witch'." She hobbled through the house. "Names are pointless in the grand scheme of things. And these hips- they aren't what they used to be. May I sit?"

Johnny took the computer with him and offered his seat. She plopped down with an appreciative nod. "Thank you. You're Lear's boy, aren't you? Where is that old ruffian?"

His curious eyes darkened. "He was killed by parasites." Aurora drew him to the loveseat and sat him down, leaning her head on his shoulder.

Moira spoke first, "We've had more than enough loss, as of late. The world seems to be running out of space for us. Without Kane, we'd probably be in Vorrin's position, right about now."

The witch nodded, a touch of pity in her features. "It was the humans. They're growing desperate. It's good you have a blood-wolf on your hands, I suppose."

I puzzled at her words. "A blood-wolf?"

Kane, Kyren, and Moira turned to me with different flavors of consternation.

The witch glanced at each of them. "So, you *haven't* told her, then. Don't tell me you forgot to mention the prophecy as well? Did it slip your mind?"

Kane grew unnaturally defensive. "She's got nothing to do with it. Amy is not a pawn in this fight. We're keeping her out of harm's way until it blows over."

My heart skipped a beat. I pulled away from Kane as betrayal seeped into my heart. "What are you talking about?"

He's hiding something.

"He most certainly is, Amy," the witch admitted, not looking pleased to tell me. "Every natural-born shifter is raised knowing the prophecy before even their own name. The mystics have kept the word of the Goddess alive through three generations since it was uttered by one of my kind. It cannot be circumvented." The witch seemed to swell with energy, her eyes boring into me. "Amy Ryker. We foresaw your coming, and the path you must take. When the Beltane blood moon rises in two days, our futures will be laid out before you. Your choice will determine the survival or annihilation of our world. Choose carefully, now, for you hold all our lives in your hands." The witch deflated, settling back into her chair. "Beware of your father, child. His loyalties run thin," she said, the lines in her face deepened with exhaustion.

243

The pack was stunned, all eyes were on me. Kane's look held a note of shame, but he did not deny her words. "Then, it wasn't an accident. You saved me, knowing all this." I stared into Kane's cold eyes, where I'd found comfort just this morning. "The mark that appeared on my arm, my father abandoning me, Danny, this whole *charade*? It was a lie." I let the bitterness eek into the words.

Kane's guilty expression deepened. "Amy, it's not a lie-"

"I don't want to hear another word!" I stood, an unfettered rage writhing in my stomach. "You knew, you *all* knew and you kept me from the truth."

Serena was about to say something when I cut her off.

"Fuck this, fuck your prophecy, *witch*, and fuck this motherfucking pack!" I screamed, storming out of the house. I'd been right, that first day that Kane brought me here. *Remember what happens when you trust people...*

"Amy!" Moira hollered from the porch. "Please wait!"

The wolf spread into my limbs as reason abandoned me. I barreled past a battered Honda pulling into the driveway, ignoring the driver's gaping stare and let my legs carry me far away from the farm.

The wind teased my fur as I cut through the air, faster than I'd ever run before.

Let them try to keep up, I snorted. *Let them try.*

Chapter 32

Morgan Lazaro pulled into the driveway as a bolt of white fur blitzed past the car. She was huge, larger than the video recording suggested, but unmistakable: Amy Ryker.

Before he recovered from the encounter, a hulking, dark form burst from the farmhouse, chasing after her.

If he thought she was formidable, this wolf was absolutely massive. Its bright blue eyes shot him a murderous glare before pursuing her into the woods.

He parked and waited to see if anything else decided to erupt from the farmhouse. When it seemed all clear, Lazaro stepped out of his car and ascended the porch steps, keeping his eyes peeled for any new and unexpected development.

A woman's voice rang through the open doorway before he had a chance to knock. "Come on in, we've been expecting you."

He entered, one hand resting on his sidearm in case things took a turn for the worse.

A man with a buzz-cut stepped into the hallway, watching him through narrowed eyes, and waved him grudgingly into the living room. "The name's Kyren. You're on our property now, human. Best to watch your step. Got it?"

He hesitated before following the stout man, finding himself at the doorway of the large room, filled with a collection of weatherworn, unnerved people... or were they werewolves?

His escort shook his head after eyeing an older woman in bright skirts. "Quick introductions, I guess. Moira." A weathered, older woman in jeans and a sweater waved, shooting him a cautious look. "Serena." a young woman in a beige blouse nodded, looking too tired to care. "Johnny, Aurora." Kyren waved at a couple, snuggled up on a couch, the young man had a laptop with him. "Gary, Jean, Crystal." A lean man with dark skin affirmed, as well as a tall, pale man cradling a petite Latino woman, whose stomach bulged slightly with pregnancy. "Maxwell." Kyren pointed at a younger man with a curly mess of hair who waved lamely from the couch. "Evvy and her siblings, Scarlet and Quill." He pointed to a group of redheaded children in an oversized chair. "That's Xander, Martin and Jessica." Kyren concluded, pointing to a little girl and her two dark-haired brothers.

"Emily is hiding somewhere with her kids, Solice is in bed, and Amy and Kane, well, you saw them leaving just now, I'm sure."

The older woman in bright skirts, who hadn't been introduced stood out from the group. "And I don't exactly have a name. Or, if I did, I wouldn't share it with any living being." She shot him a wink. "You can call me witch, for that is my title and profession. You have news for the pack?"

Peering around the group, a one Daniel Crichton was nowhere to be seen. But he did notice something peering out of a lamp. Something that looked terribly familiar. "If you'll forgive me, one moment." He picked up the lamp and tore the small wire and microphone out. The group watched, speechless, as Lazaro continued around the room, finding and removing the bugging devices until he was certain there were none left within earshot.

He used a knife to disabled them so they'd no longer transmit a signal. "Sorry about that. Looks like agent K was listening in on your conversations. Your Daniel Crichton is a mole. He's working for an agent K against his will and has been assigned to kill Amy. I'm here because I've seen first-hand what K has been doing to you, and to Amy." He held up the inert cords as if they were venomous snakes.

The young man, Johnny, put out a slender hand. "Can I see those, please?"

Lazaro let the boy have them and Johnny sat down, pulling the microphone heads apart, then fiddling with the innards. "Jesus, he's right. How did I miss these?"

Lazaro smiled half-heartedly. "You have to know what to look for. I've been debugging longer than you've been alive."

Kyren laughed, rubbing the back of his neck with a measure of embarrassment. "For that, you've got our gratitude. But why didn't you contact us before today?"

"I would have if I'd known. Daniel all but gutted me several weeks back and I've been healing in a military hospital ever since. I only returned to the field two days ago, and agent K told me about the 'prophecy' regarding Amy just last night."

"What do you suppose is going to happen if Amy fulfills it?" The old woman – the *witch* – asked, a knowing look dawning on her face.

"He said the human race would go extinct in a matter of weeks, because of one werewolf-"

"Shifter," Kyren corrected.

"Er, shifter," he amended. "But how is that possible?"

The witch smiled. "How, indeed. It is puzzling where he got that notion. But I can guarantee you, Lazaro, that will not happen if Amy is successful. There *are* still pitfalls ahead, and Amy is racing toward her destiny to fix what humans broke whether or not she *knows* it." She accused, panning around the room. Moira glanced at her feet. "It was your duty to prepare

248

her. But-" She stood, fighting gravity on the way up with a grunt. "I'm here to salvage the situation. Amy may not be ready, but she must be soon. We'll defend her against her father, who is attempting to control what will be released. The portcullis that Ryker has erected will have to be seized, and Amy *must* be protected until the convergence at dawn. But it's up to her to bring an end to this, after all these years."

"What does that mean?" Serena asked. She was rather pretty despite the tired stains beneath her eyes. Lazaro noted that they all seemed weary, and felt a pang of pity for them. It must not have been easy for them to hide their true natures, and now, with agent K on their tails...

"You've heard the prophecy. If all does not go as planned, chaos will reign, and may very well fulfill 'agent K's' greatest fear. He is naïve to try to stop us, though. Every species on earth is in danger if Amy doesn't open the portcullis."

Kyren folded his arms across his chest. "What can we do?"

"The best we can, really." The old woman sighed. "Events are quickening, it was no accident that Lazaro or the vampires have become involved. Don't bar Ezekiel's entry when he arrives. Convergence will begin tomorrow as the blood moon sets. All parties must be present." She teetered to the entryway on heavy limbs. "I will gather the others we need for the ritual. Kyren, you'll hear from me soon. Lazaro." She patted his arm, the skin of her hand sent electric shocks through him. "Go see your doctor. Ask her what she knows about Project Blackmoor." With a nod, she hobbled out. "One day!"

They watched as the old woman vanished from sight.

Lazaro roused, pulling out a business card. "Kyren, if you need anything, call me. It's a secure line. Since I pulled the bugs, it's not safe for any of you to be here until this whole thing is over. I suggest you find somewhere more secure." A young girl watched him with bright green eyes, following his every move. These were *children* K was waging war on, Lazaro thought with disgust. "I'll do what I can on my end to stall agent K's advances with the resources at my disposal."

"We're all fighters here. We'll figure something out. Thanks for coming out here to warn us, though. You're already risking a lot for strangers."

Lazaro shrugged. "It's the right thing to do."

"We're grateful for it." Kyren clapped him on the back, jolting his wound. "Now get the hell out before Kane comes back. He's not fond of agents, no matter which side they're on."

Lazaro had no intention of running into the massive creature that crossed his path when he arrived. "Will do."

The meeting with agent K was tonight. After that, he'd know more about their plans and how to stop them. Then he could ask Dr. Warren about 'Project Blackmoor', as the witch suggested.

How did she know about the doctor? Lazaro started the car, idling a moment before putting it in reverse. *And how the hell was Samantha involved?* His answers lay at headquarters.

Chapter 33

After agent Lazaro and the witch left, the pack hummed with questions. Kyren tried to alleviate the upset to no avail.

Gary spoke first, his tone dark and troubled. "What did she mean? Of course, we know the prophecy. But I was told it's just vague nonsense the mystics made up."

Moira's cheeks were still flush. "No, unfortunately. It was always coming. I just didn't think I'd live to see it."

Serena looked to Moira. "Did you know it was Amy?"

She pursed her lips and nodded. "Just Solice and I, at first. I had to tell Kane when I was certain. We should have told Amy when she arrived, but she was so damaged. It was too much pressure for a fragile mind."

Kyren shook his head. "She's not that fragile."

"And look how she reacted." Moira stared through the window at the woods edge. "How do you think she might have taken it before she knew any of this? I thought we had more time to prepare her. Give her a few years to come to terms. But the witch isn't known for her good humor."

Kyren glanced to the door, where he'd last seen the strange woman. "Who the hell was she, anyway?"

"The witch is talked about in many circles, but she's evasive, disappearing for years before anyone sees her again. Sometimes she helps with curses or births. She'll sell a potion or two if you have what she needs. She is a priestess in essence, and in practice. In all the years I've known her, she's barely aged a day. I honestly don't know what her role is in the convergence. But she's got everyone's best interest at heart. Don't doubt it." Moira wagged a finger at him.

Kyren regarded Moira as the mother-figure of the pack, but in this moment, he was disgusted that she would keep secrets from him, Kane's second in command. "I should have known about this whole thing years ago. Kane may be the Alpha, but I've led this pack many times when he dealt with other matters. Did you know it was coming?"

As Moira opened her mouth to speak, a firm rap at the door interrupted their conversation.

Kyren stormed to the door. "Fucking, what *now*?"

Peering out the spyhole, there was no one in sight. He opened the door and looked both ways, nearly stepping on a package left on the doorstep. Kyren picked it up and inspected it: no postage, no address, just a name in long, spidery writing: *Serena Barrow.*

The package wafted a hint of flowers.

Looking around one last time, he brought it inside and locked the door. "Serena, there's something here for you."

She eyed the parcel with a tired expression. "What is it?"

Kyren handed it over. "I don't know. Be careful with it."

She waved him off and set the parcel on a coffee table, gently folding back the thick butcher paper. When it didn't explode or fume, she plucked open another side until a small wooden box was revealed. Serena hesitated with her fingers on the lid, then eased it open.

Kyren, Moira, and Gary leaned in to see the contents.

A simple needle with clear fluid rested in the case, along with a letter. Serena picked the paper up and unfolded it.

As she read, tears sprang to her eyes.

Moira rubbed Serena's shoulder. "What's wrong, sweetie?"

Serena swiped at her cheek. "Nothing."

"Well, girl, what does it say?" Moira was not afraid to say what the others were thinking.

"Did you see who sent it?" Serena's watery eyes glanced up at Kyren, who shook his head. "Whoever did, says it's a cure for rabid shifters. But there isn't one. Right?"

Moira stood rigid herself. "As far as we know. It has to be a trick. I don't trust it."

"Why'd they go through the trouble explaining how to use it?" Serena waved the paper in front of everyone. "What have I got to lose? What would they have to gain? Owen is already caged. He's not a *threat* to anyone."

Gary gave a firm nod. "Damn straight."

"It's up to you, Serena. He's your mate." Kyren gave her his blessing. "Do you want to try?"

"I-" She hesitated, touching the needle. "I don't know."

"Well the world's only going to end in two days, take your time," Kyren mused, then sobered. "But seriously, give me a heads up before you do. I need to be there to make sure nothing goes wrong."

Serena offered a tearful smile. "I'll think about it."

Kyren could only imagine what she was feeling right now. She'd come from a life without a true mate, the rabid wolf who they believed would remain such until he died, and now, she even had the slightest chance to learn about the creature she was bonded to. Kyren always thought it a cruel god to curse them with one shot at happiness, no matter how lucky he'd been.

That one shot could be taken away in the blink of an eye as Serena knew quite well. First, the late Gregory, then Owen.

Kyren silently thanked whoever had delivered the package.

Even if it didn't work, it had given her hope.

Chapter 34

I ran as I should have many weeks ago. My inner voice taunted me as my paws sped over the rough terrain; *I told you so; I told you so,* it leered, refusing to be ignored any longer.

Kane lumbered behind me, likely waiting for exhaustion to wear me down. Little did he know how far I could travel on contempt alone. If I had a mouth made for speech, I might have shouted at him, screamed for him to leave me alone. Without one, I focused on being as aerodynamic as possible, speeding between the trees, trying to lose the feeling of betrayal that clung to my fur like a shroud.

I should have known. I blinked away tears. *The farm, the pack – Kane – all of it was too good to be true.* The walls of my new life crumbled away to reveal the ugly truth.

They wanted me for their own benefit, to dictate the terms of my life. Why had I been so blind? It was there, just beneath the surface if I'd paid attention: their conversations that ended abruptly when I entered the room, the guilty looks, the silence. Perhaps I hadn't wanted to see it.

My heart was shattered in a million pieces, throbbing in its cage. *Does he even love me? Or am I just a trophy?*

I ran until my heart was ready to burst, then I ran some more. We were deep in the woods by now, and all *I* wanted was to escape Kane's pursuit.

And then silence followed my step. Slowing to a stop, I looked around.

Kane was nowhere to be found.

I stood alone in a small valley of the forest. A rock formation lay ahead, one that would provide coverage until I could come up with a better plan. Sniffing at the entrance made it clear the last occupant had departed several months ago.

The air was moist and chill, preparing for rain.

I squeezed into the tiny space and found a nook to curl up in. From the outside, even with my shocking white fur, it would be nearly impossible to see me.

I sighed, a plume of dust rising from the parched dirt floor. As I drifted off into a troubled sleep, the weight of exhaustion bore down and lured me into a strange dream.

I'm here now, on two legs. Watching. Terrible shrieks of battle, clashing of claws and teeth. Gunshots blast in all

258

directions, a child's scream. A figure drops to the ground in front of me, dead. Blood gushes from his neck as he stares glassy-eyed at me. I lose myself in his hollow sight, falling in until the sounds of the fight dissipate. I'm in a darkness, unable to feel my limbs in this void. A rumbling voice echoes around me, a booming message I cannot understand. Something clicks, the pitch changes, and I comprehend:

"I release you."

In that instant, there is no darkness.

I am on my knees in a tent, tears streaking down my face as fire laps at the entrance. A man barrels through and lifts me into his arms. "It's okay. Your mother and sister are safe. We're getting out of here," he whispers in my ear. I know to trust him, letting him carry me to the back of a truck where he shoves me under a tarp. "Don't make a sound." I catch a glimpse of the hellfire he saved me from: men in helmets tearing my friends from their tents, gunfire tapping an unholy rhythm into the night. The truck beneath me rumbles to life and speeds away from the inferno, the scent of burning flesh on my tongue.

The rumbling changes into a rushing heartbeat, throbbing in my ears as I inhale. Mother lies on the bed, caustic copper tinges the air. "Mama," I hear myself say. "Get up, father is leaving." She doesn't respond. I hold her hand, pulling away quickly as her fingers are cold. Blood is pooling up in the

259

bedding. Father will be mad if it stains, I think. I peer over the bed and see that her face is in two, one half resting on the comforter, the other staring past me.

My scream tears through the house.

The scene fades.

A calming light blossoms in front of me, for a moment I imagine it's the sunrise, but the color is wrong, it's too bright. From within the glow I see someone approaching.

"Amy," the woman says, outlined in the light so I cannot see her face.

"Who are you?"

The light softens, revealing a young woman, short with a severe bun. "Your memories are returned to you." Her voice is familiar, and I strain to remember the source. "The journey is rough, but you have allies. Now is the time to remember, to heal the old wounds and forge ahead into your destiny."

I recognize her now, but she's much younger. "Witch," I accuse. "Where were you all my life? If I was so important to your prophecy, why was I alone?"

"I came to you twice, once when you were born to conceal your mark, once more when you were young to seal away your memories. If I could have taken you with me, I would have. But your fate was determined long ago, and you cannot avoid your role in these events to come."

"Why couldn't you tell me in the garden?"

"If you knew, it would have changed everything. I'm sorry it had to be this way. I can divulge no more."

"But wait!" I shout into the empty space. She turns from me and walks into the light as I'm torn away from it.

"Amy?" another familiar voice called out.

My head shot up.

"Amy, where are you? I know you came this way."

I tried to shake the strange vision, the light fading gradually from my blinded eyes.

"Can we talk? It's really important." I caught sight of Danny through a gap in the rocks. He wore torn up jeans and a grungy tee, looking bedraggled as he turned to face me. "I'm sorry about the vamps, I- didn't have a choice. Please believe me, Amy." My name escaped him with a whine.

I growled, backing further into the crevice.

"Your father wants to see you."

A crunch of old leaves warned me of another shifter approaching, the wind carried the smell of metal and stone dust.

"Back off, Danny." A baritone voice cut through the air. "Amy, it's me, honey. It's been so long. Won't you come out?" He peered down to catch my eye, his own brown eyes widening. "You *have* changed. If I'd known, I'd have taken you with me. Will you forgive an old man?"

The look he gave compelled me to wiggle free of the crevice, ignoring Danny, who shifted anxiously at his side.

Father looked the same, except the lines under his eyes had deepened, and his once-dark hair had streaks of ashen gray. His face softened when I emerged.

"You're so beautiful, my girl. Don't be afraid." He stayed his outreached hand. I could have bolted, but instead my second form fell away, leaving me vulnerable and naked. He tugged off his overshirt and offered the plaid fabric to me. "Put this on. It's going to rain soon."

I shrugged on the shirt, overwhelmed by his smell. "You left. Why- why did you leave?"

"I had no choice." Father's eyes were concerned, ashamed. "Your sister- she killed your mother by accident. I had to hide her away. Humans are dangerous. They steal our kind, abuse and use us for their own gain. I didn't want that for her. I thought you weren't a shifter. But how wrong I was." My father shook his head in disbelief. "It's been so long, come give your old man a hug." He reached out to me, welcoming me home again.

Despite myself, I closed the gap and hugged my father.

The warmth of his grip disappeared once I was within it, he twisted me around by my neck so I faced Danny.

"Does she have it?"

I remembered instantly that cruel voice. I was the fool to believe anything he said. The witch was right.

Danny yanked open the shirt and gripped my arm with a dirty hand. "It's here." He squeezed my flesh tightly. "She's the conduit." Before father could react, a flash of steel exited Danny's pocket and entered my ribs.

I choked and doubled over.

My father caught me as Danny raced into the woods.

"Brody!" my father barked. Several men barreled from a hiding place nearby. "Get that traitor and bring him back alive!" They chased after with barely a nod as my eyesight grew watery.

Father laid me on the ground gently, the knife jutting awkwardly from my ribs.

I reached for it and he slapped my hand away. "Don't touch it." He lifted me like a child into his arms, but I was in too much pain to protest. I was carried to a military truck parked nearby, hidden by the trees. "Sid! Start her up, we're heading back!"

A burn coursed through the wound, worse even, than the noxious parasite blood.

It clenched the flesh and spread into my limbs.

"It's poisoned, we have to get it out," a woman's voice muttered over the engine as the vehicle jolted forward.

Someone gripped the handle and teased the blade out of my rib cage. I cried, trying to curl around the wound, but firm hands held me down.

"Don't move," my father commanded impatiently. "The poison will only spread faster."

A rattling breath escaped my lungs and darkness enveloped me, dragging me away from the waking world.

*

I woke on a narrow cot with a young woman taping my wound shut.

She caught my eye and gave me a conflicted look. "We got you an antidote in time. You're lucky." From her tone of voice, she didn't sound certain about that.

I pulled in a shallow breath. "Where- am I?"

"Ryker's camp. We're close to-"

"Tina." Father's words were sharp. "That's enough. If you're finished, get out." He held a flap open, and she ducked through without a backwards glance.

I was strapped to the cot, unable to lift my arms or legs. I glared at my father, who stood over me impassively. "What the hell do you want?"

"Haven't you heard?" His eyes glowed with purpose. "You're the conduit, the 'Chosen One'. Poor Celeste was heartbroken when she learned it wasn't her. Thanks to that *witch*. But its better this way. Your sister has made me proud. You, on the other hand…" Father trailed off, reclining in a deep couch.

I tried to lean forward, the pain making me suck in a gasp. "I was eight!"

"And a useless runt. If Lily hadn't begged me not to, you'd have been sold the day you were born. Lucky for both of us, I suppose."

"You left me alone with mother's corpse. You let them take me away and never looked back!"

"I would do it again if I didn't need you. But you have a great purpose, Amy, your death will spare countless shifters from being murdered in the name of science. With our army, we will eradicate the humans, and everything they created."

"But, *why?*" I hissed past the pain.

"We have lost too much because of them." He stood and strode towards the exit. "I only need you alive until tomorrow morning, then you can die like your whore mother." He left the tent. Breathing was still difficult but couldn't compare to the burning apathy of my father.

Danny tried to kill me, I realized, *twice, including the damn vampires*. How long had he known my father? And how had I been so naïve as to trust either of them? Berating myself for running from Kane, from the pack. *So stupid, what an idiot you are. Trusting any of them.*

Another memory surfaces: *My sister twirling in the yard. Her dress reflecting the sun, shattering it into a million pieces. My father watching, smiling at her as I dash into the house. Mother in the kitchen, scrubbing a pan until her hands are raw, warning me from disturbing my father. "He doesn't care about you, you changeless shit." She glares at me, scrubbing away at the dish. "Why couldn't you be more like your sister?" My five-year-old shoulders shrug, I can't understand why she is so mean to me, why my father is so dismissive. But that's just how it is. That's how it's always been.*

He hadn't changed a bit.

Someone slipped into the tent, smaller and more agile than my father could ever be. Her voice was high, lilting and sickly sweet. "I didn't believe it when Rosa told me." Long blonde hair framed a face that was also mine. "It's been a long time, *sis.*"

Chapter 35

Kane lost track of Amy around a huge redwood. What she may have lacked in strength, she made up for in speed and agility. That, he couldn't deny. As frustrated as he was, he had to admire her determination.

A flash of white zoomed past from a different angle than he'd last seen her. She was certainly trying to lose him.

He changed direction and charged after her.

Amy was upset, of course. He should have explained everything the first day at Bob's. But Moira told him to wait.

He'd waited too long.

Kane didn't expect the witch – someone he'd only heard about from his father and the elders – was both quite real and as tenacious as he'd been told. If she'd been a pack member, he might have banished her for the infraction, and for putting Amy in such a position.

All he could do now was explain, if he ever managed to catch up with her. Kane pursued her bobbing white tail, teasing as she retreated. After a time, Amy finally slowed to a stop.

Perhaps she'd finally exhausted herself.

Her limbs lengthened again, but the flesh tone was wrong, darker. Tumbling blonde locks cascaded over her shoulders, not Amy's beautiful black mane.

This wasn't Amy.

He stopped short, leaving fifty feet between them. The woman turned around, her face a rude imitation of Amy's, but not hers. He'd know his mate anywhere.

The woman drew out his name sardonically, her voice higher than Amy's. "Kane Blackmoor."

Kane let the change fall away from his form, keeping the strength coiled in his limbs. "You're her twin."

"You're a bright one, aren't you? I'm actually just the decoy. Father wants to speak with Amy alone, you understand." She sauntered around him in a wide circle, sizing him up.

Before Kane retorted, a heavy iron netting landed on him from above, forcing him to the ground. Kane let the change consume him again, if nothing but for the sheer power it possessed. But they seem to have anticipated his strength and overcompensated with the weight of the mesh.

Struggling did nothing to free him.

"And they said you'd be hard to bag. Good job, fellas." A dozen shifters emerged from the trees. "Let's load him up. Ryker's waiting for us back at camp."

Kane's rage boiled over, but he could not help himself or Amy, wherever she was.

Locking chains around his midsection, it took most of the shifters to drag him to his feet with the weight of the metal and his own size. Kane tried snapping at them with a partially formed snout, but the mesh constricted his movements.

Amy's twin approached, a ghost of her sister.

He tried to pull away as she slipped a thin arm through the mesh and into his tangled hair. "You're cute, though. It's not fair, keeping you *all* to herself like that." She pouted, using the hand she'd tousled his hair with to rub her own bare chest. "Too bad you won't be around for the finale." She ambled back to a concealed truck as the other shifters shoved him forward.

He let his second form sink back under his skin. "Where is she? Where is Amy??"

One of the men chuckled. "You ain't gettin' her back from Gabe. He's got big plans for that-"

"That's Ryker to you." Amy's twin peered back with a menacing glare. "Shut your fucking hole, Ryan, or I'll tell father you were talking about him behind his back."

Ryan's face froze. "Yes, miss." He mumbled an obscenity under his breath and shoved Kane harder. Kane stumbled over the netting, hitting the ground face first. Several of Ryker's pack hoisted him onto the bed of the truck.

He couldn't get through the mesh to bite them.

When they let him go, someone sucker-punched him in the gut, a solid hit. He peered up at the attacker, the blood-wolf roiling just beneath the surface. "I'm coming after you first, *Ryan*." Kane glared at the man, who hit him again square in the jaw. A trickle of blood seeped from between his lips.

Amy's twin shouted like a mirthful child playing at war, pointing dead ahead. "Let's move out!"

The engine rumbled to life, and the truck began its ascent over the rolling hillocks. It picked up speed as the driver found a niche in the woods where the trees didn't grow.

Kane had accepted his own death a long time ago, and he knew the pack could survive without him this time. But Amy's face flashed through his mind. No one knew where she was but him, and he was immobilized by the blonde bitch.

Somehow, he'd find a way out.

And when he did, nothing would stop him from exacting bloody retribution on their captors.

Chapter 36

"*Celeste*," I said in disbelief.

She inclined her head. "Amy." A familiar scent wafted off of her, and she waited for me to recognize it with a grin. "So funny how difficult everyone made it sound, capturing your mate. I had no trouble at all." Celeste shrugged with a smirk. "The only question that remains is, why did he choose *you*?"

A quick inhale made my chest contract painfully. "What did you do to him?"

"Nothing, yet. You'll be staying with us a little longer, *conduit*, until it's time to fulfill the prophecy." Jealousy colored her words, and she loomed over me with a murderous glare. "You know, I've worked my entire life to live up to father's expectations, and only because you've got the mark, do you matter more? It was *my* glory you stole!"

"Fuck you, Celeste." I turned away. Unable to move, breathe, or even defend myself, there was no point arguing with my twin, who had apparently gone insane in her pursuit of father's approval. "What would mother think of you now?"

"Mother was a dirty human."

I smiled, realizing I'd hit a nerve.

"*You* didn't grow up afraid of being captured. *You* didn't have to claw your way through the ranks, getting beaten until blood came out your ears. You didn't have to-" She stopped, unable or unwilling to form the words. The redness in her cheeks faded as a smile spread. "But it's not my burden to bear anymore, it's yours. Good riddance." Celeste stormed out of the tent. A muffled silence from the outside world was cut short by an agonized roar.

I pulled against the straps, listening helplessly as my mate was tortured. A chorus of laughter followed each howl that ripped from Kane's throat.

The change unfurled, realigning my breastplate as I writhed with newfound energy. The restraints were obviously shifter-proof, but I managed to topple the cot over in my struggle.

Two guards rushed in, one brandishing a cudgel, a jagged scar sliced across his cheek. They hoisted the cot upright and the big man raised the club, connecting with my skull. *Kane*, I tried to say his name as my vision faded.

Chapter 37

The farm came alive with a flurry of activity once nightfall arrived. Kyren instructed the adults to gather supplies and pack any and all necessities. If they had to leave quickly, they'd be ready to go.

Serena slipped into the room as Kyren listened to Crystal's concerns regarding the upheaval; her stomach was growing noticeably larger by the day. Jean was arguing against leaving so late in the pregnancy.

Kyren groaned at their protests. "We may not go *anywhere*. I just want us to be ready in case we need to. Kane and Amy haven't returned yet, and what with this prophecy business, I don't think it's safe here. Think about the kids." He motioned to Xander and Quil rolling on the floor in play.

Jean bit back with his own logic. "The farm is the safest place. We can hold off any enemy here, we know the layout. The advantage is ours."

"The loss would be ours if they come to our door with guns and explosives. Go pack your things," Kyren commanded, leaving no room for argument. He turned around and almost ran into Serena. His mood was already soured from dealing with the others. "You come to complain as well?"

"I want to try it," she confided quietly.

"You want to- Oh." He realized she wasn't talking about leaving the farm. "Of course." Kyren hadn't considered the logistics of the task at hand. He wondered who a good spotter might be, in case it didn't work as expected. "Gary."

Gary stopped shoving clothes into a suitcase and stood up. "What's the problem now?"

"Serena wants to… try the 'thing'."

He scoffed, then smiled down at Serena. "Okay. What do you need from me?"

Kyren glanced to Serena as well. "I need you to let her in the cage and be ready to drag her out if it doesn't work. You've dealt with his confines the most."

"Sure," he said. "Happy to help."

They met at the entrance to the garage after Serena grabbed the small wooden box. No one was allowed inside before now except for her and Gary, so Kyren had no idea what to expect.

The pungent aroma of wet fur blasted his senses, tears stinging his eyes on contact with the sour air. He turned on the light, which flickered before humming to life. A menacing growl rose from a dim corner of the confines.

Two mad, yellow eyes watched his every move.

Serena bent forward, reaching a hand fearlessly through the bars. "Owen," she whispered. "I'm going to try and make you better, okay? They're friends."

Gary unbolted a single bar, enough for Serena to slip through but not enough for the rabid wolf to escape. The creature lunged at Gary, smashing into the cage with a violent snarl.

So, this is what 'rabid' looked like, Kyren thought, disgusted. He'd helped carry the shifter to the garage himself, but the creature had been unconscious, without the heat of insanity pulsing off him. Kyren had noticed his dulled fur and marred skin, torn countless times by teeth and claws.

If Owen the person ever resurfaced, maybe they'd find out what had happened to him in Vorrin's camp.

Kyren watched Serena slip through and console her mate, ever fearless of its bared teeth. The creature paid her no mind, glaring and snarling at Gary. Serena linked her arms around Owen's neck and bore the needle deep into his pelt.

He yelped and bit into her shoulder as the shot entered his veins. Serena never once flinched as she depressed the lever, screwing her eyes shut. Blood spread across her blouse, but she held tightly to his fur.

275

In that moment, Kyren could not imagine a more amazing woman. How had he never noticed her strength and perseverance? She was braving the impossible to save someone she didn't even know? He hoped, for her sake, the drug worked. Serena, above all others, deserved a goddamned break.

The next few moments would determine if Kyren needed to use the concealed handgun he brought with him.

Owen's teeth released Serena's shoulder as he slumped in her grip. She slow-fell with him to the ground, her delicate fingers tightened in his ruined pelt.

Kyren watched as nothing happened. Owen's mouth lolled open, his tongue hanging out as if he were dead. The only sign he was still alive was that Serena hadn't pulled away.

Gary hunkered down and looked her in the eye. "Serena, come out and I'll shut the cage. It's not safe in there."

She merely shook her head, her eyes still closed.

Serena and Owen laid that way until Gary put a hand on her good shoulder. "Please, we've done everything we can, just-"

Owen's paw shot out and grasped Gary's hand, losing its secondary form as long, scarred fingers emerged. His eyes glistened as cognition returned. Gary pulled away as the creature rose, shedding pelt and teeth, cradling his mate. Owen ran his newly formed hands over Serena's back and stomach, seeming to marvel at the sight of her. She choked back a sob of delight, touching his scarred face and chest.

Kyren shifted uneasily. "Are you okay, Serena?"

They both looked up at him. Owen's eyes were still glowing yellow, but free of the hatred that had ruled them.

She rested her head on her mate's shoulder. "I'm fine."

"Moira should see to your wound-"

"Kyren." Gary stopped him, slapping him on the back. "Let's let them alone, yeah? She'll be fine."

Kyren didn't budge, turning all his attention back on the strange shifter. "Owen. I don't know how long you were out, or if you know why you're here. But if you hurt Serena ever again, you're fucking dead, do you understand?" His gaze bore into those bright golden eyes. Kyren couldn't tell if Owen nodded, but they seemed to have a mutual understanding.

Gary dragged him to his feet and out the garage door. "Alright, alpha. Calm your shit down."

Once they were out of the garage, Kyren protested. "We don't know the first thing about that guy. Who knows if he'll change back and get stuck again? Then we'd have to-"

"Excellent show," a sinister voice called from the shadows, the dark figure clapping slowly. The vampire was back. "Heartfelt and all that superfluous rubbish."

Kyren's claws extended on their own accord. The witch told them not to bar his passage, but he was happy to disobey. "What do *you* want?"

The vampire straightened, smoothing out his lapels with a grave countenance. "Ryker's men stole away with my wife."

Kyren scoffed at the bastard. "A little ironic, seeing as you almost killed our alpha's mate last night."

"Entirely different," Ezekiel countered dismissively. "They intend to sacrifice my wife for their wicked alchemy, and I would rather like to keep this one." He nodded curtly. "Your alpha is in their clutches as well."

Gary's eyes widened. "They have Kane?"

"In the flesh. He was making such a racket. It's also possible they've set him on fire." The vampire's black eyes gleamed in the moonlight, as if he enjoyed giving bad news.

Kane's blood-wolf, Kyren thought. His heart dropped into his stomach, "What about Amy?"

"That rude little whippet? Never saw her." Ezekiel offered a light shrug. "I did see her doppelganger, though. More than a little cracked in the head, that one."

"Coming from *you*?" Kyren stared at the vampire dully. "What do you want from us?"

Ezekiel folded his arms across his chest. "I need your help."

"*You*. Need *our* help?"

The vampire rolled his eyes. "Perhaps I may have overreacted the other night. The artifact has a special meaning to me, as it's- regardless." He shook his head pushing back his peppered hair. "You do not have enough power to collect your own Alpha. In that I can assist, as long as saving my wife is also part of the plan."

"I'm still getting over the fact that *any* woman would want you." Gary prodded their guest with a grimace.

Ezekiel's eyes iced over. "Hilarious, *dog*." He turned to Kyren. "I spoke to the witch. She is gathering a small army to usurp Ryker's pack before he makes his move. Will you be joining us?"

With Amy and Kane on the line, he had no choice. "Do you have enough able-bodied fighters?"

"There are no fighters residing in my home. *My* children are killers. Come tomorrow night, they'll follow my lead." Ezekiel stood tall, readjusting his lapel once more.

"Good." Kyren nodded at the vampire, grudgingly accepting the truce. "Where should we meet?"

Chapter 38

Secret agent Lazaro had rifled through the filing cabinets for hours with absolutely nothing to show for it.

Five minutes before his meeting with the agent K, and he couldn't find a scrap of information regarding Project Blackmoor, or anything of the sort stowed away in the archives.

As if it never existed.

He could speak to Dr. Warren after the meeting if she was still around at this hour. Perhaps she'd heard of it or had additional files elsewhere.

Lazaro's watch chimed. Time was up.

Climbing the stairs, he passed by the security desk and turned into the long hallway. As he reached for the door handle, a calm, familiar voice entered his mind: *Don't touch that door, Lazaro.* The old witch spoke slowly. *A trap is set for you in there, Kipling means to ensnare you. Keep walking, return to the basement, and speak with your doctor. She has the information you seek. When you're finished, leave the building and don't return home. Go somewhere unpredictable. I'll be in touch.*

Though her voice had been perfectly clear, Lazaro felt a little insane. He took his hand back and kept walking.

Agent K, *Kipling*, he corrected, was bad news. He didn't need her warning to know that. His only regret was that he couldn't gather additional intel for the pack.

Lazaro sped down the west stairwell, taking a quick left at the bottom to the lab. Flashing the new badge he got from director Aldridge, the door clicked open. He passed through the lively group of scientists filling test tubes, working with slides and analyzing gathered samples. Lazaro tapped on the humble brown door, waiting for a response.

"Come in!" Samantha's voice called.

He opened the door, relief coursing through him. "I'm surprised you're all still here this late."

She straightened a stack of papers. "We work when the work comes in. Are you ready to get out on the field?"

"Actually." Lazaro closed the door behind himself. "I have a question for you. It's- regarding a project."

She gave him a skeptical look, her mood still easy. "We have many 'projects' we're in the middle of, at the moment. Which one in particular?"

"Project Blackmoor."

The smile fell from her face. "Oh, *that* project."

Lazaro took a seat across from her. "What happened?"

She didn't respond immediately, standing from her desk with a sigh. "How did you find out?"

Lazaro didn't know where to begin. "Well, um." He rubbed his five-o'clock shadow, not having bothered to trim it before racing towards the farm. "It's- hard to explain." Many events in the last twenty-four hours would be hard to explain, least of all an old woman's voice in his head.

As he opened his mouth to speak, the doctor held up a finger and rounded her desk, locking the office door. "Before you begin," she said conspiratorially, "realize that there are some things even the director isn't aware of. You can't breathe a word to anyone about what you might hear in this office. Do you understand?" Her eyes flashed bright in the florescent light.

"Of course." Lazaro would never dream of betraying her confidence. "So, you know that I got attacked by a werewolf – um, a shifter."

"A 'shifter'?"

"Yeah, that's what they prefer."

The doctor's eyebrow rose slightly.

"Anyway, this Danny Crichton was the one that did it. He's been living with Amy Ryker until recently. She was my target on the last mission. An agent K showed me files on some of them, but nothing on her partner, Kane, in the records department. Nothing on any sort of project, either. Shouldn't there be *something* if it was funded by us? Is there a connection between Kane and project Blackmoor?"

Dr. Warren's face went through a rainbow of emotions, finally resting on 'dirty secret'. "They aren't in records because I pulled them years ago." She flitted to an adjacent cabinet and took out a huge file. "They're too dangerous for even our agents to have access. Clara's life would be at risk if anyone knew." He remembered the doctor saying something about Clara coming from a lab. "She's Kane's little sister." Samantha confirmed his suspicions, dropping a file onto the desk and invited him to examine it.

He opened it, and a mugshot-style image of a young man in his late teens glared up at him. The youth, Kane Blackmoor, had a furious gleam in his eye that even the camera couldn't conceal.

Document after document was written out in cold, calculated detail of every test they conducted on him. "Jesus. What happened there?"

"*He* happened." Dr. Warren tapped the picture. "They managed to inject him with something powerful, something all the previous subjects rejected. He survived. As far as we've gathered, he killed every single guard and doctor in that lab before freeing the others. Clara was only recovered because the reinforcement bars closed before she could escape. A backup team went in to do damage control, and those numbnuts put four bullets in her." She huffed in irritation, as if the memory was still fresh in her mind. "Some trigger-happy rookie, no doubt. I had to dig them out of her, myself."

Lazaro recalled the bright blue eyes of the creature that passed mere inches in front of his car. Looking at the image of Kane, he was certain they were the same being.

What would Kane do if he knew his sister was still alive at a government site? Lazaro shuddered, refusing to be the first to tell him. "What happened to the lab, then?"

"It was abandoned. They gutted the place of any incriminating evidence, and it's still sitting in the woods somewhere." Sam shrugged, then asked, "why did you visit them? The 'shifters', I mean."

Lazaro rubbed the back of his neck. "I *had* to warn them. Agent K has tried to kill Amy twice that I'm aware of. He thinks the world is going to end because of her. When I arrived, they were already expecting me. A strange old woman was there, planning with the pack. Both K and Amy Ryker's father are apparently trying to manipulate the situation. The woman assured me the world won't end if Amy fulfills the 'prophecy'."

"Prophecy..." Dr. Warren sampled the word. "Interesting."

"Do you know what that means?" Lazaro leaned over the file, watching the doctor's features for any clues.

"Well, Clara kept repeating something to herself when she was brought in to my care. I wrote down the words years ago. But when I bring it up, she claims she doesn't remember. I believe she's suppressed the memory." The doctor rifled through a drawer and snatched a yellowed scrap of paper. "Here it is."

It read:

> *A child of the wolf that hath borne the mark,*
> *The essence of five, doubled and bound,*
> *'Neath Beltane's blooded moon,*
> *Secures the conduit to their fate.*
> *The gates long closed by hands of men,*
> *Shall open once more.*
> *So that providence, chaos,*
> *Or annihilation may rein.*

Lazaro read it over twice, memorizing the lines before looking back up. "What does it mean?"

"It's a sort of nursery rhyme, I thought. Werewolf children repeat it, though I've only been able to observe one, obviously. But 'prophecy' makes more sense. It's too bizarre to be a child's game, you'd think."

"A little macabre at the end. No wonder K is worried. What decides between 'providence, chaos or annihilation'?"

"We've only got the direct script, but we're missing something that I think your mystery woman knows." Dr. Warren grinned.

"From what I gathered, Amy had no knowledge of the prophecy until today, and she's the one that supposed to fulfill it. The woman knew of you, too. She told me to ask you about Project Blackmoor. That's why I did."

The doctor looked stunned. "What did she say?"

"She just called you 'my doctor', but I knew who she meant right away." He hesitated, worried that she might be put off by his next words, and not wanting to sound like some sappy youth. But then he wondered when he'd become so self-conscious and spoke despite himself. "You've been on my mind since the hospital. You were there before the surgery." Lazaro touched the muscle of his stomach. "And you were kind to me when everyone else treated me like a burden. I was human to you, even in pieces." It was difficult for him to admit, remembering how she'd encompassed his fever dreams.

A red flush overcame the doctor's cheeks. "I guess I understand what it's like-" there was more to the statement, but she did not say it.

Lazaro stood from his chair, and leaned over, brushing her heart-shaped cheek with a kiss. His heart fluttered in his chest, but he would have been a coward if he couldn't show her how he felt. "You're amazing, Dr. Samantha Warren." He righted himself and an instinctual urgency made him hurry. "I have to go before K suspects I won't be meeting him. *Thank you.*"

The doctor's eyes widened with surprise and mild disappointment. "Sure." She brushed a hand across her cheek, which reddened further. "Please don't say anything about Project Blackmoor. Not to anyone, especially the director."

"I promise." Lazaro gave a slight, uncharacteristic bow. Goodbye, Sam." He truly hoped it wasn't the last time.

"Goodbye, Lazaro."

He opened the door and stepped out, hesitating as it shut behind him. Lazaro caught one last glance of her through the narrow slit, and saw the doctor's shapely lips curving into a smile.

*

As the agent left her office, Dr. Warren shifted in the seat, rubbing her cheek thoughtfully. *Were* humans going to go extinct? If so, could she allow herself these feelings blossoming inside her?

287

She thought of Morgan Lazaro, not regretting a moment of her brief time with him, and still wishing they had so much more time to explore this new – strange – thing between them-

The desk phone's shrill ring cut through her thoughts.

It never rang. *Ever.*

She let it ring once more before picking it up. "… hello?"

"Samantha Warren?" An unfamiliar woman's voice crackled through the bad connection. Was it someone's secretary from upstairs? Or maybe it was one of K's people.

"This is she. May I ask who's calling?"

"Our common acquaintance just left your office, yes?"

Sam remained silent.

"I'll assume that he has. Listen, it's crucial that you meet us at the gathering point by three this morning. Bring the Blackmoor shifter you've got stowed away, along with your horned gorilla. Tomorrow by sunrise will be too late. Write down these coordinates, dear."

"Are- are you the woman he mentioned?"

A pause. "Samantha, the things you know is vast compared to most of the human race. You've lived an incredible, terrible, wonderful life. Now the world desperately needs change by people like you. Do what I ask now, without question, and I guarantee you a better explanation when this is all over." The woman's voice softened. "Are you ready to write it down?"

Dr. Warren pressed the phone to her ear and fumbled a paper and a pen from her desk drawer. "Ready." She wrote the numbers as they were read.

"We'll see you tomorrow, before sunrise." The line went dead. She set the phone gently into the cradle and stood, clutching the parchment.

How on earth was she ever going to get that gorilla out of containment?

Chapter 39

I woke to having been unceremoniously dumped into an ice-cold metal cage. My head throbbed worse than any hangover, a tender lump swelling above my temple.

Everything flooded back simultaneously, from my father's betrayal to Kane's capture and torment.

They left me naked, save for the necklace that seemed immune to getting lost or broken, though it was a little comfort in my confines,

I curled into a ball and squeezed my eyes shut.

The cool evening wind sapped the heat from my body and I shivered, my teeth chattering madly.

So stupid, so fucking stupid. My mind reeled. I'd run away from the only ones who ever gave a shit about me.

The witch came to us, told the truth, and I spat in her face. The pack should have explained everything, but would I have listened? If Kane told me in my apartment, or at the restaurant? I never would have returned to the farm with him.

No, of course he waited.

"Amy, is that you?" A man leaned over my cage, one good eye peered down at me, the other a balled knot of scar tissue he didn't bother to conceal.

I recalled the voice from my memories, the one who saved me from the lapping flames: father's second in command. "What happened to your eye, Duncan?"

He smiled wearily. "An accident." Duncan could never lie to save his life. Not then, and certainly not now. Shrugging off his coat, he pushed it through the bars. "Here, take this. It's cold tonight." As I wrapped it around myself, he hunkered down to look me in the eye. "I'm so glad you're alive. We didn't know what happened to you or your mother after the raid. I did the best I could for both of you." Pain seemed to weigh him down more than age. "I have to go now. Just know we don't all agree with your father." The sentiment rang hollow in his absence.

I wondered if it was my father who pulled his strings now. No doubt he was made example of with that eye of his.

Father enjoyed striking fear into his pack, I remembered, what better way than to leave a living example. Duncan seemed to have fallen from his mantle some time before. I only hoped his mate and child hadn't paid the price.

291

A roar burst through the camp, sending my hairs on end.

I craned my neck to see them hoisting a cage onto one of their trucks. My mate was fully changed, violently battering the confines with his bulk.

Father's men surrounded the vehicle in an attempt to manage the situation, but Kane smashed against it so hard, it fell to one side, crushing several of father's pack members. The top of the cage, in its weakened state, gave when he shoved against it, and he burst free.

"Kane!" I screamed, my heart racing with a fevered panic.

He didn't seem to hear me, barreling through the gathered crowd and catching one in his jaws, rending head from shoulders. Father's pack split, shifted, and reformed in an attempt to contain my mate.

One leaped onto his back and he flung them off, smashing them into the truck's window. Another went for his throat, but he swiped the shifter away before he made contact.

Billy-club went in for a kill shot, but was tossed aside like a doll. One of father's pack had a gun, and was loading it up.

"Kane! Watch out!"

He saw me then, and his wild eyes glistened with a golden light.

I stopped breathing as he approached my cage, realizing for the first time that fire lapped over his fur and consumed his skin without burning.

Blood-wolf.

No other shifters attacked as he stood over my cage, his eyes – hot coals of preternatural energy – stared at me with slow recollection. They began to fade to a familiar blue before the first of many darts burrowed into his coat.

A howl tore from his throat and he turned on the shooter.

Another feathered dart struck home. He lunged at the attacker, crushing him beneath his bulk. Two more men with dart guns began to shoot.

Kane stood tall from the kill, blood soaked his front as he wavered, lost his balance, and dropped to one knee.

"No!" I screamed at my father's men. "Stop it!" They didn't stop, hitting him with ten more before he crashed to the earth, unconscious under the weight of the tranquilizers.

The survivors gathered around my mate and hoisted him into an empty cage. Billy-club stood from the ground and wiped blood from his mouth.

He shot me a hateful glare. "Load 'em up!"

Several of his men hoisted my cage up, staying clear of my reach. I lost sight of Kane as they carried me to a huge van.

Squealing of metal on metal made everyone cringe as they shoved my cage into the compartment.

Once situated, they pushed in another cage with a tawny sheet draped over it. Billy-club gave me one last nasty look before the van doors slammed shut, leaving me alone with whatever inhabited the other cage.

The van rumbled to life and started moving.

A pungent stench filled the cramped space as a thin arm tore through the sheet. It was the young woman from Ezekiel's mansion, who'd stood next to him during the trade. Her beautiful dress was torn and filthy, her movements wild and erratic.

"*You*," she hissed, her eyes coal black.

I snarled in response, my instincts told me she was a ruthless killer, and to destroy her before she did the same to me.

She lashed out, trying to catch me in her iron grip.

I barely saw her movements and dodged just in time. The wolf inside me wanted to escape and tear this creature a new hole. But I had my senses, and it would help neither of us if we attacked each other now. "We aren't enemies."

The vampire's eyes glanced up at me in hateful surprise. She appeared younger and more vulnerable as reason returned to her doll-like features.

"*We* are not enemies," I repeated, "*they* are our enemies." I tilted my head towards the van door. "Do you want to get out alive, or not?"

The vampire paused before nodding, her eyes returning to a muted blue in the darkness. "How do you propose we escape?"

Without the threat of attack, I could assess the situation with my full attention. Each cage had an industrial padlock, not expensive, just impossible to pick. "I don't know."

"What's the use, then?" She sat in a corner, red tears welling up in her eyes. "They're going to kill us."

I grabbed the bars of her cage. "What's your name?"

She looked up, misery drawing her face long. "Elizabeth."

"Listen, Elizabeth. I don't know how, but we're going to get out of here soon, okay? If we can escape, you run straight home and don't look back."

Then at least one of us might survive, I thought.

Elizabeth's eyes lightened to a precious blue, intensified by the red tear stains. "Ezekiel will kill them all." Her laugh cracked miserably. "They're not going to get away with this."

I leaned back onto the cage wall and shoved my hands in Duncan's coat pockets. "We've got to-" My finger touched something cold. Small, but promising. I pulled out a set of keys on a cheap ring.

The keys to the locks.

Without a word I set to work unlocking the cages, first mine, then hers. Elizabeth's eyes were filled with hope as she exited the confines.

We stood, shifter to vampire, and hesitated before hugging each other with relief. I didn't know if I might ever consider her a friend, but we weren't enemies, not after tonight.

Her guy, on the other hand...

Someone turned off the engine and voices rounded the vehicle.

I hoped she was able to fight. "Get ready."

One of father's men swung the van door open. "What the hell-" The shifter had not a second to react as Elizabeth mounted him, burying her face in his throat.

They fell back onto the grass. He bucked and writhed beneath her iron grip. If he had a moment longer, he might have changed, and she'd had a run for her money. As it were, his protest grew faint until his limbs went limp on the grass.

Elizabeth pulled away with a satisfied grimace, her long canines glistening vermillion in the moonlight. "You wolves taste terrible."

Several more were coming.

I threw off the jacket and fell on all fours, the change consumed me, unfolding into my limbs.

Two men who'd clearly gotten wind of the bloodshed dashed around the van half-changed. One leaped onto Elizabeth and began tearing at her face and neck, the other watched me with sharp eyes. "Where are you going, *princess*?"

I ignored his taunts, dodged, and charged at the shifter on top of Elizabeth, barreling into him. Catching his jugular in my mouth, I twisted until his neck crunched impossibly. She rolled to one side as I stood above my kill.

"You're *not* getting away." He hunkered to the ground with a gleam in his eye. I teased him away from Elizabeth while she recovered, silently praying vampires healed faster than shifters.

After I dodged his claws twice, I wasn't disappointed.

Elizabeth – fully regenerated – flitted into view, and clocked the shifter square in the jaw. The hit flung him ten feet away, and when he got up, his jawbone hung awkwardly on one side. He shot us a fearful glance and bolted.

She took a triumphant breath, blood speckling her shredded dress. "There will be more."

I stood on hind legs, letting the change fall away and scooping up the coat. "Get out of here, Elizabeth. I have to find-"

"Gotcha!" Sturdy arms linked around mine and dragged me backwards. Elizabeth stole one last, desperate glance before dissipating like a mist in the darkness.

Two more shifters ran up to my captor, who spun around with me in his arms. "Where did she go?"

"She's a vampire, you fucking idiots." Billy-club's voice rumbled as he dragged me out of my captor's arms. I kicked and struggled, but he got me in a lock before I could wiggle free. "Jeb, follow that bitch! She'll lead her friends straight to us." I bucked against him, trying to escape his grip. He took it as a challenge and clenched my pelvic bone. "You're not going anywhere." Billy-club breathed in my ear, barking at his subordinates. "Grab her legs!"

They hoisted me up and carried me towards a tall building erected in the middle of absolutely nowhere. The structure was illuminated from within, high slats sent rays of yellow into the night sky. The blood moon hung low on the horizon, almost entirely eclipsed now.

Father stood at the entrance; his arms were crossed in what looked like irritation. "Where is the vampire?"

Billy-club gave an audible sigh. "She disappeared, sir."

"Brody, you son of a bitch. I told you to leave them caged!" He peered at me over Billy-club – Brody's – shoulder. "What happened?"

"They were both out of their cages when we arrived. They killed Liam and Gideon before we got there."

"Incompetent, the lot of you." Ryker led us into the building. "We have to find her. *Two* vampires are needed for the ritual, as you idiots seem to have forgotten."

"Jeb's chasing her down. We'll get her back." Brody cursed under his breath, depositing me onto the cement floor and shackled me to a string of thick chains.

They were yanked backwards until I was wrapped around a cold, cement pillar, overlooking a heinous scene. Father's men were slitting throats of two humans and a vampire.

Bowls rested beneath their gaping necks to catch the blood.

Once the blood was collected, the bodies were discarded in a far corner of the room.

Duncan was next. He did not fight, merely kneeling over the bowl with resignation.

"Father, no!" I screamed, but it did not stay the knife.

Duncan smiled up at me before the tool bit into his neck, drawing a stream of blood from the artery. One of father's men caught his body before he collapsed into the bowl.

I looked up at my father, who watched the scene impassively. Celeste was by his side with a cool smile. *How could you? Why would you do this to your own kind?*

I couldn't watch as they brought two more people – blinded, gagged, and bound – to the knife and sliced them open.

Magic tinged the air, *witches*.

Father ushered his men with a wave. "Bring the descendants in. But be careful."

A woman and a small child were escorted towards the executioners. They appeared human in all respects, but the woman's eyes flicked around the room, glowing like coals in their sockets. The child – a little girl – clung to her leg, following wherever they led the woman.

Brody snatched the girl, and another took the woman. She shrieked in a language I'd never heard before. The child cried out for her with outreached arms as they were torn apart.

The woman mumbled to the girl even as she was bent over a bowl, words of consolation in her last moments.

One of father's men brought the knife to her throat and sliced. The child's scream pierced through the chaos. My heart ached to protect the child from the monster my father had become in his quest for power.

Brody lifted the girl and replaced the corpse with her.

"Stop it!" I writhed against the restraints. "Leave her alone!!!" My voice was lost on him as he ordered the child's death, too.

The knife slipped effortlessly through the girl's jugular, the easiest kill. Any words I may have had were caught in my throat.

They discarded the tiny body like the others, without reverence. Shifters carried away the bowls of blood, eight in all. One had less fluid than the others.

Father spoke to his pack, but I couldn't bear to listen, wondering how Celeste could watch on passively the way she did as he committed these atrocities.

In the corner of the room, I spotted a massive cage, with a mound of dark fur. Red feathers protruded from his coat. *Kane*.

I hung my head, unable to bear another loss. My heart was shattered into a thousand pieces after the carnage. Duncan, the nameless innocents, that child…

Amy, a voice fluttered into my mind.

I squeezed my eyes shut. *Go away, little flies*.

Amy, this is the witch. We're on our way. Elizabeth has reached us and we'll be there soon.

Your father can't start the ritual before the blood moon sets. Don't give up hope, dear, the voice whispered. Little did they know what father had already done.

What could they *possibly* do to rectify his crimes?

Chapter 40

Dr. Samantha Warren paced through the emptied lab. Clara would be easy to escort out if she donned the generic blue scrubs of an intern. But the gorilla? Who could she trust to stay quiet?

No one on site at this hour, that was certain.

The techs had finally closed up for the evening, so Sam was alone in her task. She sighed and punched in the code to the reinforced door.

The air pressure lock hissed open; her menagerie was too-quiet. Sam stepped inside curiously, shutting the door behind her and taking inventory of each beast. All were accounted for until she reached the gorilla's confinement.

A young man inhabiting the gorilla's cage nodded at her. He was short-statured with a deep tan, and completely nude. There was no gorilla in sight. The youth's eyes, however, were deep brown, his whites black. "Doctor."

She gaped at him, more curious than embarrassed. "You changed back. Have you been able to this whole time?"

He glanced away. "A little voice reminded me how. Sorry about the mess. I sort of forgot who I was for a while."

The doctor shook her head. "You aren't going to change back if I let you free?"

"I'd be rather grateful, actually. Any reason in particular?"

Sam jangled the keyring at him. "We've got to be somewhere in an hour. Do you want to come?"

He stood and stretched. "Don't see why not."

The doctor trained her eyes on his youthful face, his nudity hardly a distraction. "Do you have a name?"

"Before I escaped the zoo, they called me Hercules."

She smiled at the boy, surprised he accepted his given creature name so readily. "Alright, Hercules: behave and I'll get you out of here for good. Let's go get Clara and we'll hit the road." He followed close beside her as she punched in the code, then eased into the room. "Clara," Dr. Warren called into the tiny apartment. "It's time to go."

Silence greeted her. Usually the girl was asleep at this hour, but the place appeared empty.

Clara peered out from behind the metal door at the boy, her blue eyes wide. "Who is that?"

303

"His name is Hercules. We don't have much time." Sam took a melancholy breath. She knew that this was more important than anything she might learn from their studies. And when they were done, Clara had to return to her own family, as it should have been years ago.

Clara seemed fascinated with the prospect, fiddling a fingernail in anticipation. "Where are we going?"

"We're taking a little drive, but we've got to go now."

Clara swished her dress and beamed at Dr. Warren. "That'll be fun. I've never been in a car before!"

Samantha shot her a sad smile.

They made for the exit after she dressed them in utility scrubs. She stole a pair of intern's shoes that fit the youth well enough. Hercules squirmed uncomfortably in his new clothes. Clara, on the other hand, could've easily pass for an intern, just as she'd thought.

Dr. Warren led them through the front of the building with little more than a sidelong glance from the night guard.

Opening the door to her car, she stopped. "Neither of you better change in this car, or we'll *all* get squished," Sam warned with a stern shake of her finger.

Hercules entered the vehicle first. "Got it."

"Of course! It's rude to change without permission." Clara scooted in next to Hercules. Samantha Warren wondered where the girl had picked *that* gem up.

No. The lab was most certainly not the place for her.

Sam had done what she could for the girl, kept her alive and safe. But Clara was not her child. She was a wild thing and had a family that loved and missed her.

Dr. Warren glanced back at headquarters before starting the Mazda and puttering out of the security gate, not exactly sure how she felt about this.

She was putting everything at risk, her career, her work, her *life*. But she knew, deep in her heart, that this was the right course of action.

There would be no going back after this.

Chapter 41

Agent Kipling swept a stack of books from his desk and took a heavy breath, realizing the action did little to stifle his rising fury. The backstabbing Lazaro hadn't shown up to the meeting that evening.

Somehow, he'd bypassed security and disappeared without a trace. They were out of time, and he didn't want a rogue agent fucking up his plans.

He picked up the radio, barely able to grip the thing without crushing it. "We have to move the raid team out there *now*. Gabriel Ryker is already setting up the blood ritual," he spoke into the radio.

The dirty heathens. He'd have preferred to bomb the building and be done with it, but the portcullis was the only thing holding the ancient evil at bay.

Director Aldridge refused him heavy artillery weapons, so he had to make do with two military vehicles and twenty-some

Marines with automatic rifles. Without divulging the real threat, it was difficult to persuade the director to his cause. That, along with Dr. Gray's 'favor', it might be enough.

Might.

"*Yes sir*," the speaker's voice crackled back. The team knew the plan, they had their orders, and they would be at Ryker's front door in thirty minutes.

Kipling couldn't stand to let them go without seeing it for himself. He'd watch history unfold, whatever the outcome.

The agent had purloined a small bulletproof truck from the lot behind central. After tonight, it wouldn't matter what happened to him. They just had to stop the ritual.

Dr. Gray rode along with him, the sweet waft of her perfume tickling his nose as he turned to gauge her conviction. "Can you believe we're almost done?"

She shifted the metal case in her lap. "Indeed." Althea's perfect mouth pursed in a tight line. She seemed disappointed about something. "Did the Dame really want us to use the V-2534 strain? It seems rather extreme for this level of infestation."

"That's what she said. It's more important that we eliminate the threat first, then we can contain what remains of their party."

She gave a heavy sigh. "But there's nothing like having a live, unaltered sample."

He glanced at her again, then his eyes flickered back to the road. "We'll isolate at least one before the night is over. For your research, of course."

Althea's severe features softened. He had always wondered why a bombshell like her decided to work for the government in the first place.

Althea could have been anything she wanted, with both beauty and brains, but she settled for this dead-end job. *But*, he amended, *we all got here by seeing something we shouldn't have.* There was no denying it.

The trucks turned onto the main road. Cars slowed to the shoulder when they saw the military parade. *One small perk in the shit position*, he thought as anticipation rose in his gullet.

Their work was coming to a close tonight.

For better or worse.

Chapter 42

Morgan Lazaro waited in a dung-heap motel off the interstate, a place without cameras or any real security to speak of. The bloody eclipse had already consumed the pregnant moon, and he wondered if they'd forgotten about him entirely.

He fiddled with his phone and decided to call the doctor, then thought better of it. After leaving headquarters, he was certain agent Kipling was aware that he'd visited Dr. Warren. He didn't want to implicate her further.

Lazaro knew Kipling would take any means necessary to finish his mission and eradicate whatever obstacles that stood in his way. Tonight, that would be Lazaro.

He lounged on the on the comforter, the infomercials nearly lolling him off to sleep when word finally came.

Lazaro. The witches voice cut through the sleepiness. He didn't think he'd ever get used to her means of communication. *Meet us within the national forest to the northeast section of the Jackson river. There's an unmarked facility that doesn't belong. It will be upstream on the west bank. From your location, it should take twenty minutes to reach us. Don't be late.* Her cantankerous voice droned the last sentence, as if he were known for his tardiness.

He knew the area but hadn't been so far north on that river before. Stretching the exhaustion from his limbs, Lazaro stood from the cheap mattress. Despite his wrists, he brought both sidearms. One shot per hand, he estimated, until they refractured. He hoped it wouldn't have to come to that but he was willing to make that sacrifice.

Lazaro wasted no time checking out and getting into his car. The engine started easily, despite the unusually cold night. His permanent government plates would deter any bored beat cops from pulling him over. If they did, he'd merely flash his badge.

Lazaro zoomed down the street at almost twice the legal speed, shouldering past slow and obstinate drivers. A random song blasted from the radio, the only thing keeping him awake and alert at this hour.

*

Lazaro crawled along the dirt road in his car looking for any sign of life. The location couldn't be much further up, or he'd run into the steep hills across state lines. Unease built in his chest, tangling with the scars of his stomach.

Time was almost up.

A bony white hand reached from the passenger seat and turned off the radio. A chilling figure sat next to him casually, as if he hadn't just appeared out of thin air. "You are going the wrong way."

Lazaro slammed on the brake and released his service pistol from the clip, aiming at the pale intruder.

The aging man with peppered hair in a too-expensive double-breasted lapel jacket looked over the barrel at Lazaro with amusement, using two fingers to move the muzzle aside. "No need for unnecessary violence in this late hour, little government man." The intruder's smile widened, exposing long, pearly canines. "We're on the same side, *this* time. You're too far down the river. I suggest you follow my instructions." He nodded towards the road.

Lazaro returned the gun to its holster and watched the vampire from his peripherals. "It's agent Lazaro to you."

The intruder shrugged. "You're human. That is all I need to know." After a while, he pointed into the gloom. "Turn into the woods there."

As Lazaro parked the car, familiar faces emerged from the shadows. Dr. Warren was among them, along with Clara and a thin boy she had in tow.

A red-headed giant with a massive, unruly beard, wearing only threadbare jeans, watched him. He stood next to a youth who appeared as if he just graduated university, wearing oddly colored robes and had fair features.

Kyren came up to him. "The witch brought along a few allies to extract Kane and Amy, who are both inside with Gabriel's pack. Dr. Warren caught sight of military vehicles approaching from the East. We won't be able to stop them from getting in."

"That must be Kipling. How many soldiers?" He turned to the doctor, who looked frazzled, but thoroughly excited, like a child after a carnival ride. Who could blame her? She was in the field, surrounded by precisely the things she'd been studying her entire career.

"Two vehicles. They could probably hold ten people each, but from what I could tell, they're fully equipped."

"How close did you get?" Lazaro asked, concerned.

Her lips pursed into a naughty smile. "Nobody questions a middle aged 'mom' in a Mazda, I don't use government plates so they thought I was a civilian. I tailgated them."

"Well don't do that again. Agent Kipling doesn't care who dies on this mission." He wrapped an arm around her protectively, careful to maintain some level of professionalism, though he didn't want to. "How many, um, shifters, are inside?" Lazaro looked towards the cement building.

"Hard to tell," Kyren responded. "Based on the movements, thirty? Forty? A team of five is continuously doing perimeter checks. We killed one pursuing Elizabeth as she escaped." He pointed to a young vampire that looked a little worse for wear, her dress in tatters. "That doesn't include the victims."

"Victims?"

"Ryker's men have eight bodies inside. They've all been exsanguinated," the aging vampire who'd escorted him spoke up. "We can smell their blood on the wind."

"He's trying to begin the ritual on corpse blood." The witch approached, shaking her head. "This is not good, but I'm certain Ryker is beyond listening to his advisors. His mind is sealed up tighter than a lockbox. Wonder where he got that trick?"

"Sixty, then, if we assume the worst," Lazaro concluded. "The numbers aren't in our favor."

"No, but..." Gary, another shifter from the farmhouse piped in, glancing over at the vampires. "-we do have a few tricks up our sleeves."

"I'll say," the giant red-head spoke hungrily. His eyes glowing with an internal, warm light, something Lazaro hadn't seen in any of the shifters. "But what are *we* doing here, witch?"

"We need the five primeval species, Bear, and here we are." She smiled, looking to each of them.

Kyren glanced around as well. "There are only four: humans, shifters, witches, vampires…"

"Are you sure about that?" She panned over them all. "I'm not surprised you don't know. There's few enough of them on the Earth, and fewer still that know their true nature." She waved 'Bear' and the lanky youth to her. "Hercules, is it?"

He stepped forward warily. "Yes, ma'am?"

"What are you?"

"A shifter."

"And you, Bear?"

"A shifter, of course."

"That would make both of you quite wrong." The witch grinned, seeming pleased to tell them. "There were creatures before even shifters that had amazing strength and ability to transform. They all had one identifying characteristic: horns."

Hercules watched her, seeming disturbed by the revelation. "So, what are we, then?"

"It means you are descendants. Descendants of an old race, one that precedes humans, shifters, and vampires, even us witches. You're the first of the five, and we need you now more than ever. The ritual won't be complete without you."

Bear took a seat on the dirt floor, crossing his legs and stroking the unruly beard. Hercules only stared at the witch, glancing back at Dr. Warren who, Lazaro noticed, was stunned into silence.

"Fine and all." The older female shifter from the farmhouse stepped forward. "But we're running out of time. Have your revelations after the sun rises. We have to fight now, before they make their move."

"Moira is absolutely correct," the witch said. "Roth and I must begin the summoning. If we don't gather the energy to undo the portcullis, then Ryker's plan will prevail, and we won't live to see the next full moon." She signaled to the university man, who ran a hand through his dirty blonde hair nervously. "The rest of you, I trust you can play at strategy. Secure that building. Keep Amy alive at all costs."

Kyren lead the group away from the witch and her acolyte. Bear towered over everyone, even the bony vampire who stood a head and a half taller than Lazaro.

The vampire comforted the sodden female vampire, who was covered in gore and clothed in a shredded dress that might have been beautiful, once. Three other pale-skinned creatures loomed a distance behind their leader.

"Ezekiel." Kyren, who was flanked by several pack members, stared up at the vampire. "Dawn is coming soon. That means we have no time to make mistakes. The military team will have to be dealt with inside the building, where the fighting will be the thickest. We'll make an opening for your team."

"I had already sent Garrett to loose the air in their tires. The vehicles will not take them any further." Ezekiel bowed slightly, a sardonic grin spread across his face. "But it will not slow them down much. Let them destroy each other, and we'll sweep behind both enemies."

Kyren merely nodded, then looked up at the ginger giant. "Bear, you're a fantastic first impression. You go in first, scare the shit out of them."

"And I die first, is that it?"

"They'll be focused on Ryker's men. We can charge in and guard your flank." Kyren gave him a reassuring nod. "I'm not going to lead a friend into death, just don't crush any of us in the fray, please."

"What about me?" Hercules puffed his thin, bony chest. "I'm formidable enough."

"I'll vouch for that," Dr. Warren snorted. "I had to change your cage four times since last year, you kept ripping the bars off and throwing them at my staff."

Lazaro stared at the youth with renewed awe. "*You're* the gorilla?"

Hercules shrugged noncommittally. "It's nothin' special."

"Okay," Kyren decided on something. "Hercules, you'll go in with Bear first, then."

He and Bear exchanged curious glances, seeming to size each other up with silent reappraisals.

"We'll bring up the rear. Vampires, you slide in when we create enough chaos and take out Ryker's pack. We're going up against other shifters. You won't get confused, right?"

Ezekiel donned a look of disgust. "You doubt our ability to differentiate your stench from theirs? I am offended."

"I really don't give a shit that you're offended, vampire. There's only twelve of us, sixty of them. We'll bicker later." Kyren rolled his eyes, then turned to him. "Lazaro, where do you think you'll be the most use?"

Lazaro was glad to have the sidearms and a tactical knife he stowed in his jacket pocket, but he was still ill-equipped to join this supernatural fight. "After the vampires, I can take out any survivors. I'll find Amy too."

"One minute left, children!" The witch called over her shoulder, then resumed her focus on whatever she and her acolyte were doing.

Ezekiel looked over at the structure. "The soldiers are entering the building already. And five shifters are incoming."

Bear hoisted up with a wide, toothy grin. "Let's get this show on the road." He peered down at Hercules. "You better live up to your name, kid."

Hercules scoffed at the giant. "I hope you're ready to eat my dust, *Bear*." The boy grew in size, losing his thin limbs to hulking, furred muscle. Hercules' face puckered inwards and horns protruded from his temples until the giant horned gorilla stood in their midst.

Bear let out a belly shaking laugh and followed the beast into battle, hunkering low and growing a massive red pelt as he dashed towards the oncoming group of shifters.

Kyren and the others changed as well, multi-hued fur shuddering over their lithe forms as snouts and long ears protruded from their faces.

Dr. Warren's eyes were wide as she watched the transformations in silent awe. Clara stood on her right, looking like she was itching to join them. Samantha put an arm in front of the girl. "Stay here. It's too dangerous for you."

The hulking gorilla and grizzly scattered Ryker's shifter group. Bear gained momentum as he charged, lumbering at his target. He made the wolves look like dogs in the silhouetted light from the building, his massive form coiled over one as they tumbled mere feet from the entrance.

Hercules snatched a shifter by the scruff of his neck and threw him headlong into the building, crushing his skull on contact. He chased down another without hesitation. Lazaro shivered, glad he wasn't on the wrong side of that fight.

Kyren's group pulled in behind the descendants, making good on their promise of support and defense. Shortly, the vampires would intercede as well.

Lazaro needed to nut the fuck up and get in there, before all his training fell out the back of his skull.

He drew closer to Samantha, stopping himself from leaning in and stroking one of her many vibrant curls from her heart-shaped face. "Listen, before I go, I've- been meaning to ask you a question."

Suspense glowed in her features. "Shoot," she said, but her eyes were expectant, as if she already knew his mind.

Lazaro picked up her hand and cradled it, stroking his thumb over hers. "This is- insane, for me, at least. I've never had an inclination to do this before, but... If I had asked you out, would you have said 'yes'?"

Samantha beamed up at him. "All you had to do was ask."

He leaned down and planted a kiss on her shapely lips, caressing the back of her neck. Dr. Warren slipped her arms around his waist, returning the affection with a sweet sigh.

With the doctor's lingering scent on his lips, Lazaro could die a happy man.

Chapter 43

"Finish the North end," my father instructed, passing his hand over the macabre work as if it were a masterpiece.

His pack members used the bowls of blood to paint crude designs around the center of the building, where a wide, low grate rested, unmolested by the building erected around it. The bars didn't appear old and were made of no metal I'd ever seen. Too shiny, almost etheric in nature.

It seemed the focus of his work.

Two sides of the bloody sigil remained unfinished after the painters laid down their tools. They were missing something, and after seeing the bloodbath, I didn't have to guess what.

But whose?

"Celeste," our father beckoned. "Come here, my child."

She ascended the low steps to him, blind to anything but his approval. I realized I could have been her, in another life, if the witch hadn't intervened. "Yes, father?"

"You have done well, my girl. See your quarry." He waved a hand towards Kane's cage, where he'd begun to stir. "What a prize. His body will be the first to feed the ancient ones. The blood moon is almost set and we'll bask in the glory of *our* new world together!"

His men cheered and whooped, convening near the grate.

Our father draped an arm around Celeste casually, and a flash of obsidian was in his right hand. Celest smiled up at him, still blind. "We're almost done, then?"

"We're almost done." He nodded, plunging the knife deep into her breastplate with a sickening crunch.

My sister's eyes bulged with disbelief. Despite our distasteful reunion, it hit me as hard as Duncan's sacrifice.

Father's lackeys caught the blood with another saucer. He gripped her golden hair, so similar to mother's, until she ceased to struggle in her death throes.

The obsidian blade jutted unnaturally from her chest as she was released to the cement, glassy eyed and unseeing.

"No sacrifice is too great, no goal unobtainable. With the ancient ones at our beck and call, humans will once again hide beneath rock and soil, as is their place. Now, find Mason's crew, let's get the bloodsucking bitch and finish the ritual!"

They dispersed after another brief display of comradery. Two of the men sauntered close enough that I could hear parts of their conversation.

Father's second, Brody, thumbed back at my sister's corpse. "... a bit of a waste, if you ask me."

"Yeah, but-" His partner leaned in, shooting me a lascivious glance. "Good things come in twos."

Brody rolled his eyes. "That's 'three's' you idiot. Anyway, she'll be dead by sunrise. You a fucking necro, Mac?" He shouldered his companion with a chuckle, who didn't instantly object to the accusation.

"Well, it's no fun if..." their conversation faded out.

Kane's cage was being brought to father's side, rousing him further from his drug-induced sleep.

He gripped the cage bars and lifted himself up, still fully changed. Kane's eyes were strange, glowing like the woman and child my father had slaughtered. His beautiful blue lost in the turbulent heat of his blood-wolf.

Red embers flickered, watching my sister's killer.

My father leaned forward, maintaining a healthy distance from the bars. "Hello, Blackmoor."

Kane growled in response, the air surrounding him became a mirage of roiling heat. His fur stood on end as my father studied him.

"If only your gift were transferrable. It's a real pity," father mused to himself. "Joshua, get the tranquilizer."

The lackey balked. "But, sir. He barely went down with twelve shots last time. It will take twenty-four at least."

"Then shoot him with twenty-four." Father's cold glare fell upon the man, who cringed under his alpha's attention.

"Sir." He bowed, loading the feathers and shooting. I stopped counting at eleven as Kane's howls shook the building. He threw himself against the bars as flames danced over his fur, dampened only by the occasional flit of a red feather.

As sturdy as the cage was, Kane's fury defied gravity. The cage tumbled to one side where he could slam into the bottom plate with all the ferocity of a blood-wolf.

Fear tightened father's brow as he commanded the pack. "Defend the portcullis and contain this beast!"

Red darts kept barraging my mate's fur.

Kane threw himself once more against the bottom plate, blasting through and teetering before crashing into the concrete floor. His energy went out like a lit match thrown into water. The tranquilizer did its job.

"No, no, no," I whispered, yanking at my shackles. The change refused to obey, coiled tightly in my chest.

"Bring him here," my father demanded, seeming winded from the scare, but in control once more.

Kane was dragged, with much effort, towards the grate in the center of the room. The men dropped him a short distance from my father, and a pack member handed him the obsidian knife. Lifting my mate's head from the floor, father brought the blade to his jugular.

"NO!!!" I screamed, blood pounding in my ears.

At the same moment, the front doors slammed open. Soldiers poured into the room in full riot gear with automatic rifles. Bullets shattered the quiet shock in the wake of my father's crimes, wasting the first line of his defense.

I breathed a sigh of relief as the knife was pulled away from Kane's throat, not at all concerned about myself, or the battle growing ever closer.

The shifters that survived the hail of bullets split their clothes with the change, meeting the soldiers head-on. Father screamed orders to his men and profanities at the fallen.

"Louis, to the left! Nico, push through their ranks!" His men held the attackers off well enough at first, disarming them until no more bullets pierced the air.

But they pressed on, slicing into the shifters with knives, their human flesh concealed beneath riot gear.

A shifter near me leaped onto a soldier and ripped an arm off with teeth and torsion. To my surprise, the soldier did not scream, he did not flail, and he certainly did not bleed.

These weren't humans, at least, not anymore.

Somehow, the soldier managed to use his other arm and latch onto the shifter's neck. The helmet slid off, revealing razor-sharp teeth and sunken eyes.

Black ichor leaked from his orifices as he bit down into his throat, tearing out shreds of meat as father's man tried to dislodge the parasite. He fell backwards into the group and I lost sight of them among the flurry of blood and fur.

As the battle neared, I tried to inch away from the claws and teeth that showed no mercy.

Where are they? The sun was about to rise. The slats in the ceiling had gone from pitch black to ultramarine and were brightening still.

"Kill them!!!" father shouted over the madness.

One parasite who was dragging a broken leg caught my eye. He lurched forward and reached for me with thirsty claws. With nowhere to go, I screwed my eyes shut, hoping he'd make it quick. I did not want to live through the agony Matt's claws had wrought all over again.

A deafening roar broke the focus of the fight.

Parasites and shifters alike paused to stare at the uninvited guests. An enormous grizzly bear rose above the crowd, letting out another explosive roar. It had two thick horns protruding from its temples that jutted forward like a bull's. The creature barreled through the crowd indiscriminately.

A silverback gorilla shrieked and whooped in the grizzly bear's wake. Through the gaping entrance poured several of our pack members, fully changed.

My knees nearly gave out with relief.

A young woman appeared at my side, curtsying in yet another sundress, this one a baby blue. "Hello again, Amy."

"Jane!" I cried as she tested my restraints.

I never thought I'd be this happy to see her.

The chain snapped easily in her grip and my right arm was freed from the pillar. "It was brave of you to help our Elizabeth the way you did."

Before she could release my left, a parasite lunged at her.

Jane turned and threw a punch at its head, black matter blasting into the air. The body stumbled back momentarily, then resumed its pursuit. "One sec." She disappeared, the parasite with her. When she reappeared, she was across the room, with the creature's ichor decorating the concrete wall. But she didn't return, becoming distracted with a gnarled shifter.

The bear reared again, flinging off a shifter and three parasites. I could see several vampires flitting between enemies and disabling them in equally creative and disturbing ways.

A flutter in my heart made me look back at my father, who had picked up Kane by his braid and pressed the knife

326

deep into the muscles of his neck. A red waterfall of blood erupted from the gouge and spilled from his lips.

Time stopped.

My hearing departed though the battle raged on. White nothingness enveloped my vision with a strange disconnect, only the sight of Kane's failing body remained.

His eyes rolled back and my existence shattered. Everything that mattered to me was gone.

Then a knowledge poured into me, as if I'd always known what I needed to do. I took hold of the crystalline marble and crushed it, the orb deceptively fragile in my grip.

With a last sigh, I allowed the light to enter me fully.

It's time, the goddess' voice whispered, loosing me from the world of suffering. *Be pained no longer with this burden.*

Chapter 44

Lazaro stepped past the threshold and into the chaos behind Kyren's group. The witch and her acolyte, Roth, had finished the summoning and entered behind him, along with Samantha and Clara scooting in behind a defensible pillar.

Next to the witch, he knew they were safe.

He slipped to the side wall and skirted around the perimeter of the building. Stealth was paramount in this moment. He was no use to them in the middle of this battle.

Bear had made quick work of the crowd, leaping into the fray and disrupting the military's assault on Ryker.

It didn't take long for Lazaro to notice the marines were fighting with their bare hands and teeth. Some lacked arms or legs but pressed against the mass of shifters anyway, without fear of the claws that tore through gear, skin, and bone. He didn't have time to assess them, too busy with his own task.

Lazaro spotted Amy, chained near the portcullis at the center of the room. A pretty young vampire was already by her side, tugging loose her restraints.

Thank god, he thought. *She's still alive.*

Ryker, every bit the man he recalled from the cold case, stood at the head of the room, crouched over another man's unconscious body.

The face of the unconscious man was older compared to the photograph, but Lazaro recognized him: Kane Blackmoor.

Leveling his gun at Ryker, Lazaro held it steady. He only had one good shot.

Blood gushed from the wound Ryker inflicted on Kane's jugular at the same time Lazaro unloaded his clip. As he had expected, his wrist gave out with a sickening crunch. Agony tore up his arm and forced him to his knees. All he could do was cradle the shattered joint with a groan. Ryker had also recoiled from the shot, a drop of satisfaction in an ocean of pain.

A light flooded the room, gently at first, then brighter until he was blind and deaf. The sounds of battle faded to a whisper, then ceased altogether.

With the light brought soothing comfort to his wrist until it no longer held his attention. Lazaro peered through the glow, realizing the battle had somehow ended.

The marines, or what was left of them, ceased their pursuit, and fell to the ground as if their marionette cords had been severed. Shifters, vampires, witches, descendants, and humans stared at the source of the disruption.

Amy, or what she had become, ascended the stairs to the portcullis, her body the source of the radiant light, almost too powerful to look upon. Her father knelt at her feet, gripping a shoulder that seeped crimson fluid.

Ryker gazed up at the goddess incarnate, and fresh tears sprang to his eyes. He wept for mercy, and a glowing hand reached down to caress his cheek.

Their eyes met, and Lazaro swore he saw a hint of a smile cross Ryker's face before he doubled over in pain. The light consumed him completely, and when it dissipated, Ryker was nothing more than a swirl of ash.

The being of light turned to face them, standing above the portcullis. Lazaro had to shield his vision. But with the light came an overpowering sense of serenity.

They had won.

"Magnificent," Lazaro murmured, knowing the word did not do justice.

"*My children.*" She splayed out her hands and a comforting embrace settled over the room. The sound of her voice permeated every facet of Lazaro's mind. He could have sworn she spoke only to him. "*Fear not. Though for millennia*

We have been separate from you, no longer shall it be. Those who feared Our power have none superseding this awakening. We will be with you in spirit until night consumes the sun disk, and the world shall thrive once again."

With a last breath, power billowed into the Goddess. The energy lifted itself from Amy's body, releasing her very human form to the ground near the portcullis, her eyes remaining closed. The energy hovered above the ground for a moment before zooming through the grate. A brilliant explosion rocked the building, and Lazaro braced himself.

He stood and saw that everyone else was as shaken as he, except for the witch, and a handful of Ryker's shifters, who wasted no time retreating.

Lazaro approached the gaping hole in the ground, seeing the dazzling energy still trailing down as far as the eye could see. When the light disappeared from sight, the Earth beneath them shuddered once more.

Assessing the damage, Kyren and his group remained, all except Moira who lay near the pore of the Earth, no question as to how she died. The vampires were gone, whether to dust or due to the sunrise, Lazaro couldn't tell. The young vampire in the sundress, Jane, lay prone on the floor, completing a bloody sigil that had been painted by Ryker's men.

Kyren looked to the witch. "Is that it?"

Lazaro leaned over Amy's body, feeling for a heartbeat. Near her lay Kane, the last of his blood leaking from his carotid artery. He couldn't understand how the Goddess could leave Amy and the others in this state after they'd sacrificed everything for this moment.

The witch smiled. "You might want to step back, Morgan."

He got up, cradling his mangled wrist, and backed away.

An unearthly wind shattered the silence, erupting from the opening. A luminous beam of light emerged, blasting the humble building outward around them. Three pulses of white light burst through the group, sending with it a revitalizing tingle that went straight through Lazaro's core.

It wrapped around his wrist and soothed the agony.

As the mass of energy mounted high above, growing smaller until it might have been no more than another star in the sky. It burst with radiance, shattering into a multitude of fractals that fell softly back to the Earth.

The first to rise was Kane, the blooming slash across his throat gone. He felt his neck and face in relief and reached for Amy, who remained still on the cement floor. Many of the others rose as well, even the creatures who had been affected by agent Kipling's poison, stood human once again.

Bodies that had been piled up against the wall began to move on their own, rousing to stand, alive again.

Kane lifted Amy's body into his arms, her head lolling against his chest. He pressed their foreheads together. A tear trailed through the grime on Kane's face, and his features contorted with the strain of loss.

Someone's hand slipped into Lazaro's, and he turned to see Samantha. "We made it."

"Yeah, but-"

Amy shifted slightly in Kane's grip. "You're squishing me."

Kane looked down at his mate with wide eyes and began to laugh, cautiously at first, then louder, fuller, until the ruins echoed with his joyous relief.

Chapter 45

Agent Kipling peered out from the underbrush at a safe distance from the building, with Dr. Gray crouched beside him.

She slapped at her arm for the thousandth time. "There are *so* many bugs out here!"

He was beginning to lose patience with her. "Yes, doctor, we're out in the field. That's what field work is."

"The serum had to work," Althea continued with little regard to his mood. "I tested it myself. They should be unstoppable. It was perfect!"

Kipling pulled out his binoculars and peeked through an opening in the building. "Clearly they *have* stopped."

A brilliant light blinded him. He yanked the binoculars away and rubbed his eyes. "What the hell is going on in there?"

The ground shuddered and Althea jumped up, storming off to the vehicle. "It's certainly not worth dying for."

Agent Kipling scrambled to his feet. "Wait a minute." He chased after her, surprised she could move through the dirt so quickly in heels, and grabbed her arm. As she whipped around to confront him, a tremoring blast interrupted them both, and they turned to watch the building explode.

A huge rush of energy shot high into the sky, a long tail and- *Are those wings?* Agent Kipling blinked, but it was still there. The iridescent creature mounted higher and higher into the atmosphere until he could no longer see its long appendages.

A dragon?

It burst into endless shimmering snowflakes that descended back towards the Earth.

Kipling swept past the stunned doctor and into the driver's seat. "It's time to go." He found the concealed pistol and screwed on the silencer. The doctor got in beside him, marveling at the oncoming fallout.

Before he started the truck, Kipling turned to Althea. "It has been a real pleasure working with you." He didn't have much time to drive the point home. "But I feel we aren't exactly compatible, you understand."

The doctor tore her gaze from the sky, seeing the barrel of the gun. Her charming round eyes turned into saucers. "What are you doing?"

"I know you snuck the antidote to the Blackmoor pack." Kipling held the gun level to her chest. "And you've been working for the Dame this whole time, haven't you?"

"I don't know what you're talking about," she said, the sternness in her face mingling with disbelief.

The fallout was quickening, drawing closer. "That bitch has been stringing me along this whole time, and you've been working for her. Who is she?!" He grabbed her by the hair and shoved the gun to her throat.

"I don't know!" At least in that, she was telling the truth. "Kipling you don't know what you're-"

The silencer muffled the three blasts to her chest and he let her body drop out of the vehicle on the passenger's side. Agent Kipling started the truck and rolled away, pulling the top down to avoid contact with the poisonous snow.

He paid no mind to the speed limit as he barreled towards the bunker. They had failed, and the team he'd put his faith in turned out to be little more than a sham. Betrayal and fear wrestled inside of him.

"If humans insist on dying out, then so be it."

He would survive.

Chapter 46

After a quick stop to the pawnbroker's, Danny checked into the hotel and lounged on the penthouse sofa.

With a pocket full of diamonds and a desperate case of wanderlust, he couldn't get away from the drama fast enough. He'd lost four months of his life to their petty pursuits. But with the unexpected windfall, he'd make the most of it and get the hell out of dodge.

They'd never catch him.

Danny gazed out the picture window at the little city beneath him, bustling with early morning traffic. Though the view was fantastic, he'd only stay as long as it took to secure a flight off the goddamned continent. He stood and undressed, hoping someone was watching his sleek figure.

While those idiots squabbled over good and evil, he would enjoy himself to the fullest. Let the world end, he'd ride it out.

I always do.

A thump from the closet reminded him of his surprise treat. She'd followed him from the pawnbroker's looking to score an easy buck, finding a lot more than she'd bargained for.

He flung the closet door wide, and she fell forward, bound and gagged, onto the shag rug.

Her painted eyes pleaded for release.

Danny stood over her, giving her a good look at the last dick she'd ever get. "Well, good morning." He knelt down, toying with a curl of her hair. "Following me was a bad idea. Do you know what I'm going to do to you?" he asked, hearing her pulse spike. "Yeah, you do."

She moaned behind the gag, somewhere between defeat and another pointless plea.

Hoisting her rump in the air, with her face planted in the shag rug, he drew a line across her back with a grown nail, cutting into the perfect flesh.

She squirmed with a muffled squeal.

The room dimmed on its own accord. Danny glared at the dimmer switch, but it was untampered with. Turning to the window, a brilliant beam of light shot into the sky, darkening even the oncoming sunrise.

He stood and assessed the potential hazard, leaving the unlucky trick dripping blood into the carpet.

The blazing trail crested above the thin clouds.

It burst in every direction, causing a silent, blinding explosion. Particles of the blast cascaded slowly back to earth, dancing like snow in the window's view.

Danny paced to the window and flung the curtains shut. Whatever it was, it had better not fuck up his flight plans.

Chapter 47

Kane grinned down at me, a little worse for wear, but whole. I touched his cheek, not quite believing it. "You're alive."

"So are you." He nuzzled my ear. "I thought I'd lost you."

"You can't get rid of me that easy." I scoffed weakly, twining my fingers through his thick hair. The blooming slash across his neck was gone. I cringed and stroked a thumb over his jugular. "How did you-"

He shook his head with another smile. "I don't know."

A crowd of people, fully restored from the slaughter, stood and checked their vitals. When they realized they really were alive, they hugged and laughed, thrilled to be alive.

A ginger giant stood above the crowd, speaking with the witch and her companion. The mother and child I'd seen sacrificed embraced each other, crying in their relief.

Whatever destruction had been wrought in the Goddess' name had been mended. All but my father, who I vaguely remembered collapsing into a pile of ash, and my sister, who lay frozen in agony on the cold cement floor.

They were too broken.

"Blackmoor," the witch's voice called, tearing us from our trance. "There's someone here that wants to see you." She held her hand out to a young woman, who watched us with nervous anticipation. The girl had bright blue eyes, standing lean and tall for her age, with dark skin and nut-brown hair.

Kane set me down gently. "...Clara?"

She paused, then dashed at him. "Kane?!"

He reciprocated by catching her thin form, swinging in a circle before setting her back down. "I thought you were gone!"

"Not if I had a say in it." A stout woman in her mid-forties with wild red curls approached, holding the hand of a lean figure with short hair and watchful, sharp eyes.

Kane eyed the woman and her partner. "Who are you?"

Her man became defensive, but she nudged him. "I'm Dr. Samantha Warren, and until now have been her ward and caregiver. When you left the lab-" I saw Kane's look harden, and she seemed to as well, but maintained her stride. "Clara had been shot four times. I removed the bullets and kept her safe from anyone who posed a threat."

341

"It's true," Clara agreed, tugging on Kane's arm.

Kane scowled at the stout woman. "And you didn't return her to me straightaway? She belongs with her own kind."

"I didn't know where you were." The doctor shrugged apologetically. "Agent Lazaro connected Amy to you only last night. I did the best I could to keep Clara from being discovered from the other scientists."

"Why?" He pressed.

"Because," Dr. Warren struggled to find the words. "I love her like my own child. But I know she isn't." She turned to Clara. "I wish I could have done more for you."

Clara shook her head. "I'm glad it was you. Thank you."

"You're back with your family, that's all that matters." She leaned against the agent man.

"Amy," he cut in. "You don't know me, but we met a long time ago. My name is secret agent Morgan Lazaro. I've kept an eye on you since your mother was killed."

I shook my head. "I- I don't understand."

"They assigned me your case fifteen years ago. When the police found you in your mother's blood, they brought in my division. It was believed that your father was a mob boss. Turns out he was just a psychotic shifter." He considered the last spot my father inhabited. "Recently, agent Kipling has been targeting you. I tried to stop him. He wired the farmhouse and attempted to have you killed. Danny was his mole."

I nudged Kane conspiratorially. "Told you so."

The Agent's mouth twitched into a mirthless smile and continued. "Kipling brought in the soldiers and changed them into parasites. He made you kill Pierce and put you through more grief than anyone deserves. I know it doesn't mean much, but you weren't abandoned. I kept tabs on you even if it was from afar. Here." He dug into a coat a pocket, producing a business card. "Give me a call when things have settled down again. I'd be happy to share what I know about your case."

I took the card, curious about what he had to offer regarding my past. I didn't know what to say to this self-professed 'secret agent', but Kyren interrupted before I had the chance.

"Kane." He knelt on the floor in front of a corpse I recognized all too well. Shock and disbelief coursed through me. "It's Moira."

He jogged to Kyren's side, his eyes panning over her body. "We'll take her back to the farm and give her a proper burial."

Yet another terrible blow to the pack.

Moira, our rock-solid foundation, healer, and Kane's primary advisor, torn away from us so suddenly. *Why hadn't she recovered like the others?*

"Because she didn't want to." The witch came forward, acknowledging my thought. "Sometimes they choose not to. As for the vampire girl-" She looked back at where Jane's corpse had lain only moments ago. "Ezekiel must have taken her with them, but the Goddess's magic wouldn't have revived her."

Kane shrugged. "One less vampire to worry about."

Irritation prickled in my limbs. "I know they kidnapped me but that was Danny's fault. Jane was the only level-headed one in that godforsaken house."

Kane tucked me under his arm. "Well, luckily you won't be visiting again, will you?"

The witch's charms jingled as she guided us towards the exit. "With the portcullis open, it isn't safe to linger. You should all go home. Magics are still brewing, and the convergence isn't set to end until night falls again. There will be anomalous activity near the well until the moon rises."

The doctor's eyes brightened as if she had a brilliant plan. "I should get a team out here to study it."

"You most certainly will not." The witch dismissed the notion entirely, leaving no room for argument. "If you value your lives in the least, you'll keep everyone far away from here until the new moon."

Agent Lazaro glanced to Dr. Warren. "How on earth are we going to report this to headquarters?"

The witch looked him dead in the eye. "You don't. Tell them nothing. If you need someone to forget, give me a holler. Otherwise, I'm leaving, and I suggest you do the same." She huffed and jangled out the shattered doorframe.

Clara scrunched her nose. "She's weird."

Kane chuckled in response. "I'll say. Let's get out of here. Aurora will be so excited to see you." He grabbed both our hands and we strode to the door, followed by Kyren, and Gary. Jean and Maxwell carried Moira's corpse.

The others dispersed as well, leaving in droves through the front entrance. The redheaded giant nodded at Kane, smacking him on the back. "Been a while, brotha."

"Bear! Holy shit, what dragged you out of that cave?"

The giant grumbled under his breath. "The witch of course, I owe her a favor or two. Don't make deals with witches, they *always* come to collect."

A thin boy jabbed at Bear. "That was stupid of you."

"Shut up, you little runt," Bear grumbled at the kid's antics. "The adults are talking."

"Don't test me." The boy's thin chest puffed up comically. "I ain't no runt."

Bear and Kane shared a laugh.

"Come back to the farm with us," Kane said, eying the both of them. "We'll make it a celebration. Put this whole mess behind us. What do you say?"

Bear tousled the young man's hair, who boiled with rage underneath the huge paw. "Nah, not this time. I gotta get Hercules settled in."

"Don't be a stranger!" Kane shouted as they traipsed off, shoving each other like long-lost brothers. "Hopefully they don't kill each other first."

We exited the ruins and waved goodbye to the doctor and agent, Lazaro promising to keep in touch.

I had mixed feelings about him, but he didn't come across as insincere. Agent Lazaro could have answers to my past that still remained unexplained. But I was done with my own personal history lessons for one evening.

Whatever secrets he might divulge could wait.

Kyren had brought around the truck, so Jean busied himself with loading Moira in. I looked back at the wreckage, hoping I'd never have to see it again.

Kane pulled me aside and kissed me deeply. "Ready for life to get boring?"

"Absolutely." I could do boring. After all this, I'd had enough adventures for one lifetime.

"Good, then lets-" Kane froze, watching something just behind me. I craned my neck to look, regretting it instantly.

An unearthly tearing sound shredded the air as an ugly lesion split open in the space before us. Kane pulled me behind

346

him. The flapping maw sucked in as if trying to get a breath, taking with it Kane's bulk, and mine, and two others.

We tumbled through a void of shade and fire, linking arms to find some sort of stability in the torrential madness. Kane and Kyren wrapped themselves around us, willing to take the brunt end when we landed—*if* we ever landed.

Coarse fur rippled over Kane's skin, giving him an extra layer of protection.

This went on forever, my stomach wretched and produced nothing in this vacuum. If we weren't released soon, suffocation would consume us first.

Landing hard at an angle, our group split open and tumbled several feet before coming to a stop. The sky was bruised, the soil beneath us blood red. Plants, if that's what they could be called, pushed through cracks in the earth, pitch black and gleaming like oil.

As my vision finally stopped spinning, I crawled to Kane, who'd struck his head against a silver rock that shone with blue fluid. Clara and Kyren took less damage, rousing and choking on stale air.

"Kane, babe," I whispered, shaking his shoulder. "You've got to wake up." A burbling sigh escaped his lips, and I realized he was breathing, barely.

Kyren lifted Clara up by the elbow and pointing at the horizon. "Guys? We need to find cover. Like, *now*."

I followed his finger and saw a wall of torrential clouds, pulsing with angry electricity.

"Help me lift him!" I shouted at Kyren, who dashed to my side and helped me hoist Kane up. His head lolled forward uselessly as I noticed a nasty gash on the side of his head leaking, his red blood blue in this light.

We struggled with his body as Clara ran ahead, towards a cave entrance encrusted with silver ore. The wind pushed us the rest of the way into the cave, as if urging us in before thunder roared overhead. Kane's form collapsed against the side wall, still unresponsive.

Toxic rain pounded the ground outside, creating a stream leading into the cave that hissed against Kyren's skin before he pulled away. "Safe to say it's not potable." His laugh was strained as he soothed the injury with a fistful of red soil.

As the torrent raged outside, we huddled together, trying to stay warm in the frigid storm wind.

Pebbles clacked to the ground further down the cave, alerting us to another creature nearby. I didn't want to know what might rear its ugly head, but the storm had us trapped.

A thump and slide echoed above our heads. Crumbles of silver cascaded over us. *"Erreesshhh,"* a gravelly voice hissed. *"helessaaa trasssss… essa thisss, ese praay eeen ma heeum…"*

Two huge red eyes glared down at us from the ceiling, blinking with a second set of lids. The pupils dilated to thin slits and I could feel it readying itself to attack.

Oh. Shit.

Chapter 48

Secret Agent Lazaro walked the doctor to the edge of the woods. They had all witnessed the strange rift and saw Kane, Amy, Kyren and Clara sucked in, but could do nothing to stop it.

The doctor was upset, of course.

He did his best to console her but knew the witch had been right. They needed to get away from the portcullis, unless they, too, wished to be sucked into a spontaneous rift.

With a bit of persuasion, he managed to urge the doctor towards her car. "We'll figure it out. Maybe the witch will be able to help them."

"You saw inside of that… *thing* as well as I did. They're not coming back." She sniffed back tears. "All that time. All this effort. What the hell was the point?"

Lazaro wrapped his arms around her, unable to think of anything clever to say. Dr. Warren's face fell into his shoulder as sobs racked her body.

"Samantha, let's get out of here. We'll deal with it. We're not alone. There are others that want them back but we have to keep ourselves safe, first." He knew she would come around, she was a sensible woman, after all. "Do you need a ride?"

She pulled away from his shirt, leaving it wet with tears. "No, I- brought the car."

"Then go home, Sam, get some sleep. It's been a long day." Lazaro rubbed her arm endearingly. "We'll grab coffee when you're rested. Sound good?"

"I'm counting on it," she mumbled, then shot him a miserable smile, whisking away a tear.

They grudgingly departed to their respective vehicles.

Samantha's smell fixed itself to his nose as he watched his beautiful woman sit in her car and dry her eyes.

Getting into his battered Honda, Lazaro considered the idea of dating Samantha. His chest fluttered with excitement, making him stupid and giddy. He was too old to experience a silly thing like infatuation, wasn't he?

Lazaro put the keys in the ignition and adjusted the radio's volume before turning on the car. Lazaro noticed his wrist had blossomed an impressive bruise but was no longer shattered.

Nothing short of a miracle.

He committed the doctor's visage to memory and turned the keys into start.

The car didn't rumble to life as it usually did. Instead, something beneath beeped thrice, and a bright light exploded between his legs.

He witnessed with detached curiosity as his limbs were torn from his body. Lazaro flew high into the sky, rotating slowly as he caught a glimpse of the sunrise.

Morgan Lazaro could hear a scream as his vision faded. *So, this is how it ends*, he thought as his basic bodily functions halted, *If only I-*

Epilogue

Three full moons had come and gone since the convergence, and not a clue to where the rift had taken the conduit or her friends. The witch could use a locator spell until she ran out of reagents, but it wouldn't get her closer to finding them.

All she knew was that they were not on earth anymore, and it was a shot in the dark to guess where they ended up.

The witch tittered to the fireplace, whispering ingredients aloud. "…mullein root, valerian, mint…" With a flick, she threw the herbs into a steaming broth.

She slammed the lid over the concoction. After steeping for three nights, the mixture should produce a clear, deep sleep, allowing the dreamer to stay alert within the dream.

Zima, her huge, snow-white angora cat rubbed against her hip. She'd been an invaluable companion during the cold winter months. And as the weather warmed, the little kitten continued to grow well past the size of an average house cat.

The witch hummed a tune, long gone the words. It still made her heart leap with a strange remembrance, a relic of a simpler time, when the rivers always ran clear.

"What's next, Zima?" she mused. The cat's large emerald eyes watched her curiously. She opened a cabinet and produced a wrapped loaf and a salted fish for Zima. "Breakfast?"

The beast waited expectantly as she tossed the young carp into her bowl.

The witch slunk down in her chair, daydreaming of hot chowder as she gnawed on the crust. Perhaps the next needy customer might offer cream for an enchantment. Either that, or she'd have to traverse a human store.

A knock on the door startled her.

Impossible.

She scanned the entrance for a trace of thought; nothing. Whoever it was either knew a very powerful witch, or had no thoughts at all.

"Who is it?" Silence beckoned her to the door, and foolhardiness made her open it.

A semi-corporeal being cast a shadow over the entrance. *Grant me passage*, the creature projected, *you and my master have business.* Her guest was a sending from another dimension, the body of the creature was safely on its own world. Nothing she could do would affect it here, nor it, her.

"Come in, then. No need for such formalities."

It inclined the amorphous ball she assumed was the head and stepped across the threshold. At her whim, any manner of curses or spells could be activated if the creature was not what it seemed. Even if it was just a sending, she had the ability to banish it from the planet.

Shutting the door, the witch returned to her seat and eyed the creature, which remained standing in the middle of her small, intermediate cabin. "What do you want, spirit?"

Your allies, they threaten my master's rule.

"So? Monarchies come and go. Why should I care?" Her veil of nonchalance would allow her to pick at the creature's story. Amy was on their planet, she just had to figure out which one it was. And in what dimension.

Indeed, it considered. *Our politics do not matter to you. But the creator left the ruling to the highest born. If they are usurped, our world dies with their bloodline. Does that hold any significance for you? Or, are you so tainted by magic that you can no longer feel? Your years are evident to me, even if your friends cannot see.*

"You come into my house and speak of my age?" She feigned irritation, already getting an idea where the creature had risen from. "What will your master give me for this 'favor', *Anam Fola?*"

The shadow wavered. *So, you do know of us. We humbly entreat you to remove them from our presence, we cannot suffer it much longer. My lady offers minerals of your choosing, silver, gold, diamonds.*

She crossed her arms. "And what would an *old* lady like me do with that?"

We can offer you servants, riches, magics of our own design. Speak it, and it will belong to you, after you release us from this blight.

The witch considered for a moment and stood up. "Swear this, on your life and the Queen's life."

It swelled in size, nearly becoming corporeal. She almost saw the creature's face, its real face, not the shadowy mass it inhabited. *We swear it, on our life and that of the Queen's, that you will be rewarded for your expedient removal of your conduit and her blood-wolf.*

She smiled at her guest. "Good, I want one of your younglings. Doesn't have to be strong, or even royal. I need an extra pair of hands around here, and you are going to deliver them to me. I will, in return, gather my allies from that forsaken planet of yours."

The creature seemed to exhale in relief. *Very well.* It disappeared in a sweep of darkness.

She took a breath and fell into the chair once more. Anam Fola's had a nasty reputation, and little patience for other species that crossed them.

Well, she thought, *at least I know where they are now*.

Groaning, she stood and tossed a shawl over herself, opening the front door once more. Instead of the quaint woods she often kept the cabin in, she emerged onto a bustling walkway, where the last functional payphone sat next to a permanently closed mini-mart. Touching the phone activated it without charge, and she dialed a number.

It almost went to voicemail before he picked up. "*Hello?*"

"It's good to hear you voice," she mumbled, "-*agent*."

"*You know I don't go by that anymore. I thought you were in retirement. What do you want?*"

"I am, *Morgan,* but I have a favor to ask of you…"

Thank you for reading!

At this time, the second book is out and the third is on the way! Please visit my website at:
www.rykerchronicles.com for more info.